The 7th Jackal

a novel by J.L. Davis

Dreams are Thunder
Let Them Roar

"Wildly Entertaining"
~ Readerman's Bookshelf ~

Dedicated to the kids from Blueberry Hill, the adventures we shared on Pisgah Mountain and the many tales of the wind whispering in the trees under a full moon. Back then we were all just children discovering our lives… here's to the good old days and the times we loved best.

The 7th Jackal Trilogy
novels by J.L. Davis

The 7th Jackal
Jonas Blackheart
Isabella

Something Happened

"Remember that night back in 1993 when we wrestled the devil?" AJ asked just hours before his eyes turned dark. "That was the night I got murdered."

Those were AJ Samson's words. As things turned out, it was the last conversation we ever had. Days later I stood in a cemetery, rain dripping off my nose. A vision of my childhood friend pushing open the lid of a coffin flashed in my mind. No doubt he'd offer a playful wink when he peeked out of the crate. If mischief were a peach, AJ would have plucked the tree bare a long time ago.

AJ lifted his nightshirt. A cherry colored bruise splashed across his ribs. "Man, that brute in the forest really pummeled me."

The abrasion looked fresh and clean.

"You mean that scrape never healed from all those years ago?" I asked.

Looking up his face suddenly collapsed in despair. "Honest Keenan. Doctors won't listen but it isn't any horrible disease that's killing me." He again glanced down at the bruise painted on his skin. "Time passes but some wounds never heal. This is one of them."

I turned my head and pushed back a tear.

The medical world argued that the lesion near AJ's ribs was where the malignancy started before its unwelcome presence grew.

What experts failed to see was that AJ's grim condition had been forecasted long ago. It wasn't a medical happenstance but rather prophecy decades in the making.

"You'll get through this," I assured him, and maybe even more, tried to convince myself.

"I'm not stupid," he said. "Time isn't on my side. Take it from somebody who knows. Dying is one of the hardest things you'll ever do."

AJ shifted uneasily in his bed. His body looked skeletal, almost as if someone threw a thin grey sheet over a pair of meatless, protruding ribs.

"I'm getting tired now Keenan," he said.

"Get some rest," I answered.

AJ reached out and touched my arm. For a minute his eyes grew bright. "I need you to promise me something. I need you to tell the story of what happened when we were kids. Write it down. Even if nobody believes it, promise me you'll do that."

After a moment of silence, "I promise."

AJ winced in pain. Still that promise seemed to satisfy him and he almost managed a smile as if to say, "Now I can die in peace."

Within the hour, AJ Samson did just that.

———

Jim Thorpe Pennsylvania is a small town at the foot of the Poconos. Since last walking these streets the American Hotel, a dilapidated building in the center of town, had been remodeled to accommodate a growing tourism trade. Lured by scenic mountains, sightseers came to browse the small shops on Broadway, raft the Lehigh River and ride bikes on mountain trails. Down on Susquehanna Street, Poppa Joe's old pinball arcade had long ago been bulldozed into a parking lot. Little else had changed. After all these years, the place was still home.

For a minute I caught myself smiling then looked down at the coffin suspended above a dark hole. I thought about poor AJ rotting in there, God rest his soul. Reverend Joe prayed earnestly over the polished crate. A cold morning wind raced through his hair.

AJ's wife Becca stood in the wet grass next to the grave. Even in her sadness she was a beautiful woman. Only the faintest trace of grey tainted her dark hair. A noticeable limp that plagued her throughout childhood nearly doubled as she took a step toward AJ's coffin. Leaning down, she placed a rose on the lid of the casket and then bowed her head in a silent prayer. A single tear rolled down her cheek.

Sighing, I craned my head around. Just behind the cemetery's main gate sat the darkened woods of Pisgah Mountain. I recalled the dim shadows from long ago on that terrible night that we faced the battle of our young lives. Reflections of past ghosts and haunting memories hung all around me.

Everyone dies. Sometimes that's hard to imagine. Other times it's even more difficult to accept. You don't realize things like that when you're just a kid; dying, that is. As children we soared like eagles. I swore we'd all live forever.

Turning my attention back to the coffin, I swallowed hard as the wooden crate lowered slowly into the pit.

"A promise is a promise," someone whispered.

Startled, I turned around. Nobody was there but the rising wind sifting through the leaves of trees. Still, to this day I swear AJ Samson tried to make one final attempt to contact me before he crossed over to the other side, urging me to write down what happened when we were just thirteen years old. He had a thing about that. I don't know why.

———

I'm of the opinion that there are monsters in the world. Tugger Rhodes used to refer to them as The Willies.

"*The Willies* are restless," he'd say. "My dad told me about them. They live in dark places. Cellars and closets. They come out late at night when everything is quiet." He'd pause and breathed deep. "They come after kids, just like you and me."

You think that's crazy, right?

Wrong.

On some dark and lonely night run your hand along the bottom of the bed. Feel around. You might be surprised to find that there's something more than the gathering dust settling wearily back on its haunches. Something cold. Something not quite human.

I know. I've been there and seen it.

Maybe it'd be better if you didn't believe this story. Then again, my friend Tugger didn't believe in monsters either. He found out the hard way. Maybe you will too.

Enough talk. It's dark outside and getting late. Let's get on with it, shall we?

Get cozy.

Not too cozy.

Stretch out on the bed. That's it. Pull the covers up tight. Get ready for a long night's read. I'm going to tell you a story. I'm going to tell you about the day a monster walked into the lives of those people living in a boring little town in northeastern Pennsylvania. I'm going to tell you about the day we fought the battle of our young lives and faced off against the devil.

This one is written for you AJ. Because just as every good story begs to be told, a promise is a promise and should always be kept.

Keenan Braddock

Part One

WHEN DREAMS COME TRUE

1

A Restless Summer Night

Dressed in white and wrinkled infirmary coats, the three men perched themselves at the table. Their grave eyes stared out the rainy windowpane. It was 4:00 a.m. inside a guarded facility located on the outskirts of Allentown Pennsylvania. Fortified with concrete walls and an intricate security system, the place was designed to keep unwelcome visitors out and if need be, invited guests from leaving.

"We have to find him," one of the men finally said. His face looked stiff as a knot. "It's time to call the police."

"Are you an idiot?" his partner asked in dismay. "Even the Whitehouse is in the dark about what we do. This is Area 51 as far as they're concerned."

"It was a goddamn security breach," a G-Man dispatched from headquarters complained bitterly. He nearly paced a groove in the floor over the last hour. A strand of hair hung irritably in his eyes. "He didn't just stand up and walk out the door. Someone let the bird fly. I got a bullet with their name on it." He fingered the pistol stuffed in his pocket.

The men argued long into the night. Alan Stoner, headman in charge of operations, finally stood up. He walked over to the window and stared into the stormy night. "It doesn't matter whose fault it is. We'll deal with that later. What matters now is that we find him. And no police involvement. The last things we need is a headline in the morning newspaper."

Sam Cage leaned forward in his chair. His face drew a blank. "I'm lost. If we don't contact the authorities, what's our next move?"

"Stay calm," Stoner cautioned. "We can't do anything until it surfaces. Sure as hell we'll know when that happens."

Cage shifted uncomfortably in his chair. Picking up a pencil he tapped it on the surface of the conference table. "It'll kill someone. Do you want that on your head?"

Stoner crossed his arms. "Like there's a choice? If the police find out what we've been doing they'll haul all of our asses off to jail."

Cage slumped down in his chair. He rubbed his knuckles in his eyes. In the last few hours you'd have sworn he aged ten years.

"We need to move fast," he said. "If we don't you know what'll happen. Start piling up the body bags."

Stoner glared. No doubt about it; Cage wasn't a hero. If the authorities got involved and started asking questions, he'd crack under the pressure. Straight up, he never liked the bastard.

"You know how we do business," Stoner said. "It wouldn't be the first-time innocent people got caught in the loop." Straightening his tie, he leaned against the tabletop. "Don't be stupid Cage. If what we've been doing leaks into public view we'll all be eating bullets. Don't think headquarters will defend us when the cops read us our rights. If things go sour, they'll forget that they even know us."

Cage said nothing. A steady migraine chiseled at his head. He stared at his colleagues. They stared back. The silence was deafening.

Across the room, Harry Grimm showed no expression at all other than a constant look of irritation forever cemented on his face. He stopped pacing. Planting a foot up on a chair, he picked impatiently at his teeth.

Alan Stoner turned his head and again stared out the window. "There's no reason to panic," he said. "Dead or alive, we'll get our man."

For an instant the G-Man showed a hint of a smile but just as quickly turned back to stone.

Thunder rumbled outside and lit up the darkness. Cage listened as the rain splashed against the glass and rushed through tin spouts and gutters.

"We wait for it to make a mistake," Stoner said. "Then we make our move."

2

Night Walkers

Jim Thorpe, a town named after an old Indian athlete, was a small community that lingered sleepily in the mountains of northeastern Pennsylvania. Streetlamps cast pale reflections off the windows of old Victorian homes. Unlike the perils in the city, the place remained unhampered by the cruelties of an unfriendly world.

Heather Gold, twenties and beautiful, never considered the risk she might be taking by walking alone late at night. Like most romantic dreamers, one day she hoped to fall in love. Perhaps perform on Broadway and have a house overlooking the sea in Malibu. However, fate sometimes cracks like a whip and has other designs. For Heather Gold, every dream she ever had was about to take a dramatic turn.

———

The streets glistened from a steady rain that drenched the ground earlier that evening. Finally, clouds gave way to starlight. The air smelled fresh. Clean. A quiet breeze rustled in the trees. The chimes from Saint Mark's church echoed in the valley. Heather's dark hair blew gorgeously behind her face. It was late.

Turning off the avenue, she walked down a deserted side street. Houses thinned considerably in that part of town. The highway remained barren of traffic. Heather couldn't steady a growing uneasiness. Stopping and listening, she sensed that something was amiss. The night sounded too still. Even crickets stopped chirping.

"A wild imagination," she said in a whisper and continued on.

But the silence loomed larger with each passing step. Elongated housetop shadows shifted under a stark white moon.

For an instant Heather thought she saw something move from behind a hedge in Snowden's yard. The sudden crash of a garbage can clanged off the sidewalk and shattered the night.

Heather vaulted backwards. She stared into an envelope of uncertain darkness.

"Meow!"

A cat thumped out from behind the trashcan. Flashing its green eyes, it quickly disappeared behind some trees in a yard.

Heather sighed, giggling at her own idiocy. But her laughter was quickly mowed under a sudden and striking blade of terror. Someone else was abroad. She caught a glimpse of a dark figure crouched behind a fence. The heat of fear rose in her throat.

"Who's there?' she asked fearfully.

A dark stranger stood up slowly. His left arm swung dangerously as a gaveling hook. He studied the girl with silent deliberation.

Heather's heart pounded. She tried to run but couldn't. Criminal and black, the cold eyes of the unexpected visitor froze her to the pavement.

Slowly bending down, she grabbed a broken brick out of the gutter. Clutching at it, she stood up bravely to confront the threat.

The assailant blinked in the darkness. His sunken eyes looked at the brick. "You don't really want to hit me with that," he said.

Confusion washed over Heather. She grew woozy and stumbled backward. Regaining her balance, she looked closer. The stranger seemed to liquefy and then just as quickly reshaped.

"Eddie Dune?" Heather blinked in disbelief.

"You got it babe," he said. A runner of sweat dripped down his neck. He glanced at the brick and pointed. "That's dangerous. Put it down before you hurt someone, namely me." He laughed.

Heather's face weeded up with uncertainty. God, she wanted to believe that this was Eddie Dune. He had been her best friend in high school. Afterwards he moved to Lancaster County to attend college at Central Penn. Still there was no reason to believe he'd be hiding in the bushes on a warm May evening in northeastern Pennsylvania.

After all, he died three years ago.

———

Heather's fingers grasped the brick tighter. She studied the man with silent deliberation.

"What's wrong?" He smiled grimly. His lips grew tense as rubber bands, ready to snap at the slightest pressure. "Don't you recognize me, my little petunia? It's Eddie Dune. Man, remember all the movies we used to see?" He whistled. "We had some kicks back in the day."

"You're dead," she said flatly.

"I moved. That's not dead."

"I read your obituary," Heather said firmly. "You were killed at the college in Lancaster. There was a fire at the dorm. You didn't make it out alive."

"Really?" he mused. "I don't feel as if worms are eating me." His voice remained steady. A dirty smell of sweat and grime hung in the stagnant air. He again glanced at the brick in the girl's hand. "You gonna drop that? You're starting to scare me."

Heather held her ground. "Show yourself!"

After a pause, he giggled and took a slow step forward.

Heather's eyes widened. She staggered backward as if someone smacked her in the face with a wooden baseball bat. Not only wasn't this person Eddie Dune, he scarcely looked like a man at all. Fierce scars cut across his sunken cheeks. Mud crusted his shoes. A grimy green hospital shirt gave him the appearance of someone who just bolted over the fence of the local mental hospital. Grinning like a shark, his tongue raked over stained molars. A knife in his hand gleamed in the wake of a dim streetlamp. Running his thumb over the edge of the blade, a slight runner of blood dripped on the pavement.

"No!" Heather gave a sudden scream. Throwing the brick, she quickly fled down the avenue.

———

Yard dogs barked. House lights randomly clicked on from weary citizens disturbed out of a deep sleep. Others slumbered peaceably and unaware. The world dreamed. But for Heather Gold the dream abruptly became a nightmare that pursued her with speed and dark purpose. She ran faster.

"Help!" the girl shouted. Clammy sweat broke on her face. She dashed across open lawns. The loud trollop of heavy boots pounded the pavement behind her. The predator gained ground fast.

Turning, she hurried towards the main avenue where she hoped to attract someone's attention. But the streets were empty. She rushed across a darkened alley. Almost fell when her shoe got collared in a small rut in the road. Her own house was in sight. Only moments away. Still, her stalker moved quick. Cheetah fast. His stench, rotten as the carnal remains of aged flesh in a Mississippi swamp, caked the night air.

Heather reached the fence surrounding her yard. She frantically picked at the latch on the gate. Turning her head, she gasped when she saw the apish man nearly upon her. His outstretched arms raked the air.

"Open. Open!"

The latch clicked loose. The girl sprang forward.

Too late.

The darkman hauled her violently backwards. His one hand crunched her ribs. The other slid tight around Heather's throat. Much like the dark prep room of the mortician that nobody ever sees, his rancid breath rested in the girl's nostrils. A foul stink of sweat and blood seeped from the brute's open sores.

Heather struggled to loosen the darkman's grip but he was strong. Much too strong. Packing her slender body in his arms he carried her off into the blackened edges of town near the woods. She prayed hard that she had fallen victim to some terrible nightmare, one which would end very soon. Somewhere in that next hour on a dark and lonely night, it did.

3

The New Kid in Town

"AJ! Supper is ready," the old woman hollered from out on the porch. The smell of scrapple and eggs hung in the kitchen. "AJ!" She shook her gray head and stepped back into the house, leaving the screen door slam.

"He ran off again," she said. "That boy will be the death of me."

"Boys will be boys, Helen." The old man chuckled. Peeking through his bifocals he turned the page of a newspaper.

"Boys will be troublemakers you mean," she corrected and flipped a pair of eggs over in a skillet. "His parents are probably rolling over in their graves with the mischief he gets in." She walked back to the screen door. "AJ!" she hollered. "You get home for breakfast or I'll give you a licking you won't forget. Are you listening? AJ!"

———

1993 was a banner year. Bill Clinton was elected president. Whitney Houston topped the charts on Billboard. The blizzard of '93 hit the northeast, federal agents stormed David Koresh's compound in Waco and a bomb exploded at the World Trade Center; all of this and the bagless vacuum cleaner was invented too.

Still, to a kid none of those facts were newsworthy. More pressing issues were at hand like who could skip a rock three times over the Greenie Pond. Don't let anyone fool you. Those irresponsible days of youth are the most magic ones of our lives.

It was a warm afternoon in May, hours before the lives of everyone would be altered by the murder of a young girl named Heather Gold. Sun splashed down through the trees near the remains of an old dilapidated mansion. Destroyed by fire many years prior, the structure was little more than crumbling walls and toppled stones. Entrenched in tangled weeds that grew wildly through the ruins, the place served as a clubhouse for AJ Samson and his friends.

"NightBirds," AJ said from behind a pair of taped up eyeglasses. Sitting beside him, a scraggly mutt wagged its tail in the dirt. He reached down and scratched the dog behind the ears.

Keenan tilted his head and stared. "What's a NightBird?"

"We're a club." AJ sucked at his bottom lip and studied the kid. "You wanna join?"

Keenan Braddock just arrived in town. A little shy and backward, teenagers regarded him as an outsider. Sports might have given him some respect except he wasn't much of an athlete. Guys like him? They never got picked when choosing sides for basketball. More often than not they ended up with a 'KICK ME' sign taped to the seat of their trousers.

A local reject named Rudy Diggs, a kid with a sugary diet and complexion to match, took an instant interest in Keenan. One day Rudy walked down the hall and knuckled him in the gut for no reason. Papers and books sailed all over the place.

AJ stopped and helped Keenan pickup his notebooks.

"Don't let Rudy get under your skin," he said. "That guy is just a piss-ant, know what I mean?"

Keenan said nothing. Lowering his head, he continued gathering his books off the floor.

AJ eyed him with quiet curiosity. No doubt about it. Kids like Keenan had bullseyes painted on their heads. Man, it was hard to imagine who would take care of him if he lived. The kid also had manners. Didn't cuss either. AJ reasoned that to be Keenan's downfall. When you're a kid it just isn't kosher to be too polite.

"I'm Anthony James Samson." He nodded. "AJ for short."

"Keenan," he said and studied the tips of his shoes. "Keenan Braddock."

"I'll be honest," said AJ. "You look a little pathetic, no offense. I got a few friends," he suggested. "Why don't you meet me at the Babydoll Pizzeria after school? I'll introduce you around. Know the place?"

"Yes but…"

The class bell rang.

"Jeez, late again. See you later." AJ rushed down the hall and disappeared around a corner.

———

Keenan traveled the school halls in isolation for most of the day. He sheepishly peeped around corners and searched for enemies that might be lying in wait.

The dismissal bell sounded at the end of the day. Against his better judgment, he decided to amble down to the pizzeria. Walking towards the place he saw AJ Samson plunked down on a cement step. He was reading a Marvel comic book. A dog with a wet nose sat beside him on the sidewalk.

"Want a hunk?" AJ handed Keenan a scrap of licorice. A few minutes later he led him towards a woodsy trail where they crossed the slimed rocks of the Greenie Pond.

"Where are we going?" asked Keenan.

"Right there." AJ pointed.

Up ahead, a fat kid was seated in the dirt and eating a chocolate bar. A young girl with pigtails sat beside him swishing a lollipop in her mouth.

"This is Tugger Rhodes and Becca Abrams." They both guardedly nodded. "Keenan just moved to town. He wants to join our gang."

Tugger wiped his mouth on his sleeve and stared suspiciously. "You know the rules. If he wants in, he'll need to play *The Truth Game*."

Keenan scratched his head and looked at AJ. "What does he mean?"

"It's an initiation. Anyone who wants to join the club has to tell a dark secret about themselves."

"I don't have any secrets." Keenan studied his shoes.

Popping a purple lollipop out of her mouth, Becca jumped off the ground. Even with a smudge of dirt down her cheek and holes in her faded jeans, it didn't take a genius to figure out that one day she'd be a beautiful woman. Her one liability came in the form of a bad limp when she walked.

"You're not fooling anyone," she said. "Everyone has secrets."

"What happened there?" Keenan glanced at her leg, changing the subject.

Becca hesitated. "It's nothing. I was born that way." She straightened up and thrust her lip out. "You want to make something out of it?"

Keenan took a step back. "I was just asking. Honest."

Regardless of her toughness, Becca's face glowed with tender edges. Sighing, she settled back against a rock.

———

Recounting her story, Becca said she was first thrust into AJ Samson's world one day during gym class. The instructor insisted on the kids learning classical dancing. Shy boys paired up with equally shy girls. Together they waltzed their hearts out for fifty long minutes.

"Samson." Mr. Paddle popped a breath mint in his mouth and looked up from his clipboard. Paddle had AJ labeled as a troublemaker ever since he dusted the freshman basketball team's jockstraps with itching powder. "You're with Becca Abrams. Get moving."

Paddle cranked up a sappy love song. The music crackled over the gymnasium speakers. Miserable young boys with squeaky sneakers walked out on the floor.

"Sorry," Becca said after she stepped on AJ's toes for the third time. "My leg is short."

"What?" AJ blinked.

"My one leg is a half inch shorter than the right. I was born that way." Her face turned cherry red. For a minute AJ thought that she'd cry.

"You're not gonna be sick are you?" AJ backed up a little. "Relax," he said. "I'm no ballerina."

However, Becca couldn't loosen up. She struggled with a bum leg that genetics rather than bad dance moves had imposed upon her.

"Woof!" Zit Williams barked at the girl from across the floor. "Got stuck with a peg-leg, did you AJ? Woof!" He sniggered from behind a fresh case of erupting acne on his chin.

"Quit it Zit," AJ warned.

"Ha!" Zit grinned smartly and tried to impress Rita Martz, the flaming redhead from 8B. "Is this a school or a home for unwanted mutts?"

"I told you to stop," AJ said angrily.

Zit opened his eyes in disbelief. "Where's your sense of humor AJ? What are you, hot for the girl with the wooden leg? Lighten up. It isn't like she's human."

Becca lowered her head. The girl was tough. Still, when it came to her impairment, all defenses fell apart. She wanted to disappear. Slink away into a black hole.

AJ's face turned into an angry scowl. Marching over to Zit, he knuckled him square in the jaw. Everyone ran over and cheered the contenders on. Mr. Paddle dropped his clipboard. He rushed over and peeled the boys apart.

A trickle of blood ran down Zit's nose as he coward behind Stew Malone.

"One more minute and I would have finished things. Let me at him!" Zit smacked a fist in his hand after he was certain that the fight was over and AJ had been secured.

Becca always loved AJ for standing up for her that day. Later that afternoon he introduced her to the rest of the gang, including Tugger Rhodes, a young hoodlum with a watermelon for a belly. It was the start of a long friendship, the kind that endures.

———

"See now. Everyone has secrets," Becca repeated. "Now what's yours?"

Keenan hesitated. Shuffling from foot to foot, finally he said, "Sometimes I see things."

Tugger stopped chewing and tilted his head. "Are you crazy?"

"No," said Keenan. "I have dreams."

"Everyone has dreams," he countered.

"Not like mine." Keenan stared. "Mine come true. Before I moved here, I had a horrible dream about my aunt. She got stabbed to death, seven times. The following night a thief broke in the house." He paused and stared. "It happened."

Becca's eyes opened wide. "He killed her?"

Keenan nodded. "There have been other dreams too."

"What do you mean by that?" she asked.

Keenan hesitated. "Bad things are coming."

Tugger shuddered. "Man, this kid is really giving me the willies but that's probably as good of a secret as any I've heard. At the very least it's a great fish tale. I don't know if this is good or bad but congrats. You're a NightBird." He punched him in the arm the way all good pals say hello.

"I better get home," said AJ. "Don't forget. Saturday is *Dead Night*."

Keenan scratched his head. "What's Dead Night?"

AJ answered, "When the moon is full, we sneak out of our houses at midnight. We meet down at Jeremiah Benjamin's grave in the North Gates cemetery."

Keenan stepped back. "I couldn't do that."

"What's wrong?" Tugger sniggered. "I told you guys. He's a pussy."

Keenan shoved his hands in his pockets and sucked at his lip. "It's just that I'd be in deep trouble if I got caught."

"Don't sweat the small stuff," AJ said. "It's okay to be an angel. The thing is every once in a while, you just need to get a little dirt under your wings."

"But…"

"See you then." He whistled to his dog and took off through a path in the woods.

4

Monsters

If you lived in downtown New York you wouldn't appreciate the daily potential for violence. You'd wake up to a morning cup of coffee and then rush off to the subway for work. Liquor store robberies. Muggers. A shooting in the Bronx. It happens. Life is fast in the city and murder a predestined danger.

It's different in small town USA. Tragedies aren't as easily overlooked.

On the morning that the local newspaper reported on a murder, that old monster known as fear quickly blanketed the town. A group of hikers walking a trail on Pisgah Mountain discovered the remains of a local woman named Heather Gold. Police termed the death suspicious. Witnesses on the other hand described the scene with words like "pounded" and "multiple head and chest lacerations".

"Keep your doors locked and use caution," Chief Gunner told the public. "There could be a monster out there," he finally admitted.

That night people slept warily with visions of dark phantoms in their head and the battered face of Heather Gold invading their darkest dreams. Curfews were enforced. Sirens blared. Police cruisers hurried to false alarms turned in by frightened locals.

As for Norman Spencer, parked on a barstool at the Blarney Stone Tavern, the murder was a nightmare from which he couldn't awaken. The barkeep poured another round of JD Gold. Norman drank it down.

"I still think it was Wild Bill Finch." Parker Cain sat at his regular stool and tapped his fingers on a cold one. "That sonofabitch lives in a shack all alone up there on Pisgah Mountain. Who does that?"

"You're kidding me!" Dan Piper chimed in from the other side of the bar. "Wild Bill is crazier than a shithouse rat, but murder? It's probably some punk on dope whose brains turned to mud."

Someone tossed a quarter in the jukebox. A CCR tune wailed through muffled speakers.

"You're joking, right?" Mort Pearson squeezed a lime in his vodka. He looked pretty smug in a black suit and tie. "This was a professional job. No fingerprints. The killer knew his business. Rumor has it the dead girl's face was so battered that the cops needed dental records to identify her. The bastard strung her up. She had so much rope tied around her neck she looked like a frightened alley cat that got stuck in a mess of chicken wire."

The barkeep wiped a runner of sweat off his receding hairline. "This is scary as hell."

"You're damn right it is," Mort said and glanced over at Norman Spencer. "What about it Norm? You were on the recovery crew that picked the girl up. How bad was it?"

Norman stared at his reflection in a mirror behind the bar and took a slug of whiskey.

"Monsters," he mumbled. His zombie face looked as if it were iced up in visions of terror and never got quite warm enough again to thaw.

"You got that right," Mort agreed. "There's a killer on the loose. He's got an appetite for things that aren't natural." Taking a last swallow of his drink he tossed a dollar tip on the bar. "Keep your doors locked," he warned.

———

On the same night that Norman Spencer fought off demons in his head with a bottle of ninety proof whiskey, Keenan Braddock wrestled with a different kind of monster in his dreams, one that was not quite human at all.

Keenan zipped through tall cornhusks. Something chased after him. It gained ground quickly. He ran faster, sprinting out of the corn and into an open field. Losing his footing he tumbled to the ground and landed flat on his back. Dread washed over the boy when he looked up to see the brute leaning over him. His blemished face baked in the yellow sun.

"Be afraid," the ogre said. "I like that. I don't like this sun though. It's too damned hot." He shielded his eyes with a callous hand. Wiping away a runner of sweat, he turned his attention back to Keenan. "It's time you get what's coming to you. And don't cry on me, you little shit." He planted a foot on Keenan's chest. "After we're done here, I'll take care of some unfinished business with your mother, the miserable tramp." He pulled out a knife from underneath a dirty green shirt.

Keenan's eyes grew wide with terror. Just as the fiend was about to slice him open like a cold can of worms, he woke up. Turning on the light, he looked suspiciously around the room. The sensation of déjà vu faded. Still, his gut instinct told him that his dreams had brushed against a hidden truth.

Holding tight to thin bed sheets, Keenan shivered through a sleepless night.

5

The Allentown Facility

Alan Stoner stared at a newspaper on the desk. The headline reported on a young woman named Heather Gold. According to reports, she got murdered on a mountain in a nearby town.

"What do you think?" Sam Cage asked. "Jim Thorpe is only thirty miles north. He could have easily traveled that far."

Stoner shot Cage a stern look. "What the hell kind of name is Jim Thorpe for a town anyway." He tossed the paper on a table. "Don't be too confident. It might not be our man. It could be as simple as some moron pissed off at his wife for screwing the boss after hours."

Cage stood up and walked across the floor. "Are you crazy? We can't sit here and do nothing. If it's our guy and he isn't nailed down, the undertaker is gonna double his pension plan before the end of the week."

Harry Grimm leaned against the wall and puffed methodically on a cigarette. He was dispatched from headquarters to keep an eye on things. Turning his head, he glared at Cage. Nope. He didn't like him one damn bit. Cage was one of those moral shitheads that headquarters assigned to the project. He probably had connections with some political crony, a democrat no doubt, who requested he be taken onboard and shown the ropes. If Grimm had his way the only rope Cage would ever see would be one tied to his neck and dangling from a tree.

The same look of contempt festered in Alan Stoner's eyes. If the authorities stepped in Cage would crack faster than a stale nut.

Stoner took a breath. Looking in a mirror he straightened his tie. "Don't panic. I got a plan."

"What plan?" Cage's eyebrows lifted.

Stoner glared. Another goddamned corner of the world heard from. Cage just couldn't keep his trap shut. "Harry Grimm is gonna investigate." He glanced at the G-Man. "If our man is in Thorpe, he'll find him."

Cage balked. "One guy can't handle this. That's like paddling a rowboat in a hurricane. He'll sink fast."

Stoner tossed a pencil on the table. Clenching his fists, he stuffed them in his pockets. "We need to keep low on the radar. If Mr. Grimm finds our man is in Thorpe, we'll send a full extraction team to pick him up," he said. "With any luck we'll all avoid a stint in San Quentin."

Gathering papers off the desk, Alan Stoner headed out the door.

Seated at the conference table, silent rage trembled on Cage's lips. He wondered how much more he could take before everything detonated.

6

Something Dangerous

Ashley Braddock hadn't slept in days. Her mind continuously drifted to Heather Gold, the murdered girl found on the mountainside. The incident brought back an avalanche of dark memories.

It started back in Pittsburgh before she moved east with her son. Her sister had been staying with her at the time. A thief broke into the house. During the robbery, her sister saw the perpetrator and he stabbed her repeatedly. The police never apprehended the killer. Unable to erase the memories of that terrible night she packed up her son and moved across the state.

"We should leave." Keenan tugged at his mother's arm.

"Give me a second," she said and ruffled his hair.

It happened on the way back from the supermarket. She noticed a crowd gathering in front of Melber's Funeral Home. Pallbearers with dark and wet eyes carried the coffin towards a hearse. A preacher stood beside the wooden crate and made the sign of the cross. It was no secret. The murdered girl, Heather Gold, was being buried.

Ashley pulled the car over and got out.

"We need to leave mom," Keenan grew insistent. "There's something bad here. Something dangerous."

"Something dangerous?" Ashley tilted her head. An odd choice of words.

Turning her attention back to the funeral procession, a line of cars with bright headlights moved slowly down the street towards

Evergreen cemetery.

An unexpected tap on the shoulder made Ashley jump. A bird-like man with an irritable strand of hair in his face stood there. He dragged hard on a cigarette.

"Man, this is one hell of a funeral." The stranger wiped the hair out of his eyes. "It takes a sick ticket to engineer a murder like that," he said and looked at her. "Friends of the family?" he asked. "It's a pleasure finally meeting you."

Ashley stared in confusion. "Do I know you?"

The stranger ignored the question. He took another drag on his cigarette. Dropping it in the street he tramped it out under his shoe and looked up at Keenan. "That's a fine-looking boy you got there. Is he yours?"

Ashley shifted her attention to her son. Keenan stared at the stranger. He was focused as a man wrestling with an alligator.

"Leave us alone," Keenan said with clenched fists.

The stranger grinned. His teeth were as crooked and brown as icicles in a cesspool. "That's not very neighborly. In fact it's pretty damn rude. That's not good for a kid. It makes for a hateful mind. I'm telling you. You don't want to make enemies with me."

Ashley pushed Keenan back into the car.

"It's been nice seeing you missy," he called after them. "You can bet your ass we'll meet again."

Turning the ignition, Ashley pulled out. Keenan's dream-like face looked out the window. The stranger stared frigidly back at him until the car rounded a corner and disappeared out of sight.

7

Dead Night

The room was dark when Keenan woke up. He had been driven from the barriers of sleep by a nightmare. He couldn't recall the face of the person in his dream but knew someone was in danger.

Keenan sat up in bed. A leaky spigot dripped in the bathroom. A windup clock on the nightstand ticked evenly. It was almost midnight.

"Dead Night," he whispered under his breath.

The boy slid out of bed, fully clothed. He didn't stuff the sheets with pillows to make it look like he was sleeping. If his mother came in and lifted the covers, she wouldn't appreciate being bamboozled by a thirteen-year-old kid. A bad situation would get worse real fast.

Silent as a mouse, Keenan tiptoed down the hall. He froze solid as ice when a floorboard creaked. The boy had an impulse to snag a leftover chicken wing from supper out of the refrigerator. However, rather than risk making more noise he slipped out the backdoor.

———

A full moon cast a pale glow over the quiet streets. Stars shimmered; a thousand twinkling eyes, watchful and alert.

Keenan stood in the dewy grass of the backyard. He shuddered when he caught a glimpse of a white sheet left out on a neighbor's wash-line. It flapped hauntingly in the wind.

The thought crossed him about the murdered girl found on Pisgah Mountain. The prospects of coming face to face with a killer on a dark street corner made him shake in his sneakers.

The sudden memory of the man that he and his mother encountered at Heather Gold's funeral earlier that day also raced in his head. He had no idea why but reasoned that the stranger presented a danger.

Shaking off grim thoughts, Keenan looked up and down the street. The night was bottomless as a great canyon. Fearful of the dark, he considered calling everything off and returning to the safety of his own bed. He instead pushed the gloom out of his head and continued to move on.

———

Keenan turned the corner towards the Lutheran Church when he caught sight of a police cruiser motoring down the road. A cop with a military haircut and a toothpick stuck in his teeth craned his neck out the window. Keenan ducked behind a green pickup truck until the steady rev of the car's engine faded down the highway.

On the move again, he picked up the pace. On South Avenue he made an abrupt halt near the black-barred entrance of the cemetery. Nobody was in sight.

"Pst."

Keenan jarred his head around. His imagination quickly outraced his thumping heart. He again thought about the murdered girl on the mountain. What if the killer skulked around the streets? He'd drag him off to some secluded place in the woods, that's what. Long before sunrise he'd be salted, cooked, and served for breakfast.

"Pst."

Keenan peered in the darkness. "Who's out there?"

"Over here." AJ's head popped up from behind a tombstone. The whites of his eyes blinked in the moonlight.

Keenan yanked at the gate's latch but it wouldn't budge.

"You won't get in that way," AJ whispered. "They lock it up at night so kids won't sneak in and disgrace the dead. You'll have to climb the fence."

Wedging his sneakers in the metal prongs of the railing, Keenan hoisted himself over the top of the gate. He brushed his knees off on the other side of the gate and stopped cold. "I hear something."

AJ leaned over a tombstone. "A car is coming. Ditch it!"

Keenan ran, fell and tumbled down a small hill. He crawled over to AJ on his hands and knees. Both boys sprawled out on the grassy lawn, motionless as unburied corpses.

A police cruiser came to a dead stop in the street. Officer Lebowski was on duty that night. He held a spotlight out the window of the car and shined it in the cemetery. Shadows of marble gravestones danced in the white light. Satisfied that no mischief was abroad, he turned off the spotlight and sped away.

"That was close." AJ wiped sweat off his cheek. "The cops are jittery ever since that girl got killed on the mountain."

Keenan shuddered at the thought.

"This way." AJ pointed.

Keeping low to the ground, they hurried deeper into cemetery grounds.

8

Old Benji

Keenan and AJ moved quietly across the burial grounds. Near the middle of the graveyard they came upon a large marble statue. A carved figure of a tall and brooding man stood atop a granite pillar. Its stony eyes looked both sleepless and alert.

"You're late." Tugger popped his head up from behind a tombstone. He held a lit candle and dripped melted wax into his hand.

"The cops are patrolling," said AJ. "Ever since that girl got murdered they're ready to shoot someone."

Tugger stopped chewing a wad of gum and stared. "Don't talk about that," he said. "I can't get a lick of sleep for thinking about it."

"Are you afraid?" Becca asked. She leaned back and sat cross-legged in the grass.

"Of course not."

Becca sniggered. "That's it, isn't it. You're a pussy."

Tugger blew out the candle and stuck it in his pocket. He shot the girl an awful look. "Now you're being an ass. Who put a snake down your shirt?"

Becca quieted down. "Sorry Tugs. I've just been a little irritable lately."

Tugger eyed her carefully. "Are you in love or something?"

"That's crazy," she answered.

"Then you must have stuffed your bra." He sniggered.

"Stop it!"

"Wait a minute." Tugger's eyes lit up. "I must be an idiot." He slapped himself in the head.

"Shut up Tugger."

"Don't you guys get it?" He looked at AJ and Keenan.

"I said shut up!"

"She's having her period!" Tugger announced and raised his hands triumphantly.

Red faced and cheeks puffing, Becca took off her shoe and whacked Tugger repeatedly over the head. It took both AJ and Keenan to pull her off him.

"She's crazy!" Tugger hid behind his friends and pawed at a lump on his head. "I told you she was having her period. It makes women go crazy like that. Even my dad said so!"

Settling down, things grew quiet again. Becca sat on the edge of a tombstone. She looked miserable but at least she stopped crying, Tugger noted. He hated when girls cried. It was easier stomaching them when they were angry. Then he could pick on them without much of a conscience, but when they turned to tears?

"Just like a woman," Tugger mumbled. "They take the fun out of everything."

Finally, AJ plunked down on the ground. He put his hands behind his head and sprawled out in the grass. The sky shined a thousand stars and a big yellow moon. "Are you guys gonna sit here like corpses all night?" He blew a bubble and popped it in his mouth. "Hey Keenan." He glanced at the kid. "You're awfully quiet. You got a frog stuck in your throat?"

Keenan said nothing. His mesmerized gaze never shifted from the large statue in front of him. "That thing looks almost real," he said. "You'd swear it's staring at us."

"That's Jeremiah Benjamin," said AJ. "Old Benji for short. Rumor has it that when the moon gets full, he climbs down from that stone pedestal and searches for a woman who murdered his brothers.

Tugger shivered. "Jeez AJ, don't go telling that story again. I'm jumpy enough with a killer on the loose."

AJ pushed himself up on skinned elbows and grinned

mischievously. "Everyone loves a good ghost story. I think it's a great idea."

———

Sitting Indian-style in the grass, AJ turned on a flashlight and shined it spookily on his face.

"Years ago, there was a rich coot named Old Benji. He lived up on Rhoon Hill with his two brothers," AJ said. "One night, drunk in a bar, he met a woman named Aggie Black. Most people called her Dirty Aggie because she slept around and wasn't even fit for the company of hogs.

"Benji washed, spoiled and combed her something awful. Before long he asked her to move in with him. Still a woman like that could never be faithful. She whored around at night and even had the gall to bring local barflies home when Benji was out playing poker with his friends."

AJ leaned forward. "Now Old Benji's brothers were dumb but they weren't idiots. One night they heard a ruckus in the bedroom and flung the door open. Sure enough, Aggie Black was having an orgy and tussling under the sheets with some drunken bums. Benji's brothers kicked both her and her cronies out into the streets, skin naked. Glad to be rid of her, they slapped their hands together at a job well done.

"Aggie, however, was a vengeful woman," he said. "Not long after she came back with a butcher knife. She cut both their sorry heads clean off and hid them someplace on Rhoon Hill."

Tugger shivered and shifted uncomfortably in the grass.

AJ continued, "When Old Benji came home later that night he turned zombie white when he found the two headless stiffs. Neighbors saw Aggie Black running from the murder scene. Police searched the grounds but never found her or his brothers severed heads."

Keenan looked up at the statue towering over him. "What happened to Old Benji?" he asked.

AJ sighed. "Knowing that the heads of his dead brothers were somewhere on the property slowly tore away at Old Benji's sanity. He even told one of his bar buddies that one night he woke up to find the heads resting against his shoulders and snoring soundly.

"Then one day, rumor has it, he looked in the mirror. He swore he saw his brothers' ghostly faces staring back at him. Benji cracked completely. Grabbing a shotgun and laughing wildly, he stuck the barrel under his chin and pulled the trigger. The cleanup crew said the back of his head was splattered like greenish frog eggs thrown against a wall."

Becca grimaced.

"As was his request, Old Benji took his share of the family fortune and had this statue erected."

Keenan stared at it in wonder. "It looks almost alive."

AJ squinted. "Maybe it is," he said. "Rumor has it that when the moon gets full the statue comes to life. It climbs off the pedestal. Wanders the streets. People say it's the ghost of Old Benji. They claim he's still searching for Agatha Black, the woman who killed his brothers. If you look close enough, you can see the statue's marble eyes moving in their stone sockets."

Tugger jumped up as if bitten by a wasp. "I saw them move!"

"What?" AJ blinked.

Tugger pointed. "The eyes moved! They were staring at me as if I were a pig roast or something."

"That's crazy." AJ sniggered.

"I'm telling you I saw it," Tugger insisted. "If you don't believe me go ahead and laugh."

Everyone laughed.

"Stop laughing!" he said angrily.

"Calm down big fellow." AJ snorted and Keenan chuckled.

"You know what?" Tugger pointed an angry finger. "You guys are nothing but a bunch of piss-ants. I'm going home." Red cheeks puffing, he stormed off across the graveyard and out of sight.

AJ stood up and called, "Tugs, come back! We were just ribbing you. Tugger?"

Becca stood up and peered into the darkness. "He's really angry this time."

"He'll get over it," AJ said but abruptly turned his attention to the fence near the cemetery entrance.

A spotlight flicked on. It shined in the graveyard. Officer Lebowski had them directly in his sights.

9

Something in the Night

"Freeze!" Officer Lebowski waved a spotlight over the tombstones. Combat excitement painted his face. He chewed fiercely on a toothpick clenched in his teeth.

Keenan's jaw dropped. "He's gonna blast us!"

Gun in hand, Lebowski vaulted over the cemetery fence and ran straight towards them.

AJ raised his hands. "We're just little kids. Don't shoot!"

However, the cop had no interest in the antics of mischievous children. His attention was drawn elsewhere. Hidden in the shadows, something crouched down behind a crypt.

Keenan turned to look. Whatever haunted the night, it took on an appearance that looked like the stone pedestal of Jeremiah Benjamin. Its grayish face glowed with contempt. Shifting forward, it moved towards the boy.

"Run!" Keenan shouted.

Becca tried steering around a tombstone but stumbled. Clutching at her bum leg she struggled to escape.

"Come on!" AJ clutched at Becca's waist and he hurried towards the exit. Running beside them, Keenan turned around and gasped. The darkman gained ground, his face riveted with rage.

——

Waving his gun, Officer Lebowski fired off a shot. The bullet ricocheted off a grave marker, inches from the darkman who quickly veered left.

"Hands up!" The cop shouted. He searched the darkness for a clear target but nobody was there. The suspect had vanished into a thin line of trees that led up the mountainside.

Officer Lebowski hurried back to his police cruiser and picked up the receiver.

"Lebowski to base. Are you copying me?"

"Lebowski?" Chief Gunner's voice crackled over the receiver. "What's going on?""

"I'll tell you what the hell the problem is," he barked back and ducked behind the open door of the car. "There's a goddamned maniac running around the cemetery. It could be that guy who killed the girl up on the mountain. Wake up the cavalry. We need the state police."

———

Down the road and hidden behind a hedge, the company of three struggled to catch their breath.

"Did you see that?" AJ's heart beat like a hammer. "For a minute it looked like the statue of Old Benji. Then it changed. I know it must have been my imagination but I swore a long scar unfurled down its cheek." He turned towards Keenan. "It was headed straight for you."

Shivering, Keenan stared down the street. Police lights flashed in the distance. "I've seen him before," he said.

AJ tilted his head. "What do you mean?"

"I had a nightmare. I remember that face."

"You're talking crazy."

"Maybe, still I doubt that we've seen the last of him," Keenan said and looked at Becca. "You just about got away."

Becca rubbed her knees. "I wouldn't have made it if AJ didn't help me." She unexpectedly turned and kissed him on the cheek.

AJ crinkled his nose and pawed at his cheek as if a wasp had landed on it.

"Where did that come from?" he asked. "That's a horrible

thing to do to someone who just saved your life."

Becca laughed. Still a shadow of hurt haunted her eyes. AJ pretended not to see it. After all, he was much too thickheaded to admit that he liked being kissed, particularly by Becca.

"What about Tugger?" Becca changed the subject. "Do you think he made it home okay?"

"He should be fine," said AJ, eyes continuing to probe the darkness. "We better all go. Stay on guard," he warned. "That thing is still out there."

Dispersing in different directions, Keenan cut through a neighbor's yard. With one quick look across the darkened landscape, he sneaked back in the kitchen door of his house. Creeping upstairs, he slid back into bed. Restless dreams haunted him all through the night.

10

Vagrants

Tugger plodded up the road and looked around the streets. Even under a full moon the town was buried in darkness.

"Dirty scamps," he complained bitterly as he crossed an alley. The boy's cheeks puffed a brilliant shade of red. His friends had made a regular mockery out of him. If he wasn't so hungry, he would have marched right back down the cemetery and walloped AJ for being a wiseacre.

Tugger turned on North Avenue and took a shortcut through the woods. It was dark. Any trace of stars grew obscured by trees; their branches stretched across the murky sky like long arms of rotted bone that reached into the night.

The kid gasped when he heard the flutter of bat wings beating against leaves. The airborne night rats, blind and sightless, perched themselves quiet as sentinels around a lonely street lamp on a winding road near the bottom of the trail.

For an instant Tugger thought he saw glittering green eyes studying him from a distance. Pulling out a flashlight stuffed in his trousers, he shined the light in the trees.

"AJ? Is that you?" he whispered.

Outside of the wind the world remained silent.

The boy squinted in the dark. His father sometimes warned him about *The Willies*, not that he took much stock in it.

"They're out there hiding in the night," he once said when he caught him sneaking out after dark. "The Willies are mean as bulls. They thrive on kids that tell lies. When they catch them?" He moved his face close. "Let's just say it's a real bad day in hell."

Tugger shook the gloom off his shoulders and kept moving. Farther down the path it became simpler to see. Stars burned bright as a stream of distant lighted candles; they shined down between the trees dispelling some of the mysteries of knotted darkness. Twice he stopped when he heard rustling noises in the bushes that turned out to be small packs of rodents scavenging the ground for food.

"Nope." His heart beat faster. "No Willies out here."

Tugger hoisted himself over the trunk of a rotted tree. Suddenly he halted. He swore something grunted. It didn't sound animal or human. It just sounded plain dangerous.

The boy picked up the pace. Finally, he reached the end of the trail and turned into an alley where houses came back into view. He thought he heard noises again. Something kicked at loose gravel like a shoe being dragged over macadam.

"AJ!" he shouted into the darkness, cocksure that his friends were ribbing him. "Stop playing games. It'll be the death of us all if we get caught slinking around after midnight."

The scraping noise grew louder. Something moved in the shadows. It was near a garbage dumpster outside of the Diligent Firehouse, just across the road.

"Tugger," someone whispered.

Shifting anxiously from foot to foot he answered, "Who's out there?"

"Tugger," someone whispered again, louder this time.

A dim street lamp cast a faint glow on a stranger. Dressed in a dirty greenish shirt, the vagrant's eyes remained downcast and fixed on the ground. In the stagnant air an awful stench like the black ghost of death hovered all around him. Taking a step forward, his foot again dragged in the dirt, ever closer.

"You there, shush!" Tugger waved a fat fist. "You'll wake the dead with that racket. Did AJ put you up to this?"

For an instant the vagrant looked up. His eyes appeared gnawed down to hollow sockets. When he smiled his teeth were weathered as gravestones in an ancient burial ground.

Tugger rubbed his knuckles in his eyes. When he looked again the apparition disappeared but the vagrant still stood in front of him.

"You don't look so good mister," said Tugger. "Are you sick or something?"

The vagrant said nothing. He clenched his fists and stared at the kid..

"That's enough now," said Tugger. "It's late. I've got to be getting some shuteye."

A mechanical grin constructed across the vagrant's face. It was the smile of an inexperienced actor, a little tight and unnatural. "I don't think so. You're coming with me."

"I already told you," said Tugger. "I got to get in the house." He started to leave but the vagrant knocked him over with an outstretched arm.

Hitting the ground with a thud, Tugger got back on his feet. He started running but his assailant grabbed him firmly by the neck.

The vagrant's putrid breath settled in Tugger's nostrils. "I said you're coming with me."

Keeping a firm grip on the boy, he marched the kid through the darkened streets.

Frightened and speechless, Tugger stumbled along beside his captor. Several times he tripped over rocks and his own clumsy feet. He wondered when AJ and his mad gang of friends would come charging down the road and the insanity would stop. The joke had gone way too far. In fact, it was outright scary. It was like... like...

"The Willies," his father's words echoed in his head.

Keeping a tight hold on the boy, the darkman rumbled through the night, hastening his pace.

11

The Gates of Sleep from the Inside

Even as he slept Keenan knew he was dreaming. He floated in clouds. The colors of a rainbow were all around him. Then almost as if a rug had been yanked out from underneath his feet, he began to fall.

Bulleting out of the sky with breathless anticipation, Keenan landed in water. An ocean stink of salt and fish flooded his nostrils. He glanced at his feet as the tide sucked at his toes. The water raced back out into the ocean like an enormous pool of liquid glass.

Staring skyward, a black stain on the horizon came into view. It moved slowly towards him and gobbled up sunlight as it advanced. Black as night, something big was on the way.

"Help!" a frail voice called from behind a clap of thunder.

Keenan looked closer but his eyes couldn't penetrate the storm.

"Someone please help me," the voice echoed in the wind.

———

"Faster!" the darkman ordered.

Dragging Tugger along by the arm, they hurried towards a wooded area that led to a path on Pisgah Mountain.

"I said hurry." He gripped the back of Tugger's neck. "If anyone sees us, we'll be caught like two skunks in a garbage can." Picking up the tempo, his face grew more determined with every footstep.

Tugger stumbled alongside the darkman like a spiritless

puppet. This had to be a cruel joke, no doubt engineered by AJ and his friends. Any minute they would come dashing out of the darkness and save the day.

However, the madness showed no hint of an ending, at least a happy one. Skulking through alleys and side streets, the darkman turned left down a path and crossed the freshly cut grass of Sam Miller's baseball field. Beyond the field stood a wall of timbers that rose high in the murky sky and led up the side of Pisgah Mountain. Dusted with grey clouds, the moon cast a sunken yellow glow over its somber parameters.

"Please mister. Listen to me," Tugger pleaded and tried to pull out of his captor's clench. "I need to go home."

If the darkman heard him, he didn't answer. A malicious grin painted his face. He stared into the onrushing night all the while Tugger, his captive audience, was pulled deeper into the realm of a dark and unstable world.

The boy's heart drubbed with rattles of weariness and fear. What began as an apparent prank had quickly evolved into a fiasco of terror. Where were the police or even his friends when he needed them?

"Giddyap!" the darkman shouted again.

Tugger sensed that he wasn't only in trouble. He was in danger. He needed help. Bad.

———

Keenan listened again.

"Please help me!" A weak voice called from somewhere within the guts of the approaching storm.

Stiff fists of swirling winds punched the air. Rifts of impenetrable fog carpeted the ground. The sand grew fiery hot against Keenan's feet. Black as death, smoke poured into the air in thin reeds that rose into the sky. The ocean sizzled almost as if the water's surface turned to butter dissolving in a hot frying pan.

The storm quickly blanketed the ground. Gasping, Keenan

tried to run but the sand became pools of oozing mud, hindering every step taken.

"It's nothing but a dream," he told himself.

Looking from side to side he searched for an exit, a secret door that would lead his wandering soul back to his bedded flesh. Once there he could awaken peacefully in the land of the living.

"Help me!" a distant voice cried again.

Keenan craned his head around. He tried to take a step forward but black sludge encrusted his feet up to his ankles. He began sinking in the muck. Still for an instant he stopped and looked again. Like a lantern wagging on a faraway ship trapped in turbulent waters, he thought he saw someone in the storm.

"Someone please help me!" The speck of light flickered between black schisms of darkness.

Keenan struggled to see into the storm. Someone was caught inside the gale, alright. They were going down. Sending out a distress signal.

Still he couldn't see the face.

———

With one quick look across the landscape. Tugger's captor dragged him into the dark timbers of Pisgah Mountain.

Clammy sweat broke out on the kid's skin. His sneakers dug into loose soil as they climbed the mountainside. They hurried across the land, a prisoner and his captor, forgotten soldiers on a deserted battlefield. Slapping against twisted branches they finally approached the mountain's summit. The pinnacle was little more than a barren stretch of flatlands breached with large cavities and rocks; the excavations of coalminers who worked the land many years ago.

The darkman abruptly turned left towards a dense bank of drifting trees that climbed the mountainside. Behind a small ridge, hidden from the sights of civilization, a lonely opening of a cave awaited their arrival.

"Inside," the darkman ordered.

Tugger stumbled in the cavern and crinkled his nose. The cave stunk of musty air. Drips of foul water fell from sweating rocks. A dying fire crackled in the corner of a grotto; its red ash cast an eerie glow over the cold walls. In the far corner of the cave sat what looked like a dead animal, perhaps a rabbit or raccoon slaughtered into a careless bundle of dried gore.

Shivering, Tugger finally found the courage to speak. "Maybe we should be heading back home. We can always finish this riddle in the morning. You must be getting hungry. We had scrapple for supper. I could snag a few slices of leftovers from the refrigerator," he offered, thinking the way to his captor's heart might be his stomach.

The darkman snickered but said nothing. He reached behind the carcass of the dead animal and pulled out a knife. The blade was stained with something crusty and dark. Leaning forward, he wedged it into the hot coals of the fire.

"Willies," the darkman mumbled.

"What?" Tugger's heart jumped.

"Isn't that what your father told you?" He stared at the boy. "The Willies would get you if you didn't watch out."

Dread painted Tugger's eyes, still he held firm. "There's no such thing as The Willies," he announced.

"Isn't there?"

For a frozen instant Tugger swore he saw fangs, red as blood, unravel from the darkman's mouth. Closing his eyes and opening them again, they were gone. The boy shifted his eyes towards the knife nestled in the fire. He wondered if there was enough courage in his young guts to grab it.

"Don't even think about it!" His captor spun around, almost as if reading his mind.

"I wasn't doing anything. Honest!" Tremors of fear shook in Tugger's voice.

The darkman bent down. The steel of his knife glowed red from the smoldering ash. He held it an inch from Tugger's eye.

"You want me to slit you open from ear to ear?" Grabbing a clump of Tugger's hair, he pulled his head back and settled the knife close to his throat. "Stop whining and shut up," he ordered.

Fear pooled up on Tugger's face as he stared into the cold sights of his captor. "Please Mister. I just wanna go home."

The darkman raised the knife again but abruptly stopped. He swore someone shouted the words, "Over here!"

Confused, he looked around the shadowy corners of the cave. No movement. It didn't appear that they'd been followed. Still he was certain he heard something. A trespasser was abroad. Like the quiet steps of a master thief, someone must have slipped inside the cave and gone unnoticed.

"Over here!" a voice echoed again.

The darkman pushed Tugger to the dirt. He whirled around but saw nobody. The voice came from everywhere and nowhere all at the same time, almost as if the walls decided to start jabbering.

Bending down, he yanked Tugger up by the shirt collar. "Do you hear that, you little shit? You had us followed!" He threw him back to the ground.

Tugger listened. He heard nothing except the sound of his heart rapping against his chest.

The darkman let out a fierce cry. He stalked the lightless cave from corner to corner, searching for an invisible enemy.

"Over here!" the voice again sounded out.

Pounding a fist on the wall, the darkman screamed, "Where are you!"

———

Asleep in his bed and locked in a nightmare, Keenan watched as a distressed young victim called for help. His cries were haunted as the somber storm surrounding him.

"Hurry!" Keenan waved his hands in the air. "Over here!"

Hard and fast winds whipped Keenan's face. He doubted his own capacity for survival. By the time the morning alarm clock sounded, he reasoned that he'd be gone, somewhere underneath the earth and tramping around the country of the dead.

A sensation of falling suddenly overcame him. He began drifting back from the land of dreams, almost as if his body were a marsh constructed of human flesh.

"Please help me," the frail voice continued to call from within the storm. It sounded weaker this time. Much weaker.

"Over here!" Keenan shouted again. He reached out his hand, hoping that by some miracle he might pull the victim out of the dream from one world to the next.

The storm pulsed. Swirled as if it were a hot covered pot of tomato soup. Suddenly it exploded. A downpour of rain, blood red, slapped the ground in buckets. Keenan swore he saw black clouds overhead morph into the shape of lean jaws. They snapped like a wild dog, ready to crash down on him.

Keenan covered his head.

"Help me!" a weak voice continued to call out.

Glancing up into the storm, Keenan caught sight of a small shadowy figure. Lightning flashed. It cast a sudden and stark glow over the perishing figure. Leaning forward on hands and knees, Keenan looked into the storm. He thought he saw a face. He thought he saw...

12

The Willies

Tugger's mouth dropped open. Something dreadful began to hatch from his captor's already gruesome hide. A suitcase stuffed with sullied laundry, all the dirty little secrets spilled out on the floor. The kid swore the darkman grew inches right before his eyes. Wet with corruption, a grisly scar unfolded down the side of his pale cheek.

"Tricked me, didn't you?" He shook a firm fist. "You want to see the Willies? I'll show you the Willies." He sniggered.

Tugger backed up. Tripping over a rock he fell to the ground. The darkman looked down on him with eyes pitted in badly bruised sockets.

"We've only just begun here." He licked the edge on the blade of his knife. "It's your turn to taste it." He grinned at Tugger and lunged fiercely at the boy.

"Willies!" Tugger shouted.

Springing to his feet the boy darted left towards the cave's exit. His foe slashed the air with the knife. Tugger ducked. Running, he fled into the dark of the forest.

—

Tugger raced through dense brush. Branches splintered as he trampled fallen leaves. Finally, he stopped and hid behind the backside of a tree trunk. In the near distance he heard the angry grunts of his captor barreling towards him in hot pursuit.

Everything turned suddenly quiet. The boy peeked around the

corner of the tree. No movement could be seen.

Listening again, he thought he heard something. It was quiet. Faint. Instead of the loud crash of branches breaking or heavy boots pounding the forest floor, it sounded somehow even more frightening. A single twig snapped from the opposite side of the tree.

"Willies!" his captor shouted. Reaching an arm around the tree trunk he latched on to Tugger's shirt.

Tugger gasped and wriggled loose. He fled down the mountainside. Once his foot got tangled up in weeds. He tumbled down a rocky hill. Quickly getting up, he rubbed his aching knees and looked in all directions. An ocean of night, waters uncharted, stood before him.

Frightened but determined, Tugger splashed across a small stream that led to a densely wooded area and an open stretch of land. Huge quarries pocked that part of the mountain. It looked like the forgotten ruins of ancient kings. Breathing hard, he hunkered down behind a large stone and curled up in the darkness.

The distant sound of footsteps grew closer. Gloom overshadowed his heart. There were no clear roads to escape. Directly to the right of him stood a sizeable cliff. To the left was what appeared to be an old mining shaft. The opening had been nearly caved in. He was alone in an alien world, as good as dead.

"Tugger curled up and crossed his fingers. "Don't let there be Willies. Please don't let there be Willies."

Tying courage around his heart, Tugger inched his way through the forest. However, a long arm and callous hand suddenly emerged from behind a rotted tree and knocked him flat on his back.

The darkman grinned like an alligator. He grabbed Tugger by the scruff of the neck. Pulling a knife out from underneath his belt, the edge of the blade glinted in dull moonlight. He scraped it against the boy's throat.

Smiling, the darkman said, "Welcome to the land of the Willies."

13

Awakenings

Keenan woke with a start and bolted straight up in bed.
"Tugger!" he cried and stared into the darkness.

14

The Guy in the Green Cougar

Ashley Braddock's heart flinched when she seen the green Cougar roving the streets. She saw the car twice that morning. It sat at a parking meter when she exited the bank. Later it motored up the alley while she hung wash on the line. Dropping a letter in the corner mailbox, there it was again.

The woman recognized the driver; the same man who confronted her and Keenan at the funeral of the murdered girl found on the mountain. Seeing him alone didn't frighten her. It was the way he looked at her with those heavy-lidded eyes.

Slowing the car down, he flicked a cigarette out the window. Checking her out from toes to hairpins, he smiled and hit the gas, disappearing down the road.

The guy gave her the creeps. Hurrying in the house she locked the door. Keenan sat cross-legged on the floor. He stared blankly at a cartoon on the television.

"Is something wrong?" she asked.

Keenan said nothing.

Ashley waved her hand in front of the TV. "Did you hear me? Earth to Keenan."

"What?" Keenan shook himself out of a trance.

"You were shouting in your sleep last night," said Ashley.

Keenan hesitated. His mind drifted to a dark dream that woke him in the middle of the night. He recalled someone disappearing inside a big storm.

"Just a nightmare," Keenan said.

Ashley walked to the window. She peeked out from behind closed drapes. There were no signs of the green Cougar. "I'll put some eggs on." She ruffled his hair. "See you in ten minutes."

——

Keenan didn't recall much of anything else that morning. Sometimes it happened that way. He had visions. Glimpses as he liked to call them. He'd blackout and slip into a dream world. When he woke up, he remembered little that transpired in the moments he lost touch with consciousness.

However, he did recall the dream that haunted him last night. There was a bad storm. Someone had been in trouble. He couldn't see a face. Then the mist cleared. He recognized the person. It was Tugger, his newfound friend, being swallowed up.

Shaking off the effects of the dream, Keenan walked outside to collect his thoughts. A quiet wind blew in his spiritless eyes. Looking at the ground he saw something glinting in the sun. He reached down and picked it up. At that moment a car drove up the alley. The driver rolled down the window.

"Hey dude." The man in the car stuck an elbow out the window. "Looks like you found yourself a keepsake." He pointed at the object glinting in Keenan's hand.

Keenan stared, his mind drifting in a fog.

"What's wrong, you been smoking some of that wacky shit?" The stranger grinned. Reaching in his glove compartment he pulled out a small plastic bag. "Try some Columbian buzz. One sniff of this and you'll be on planet nine." He flipped the handle of the passenger door and pushed it open. "Come on son. Climb aboard my starship."

——

Ashley went limp when she looked out the kitchen window. A glass of water slid from her hand and shattered on the floor. The man in the green Cougar returned. He was outside talking to her son. Bolting out the door she ran down the sidewalk and pulled

Keenan away.

"Morning missy." He grinned and waved from the car window. "I see you made it back from the funeral alive."

Ashley's heart pounded savagely. She turned to look at Keenan. His eyes, bolted on the stranger, were electric. Even the man in the green Cougar shifted uncomfortably in his seat, almost as if backing away from a dangerous voltage.

"What do you want?" Ashley's eyes narrowed.

"Just being neighborly," he answered. His expression remained dry and lifeless.

"Go away." Ashley tightened her grip around her son. She glanced down at her hands and noticed that they were shaking. "My husband is in the house."

"Is he?" The stranger pulled out a cigarette, sparked a lighter and lit up. "That's nice." He took a drag. "That's real nice. Why don't you go get him?" he said. "Go ahead. Get him." Lifting his head, he blew a thin line of smoke in the air.

Ashley swallowed hard and held her ground. "Leave us alone. If you don't, I'll call the police."

The stranger laughed. He tapped his fingers off the side of the car. "Chill out honey. No laws are being broken here." He pointed a finger at Keenan. "You're even starting to spook the brat."

Ashley glanced at Keenan. War and horror painted his face. Even the man in the green Cougar scratched his chin uncertainly. "What's wrong kid? You look like you just swallowed a golf ball."

Slipping from his mother's grasp, Keenan walked straight towards the car and pointed an accusing finger. "MUR-DER-ER!" he shouted, every syllable pronounced crisply as a whip.

"Keenan!" Ashley pulled him back.

The stranger's face turned black with contempt. "We'll be talking again soon." He reached over and slammed the passenger door shut. With one last look he quickly drove off.

———

Keenan shivered as the green Cougar motored away.

"Are you okay?" Ashley asked. Bending down she held the boy's wrists. "Can you hear me? Keenan!"

The dense fog overshadowing the boy's face lifted. "Mom?" He blinked uncertainly.

Ashley looked down the road again. "Who was the man in the car? What did he want?"

"What man?" Keenan asked.

"We spoke to him at the funeral. He…" Ashley stopped short.

Keenan looked at her with befuddled eyes.

It must have happened again. The boy had a blackout. It wasn't the first time. She touched his forehead. "You don't have a fever," she said. "How do you feel?"

"Jeez mom, people are watching." The kid blushed when the mailman went up the street.

Another car drove up the alley. Ashley's heart jumped. It was only the Collins boy from down the street. Blaring music, he gunned the car as he passed by, a disinterested look on his face.

Ashley sighed. Pushing Keenan towards the house she suddenly stopped. Something glinted in the boy's hand. Taking it from him, she held it up in the sunlight.

"Where did you get this?" she demanded.

"I found it."

"Found it where?"

"In the yard."

She shook Keenan's shoulders. "Don't lie to me."

Keenan backed up. "I'm not lying. It was right there in the grass."

Blood drained from Ashley's cheeks. It was a gold necklace. She turned it over in her hand and immediately recognized it. She bought it in Ocean City last year while on vacation. It was a present for Lisa, her sister. Her name was engraved on the back of the heart-shaped locket. Lisa wore the necklace all the time, even on that dreadful night of the murder when it mysteriously disappeared.

Until now.

15

Early Distant Warnings

Keenan slipped out of the house and sprinted three blocks. Racing passed the old Elementary School he headed down Center and Pine. An icy chill gnawed at his bones. He couldn't help recalling the dream that plagued him in the middle of the night.

Not far up the street a police cruiser parked in front of AJ Samson's house. Its rotary lights sparkled in the morning sunlight. A serious looking cop hung outside the door and jabbered over a radio.

Standing on the porch, AJ watched as the police officer climbed back into the car and pulled away.

"AJ!" Keenan shouted and raced up the street.

AJ turned and looked at his friend. "What are you doing here? Didn't you hear what happened last night?" He paused and whispered. "Tugger never made it home. The police are going door to door asking questions."

Keenan's mind drifted back to the dark dream that invaded his sleep. "Listen. Tugger is in trouble."

"What do you mean?"

"I think that thing we saw in the cemetery has him."

AJ stared and swallowed hard. "You're jumping to conclusions. Maybe he ran away from home. It wouldn't be the first time."

"I'm telling you he has him," Keenan said. "I had another dream last night. Call it a glimpse from the corner of my eye. It was about Tugger. He needs help. We don't have much time."

AJ raised an eyebrow. "You want me to believe all this just because you had a nightmare?"

"You're gonna have to trust me. I told you before," said Keenan. "My dreams have a way of coming true."

AJ sucked at his lips thoughtfully. If Keenan was lying, he put on a stellar performance. But dreams that came true? It seemed like a reach.

"We need to meet again tonight," Keenan insisted.

"I don't think we can…"

"We have to!" Determination cemented Keenan's eyes. "You've got to believe me. If we don't do something, Tugger is as good as dead."

AJ hesitated. Opening the door to his house he said, "Let me think on this."

"Wait!" Keenan shouted. "Your wrist AJ. Be careful and watch your wrist!"

Tilting his head curiously, AJ disappeared inside his house.

———

Nobody ate dinner that night. AJ grew steadily worried about Tugger's whereabouts. Stories of Keenan's bizarre dreams didn't help matters. The kid's dark visions drifted in and out of his head like the restless ocean tide.

By 6:00 p.m. there was still no word on Tugger. The police even made another sweep of neighboring houses to see if they could gather any information.

"I was on duty last night," Officer Lebowski told AJ's grandparents. "I saw kids in the cemetery. Someone else was around too. A big guy. Brutish looking. I took a shot at him but he disappeared in the woods." He turned a suspicious eye to AJ. "What do you know about all this?"

"Nothing," AJ gulped.

Finally, AJ went upstairs and paced the floor. Tugger had all the courage of a mouse stuck in a cage of cats. Something must have gone terribly wrong.

"I have dreams. Sometimes they come true." Keenan's shadowy voice

echoed in AJ's head.

At about 8:00 p.m. AJ sneaked outside and looked in Jimmy Grace's toolshed. Tugger once skipped school and he found him sacked out under a green tarp draped over a lawnmower's handlebars. Today however, there were no signs of the kid.

On the way out of the toolshed AJ tripped over the lawnmower. He went down like a hammer on cement. The fall bent his wrist straight backwards. For a minute he feared the bone snapped. However, gritting his teeth he found that he could still move it.

"Your wrist AJ. Watch your wrist!" Keenan's voice echoed in his head.

Yup, she was sprained alright, just the way Keenan said it would be.

———

AJ picked up the phone at about 8:30 p.m. and dialed a number.

"I thought I'd be hearing from you," Keenan answered.

"We meet at midnight." AJ's voice trembled through the receiver. "Only this time instead of the cemetery, head for the castle."

"I'll be there," Keenan said and hung up.

16

The American Hotel

Street-lamps clicked on just after dusk. Barring a steady drone of electric that filtered in transformers along telephone poles, the avenues lingered in silence. It was late.

Ashley Braddock crouched down in the front seat of her car outside of the American Hotel. She reached in her glove compartment and pulled out the gold necklace. Keenan found in the yard. She squeezed it hard in her fist.

The necklace was her sister's. It went missing on the night of her murder. Now, three hundred miles away, it made a grand entrance. The logistics didn't add up. Someone wanted her to find it.

———

Earlier on she sent Keenan to his friend's house and went to her job at the Sunrise Diner. A long shift for sparse waitressing tips. Still before the day ended, she convinced herself how crazy the idea sounded that someone deliberately put the necklace in the backyard. Keenan had been close to his aunt. Perhaps he took it as a keepsake and was afraid to tell her.

As for the guy in the green Cougar, she saw her share of lonely creeps and drifters during the late shift at the diner. He probably just needed some company.

The issue had been put to rest. Then on the way home from the diner she spotted the green Cougar parked in front of the

American Hotel. A sudden vision of her sister rotting in a windy graveyard on the other side of the state snapped in her head. Ashley had been parked in the front of the American Hotel ever since.

———

Twirling her hair in damp fingers, Ashley stared mutely at the second floor of the hotel. A shadowy figure moved behind a curtain. She considered going down to police headquarters but it wouldn't do much good. The boys in uniform would likely pass her off as another frightened woman jamming the 911 lines, spooked by the murder of the girl on the mountain.

"You found a necklace in your yard and you think there's a killer hunting you?" The cops would smirk. In the end they might haul the guy in for questioning. Maybe even ask him not to leave town just to appease her. It didn't matter. If he suspected the police were closing in, he'd slip away on an unguarded highway.

Ashley turned her attention back to the lone-lit room on the second floor. Twice he stepped out on the terrace and looked wearily up and down the street. For a minute the girl thought he spotted her. Flicking a cigarette off the balcony, he walked back in the room.

Just down the street a gruff looking man with a baseball cap staggered out of a bar and towards the car. Bending over, he pressed his stubbly chin against the passenger window. He opened his mouth to say something but closed it again and then wobbled up the street. Clutching at her heart Ashley breathed a sigh of relief.

The girl's eyes widened when she looked back up at the second floor of the hotel. The stranger's room had turned dark. A dismal thought slapped her. Could he have seen her watching him?

No.

Yes.

No.

(Maybe)

The front door of the hotel opened. Someone walked out.

Ashley scrunched down in the driver's seat. It was the man in the green Cougar.

If he spotted her, he showed no signs of it. Lighting a cigarette, he stepped off the porch and sauntered down the street into The Molly's bar.

Ashley stared at the doorway of the tavern. Uncertainty bit at her thoughts. If only she knew his name. At least she'd have something concrete to tell the police. Grasping at thin reeds of courage she climbed out of the car. Looking up and down the sidewalk, she hurried across the street and slipped through the front door of the American Hotel.

———

A clean-cut teenager, probably a first-year college preppie, was seated at the front desk of the lobby. Chewing on a piece of stale gum he paged through a sports magazine. A telephone rested under his jaw as he fooled with his girlfriend on company time. He looked up when Ashley opened the door, more annoyed with the prospects of her intrusion than the idea of getting bagged for screwing off.

Whispering something in the phone the kid put the receiver down and shoved the magazine under the desk.

"Excuse me." Ashley smiled thinly. "I need some help."

The desk clerk looked tiredly at her and cracked a wad of gum.

"I wonder if you could tell me the name of the man who just left."

The kid said nothing. He eyed her skirt up and down.

Ashley glanced at the door. She wondered how long it would be until the stranger came trudging back up the street. "We're old friends. At least I think I used to know him," she said.

The young clerk impatiently tapped a pen on the desktop. Pausing and if for no other reason but to get rid of her, he flipped open the registry. "Harry Grimm, but I shouldn't be doing this lady. It's against company policy. He even left a message not to be disturbed. Besides, he just walked out. You had to see him go."

"He's not checking out?" Ashley asked with alarm.

The desk clerk crinkled his nose. What the hell. Did she think that he was the guy's mother? The college brat ran his sights up and down Ashley's skirt. His gaze settled briefly on her breasts and then again met her dark eyes. The shadow of a wrinkle had started to settle around them. Still she wasn't bad looking. Probably in her late twenties or early thirties. Judging by the way she was sweating the broad must have been awfully horny. For all he knew she was Harry Grimm's private backdoor screw in the woods. Yeah, he knew about stuff like that. Maybe they were gonna engage in some sick sex games that the older cronies played. He could hardly wait to get back on the phone and tell his girlfriend this one.

"Hold your shirt on lady." He smirked. "He'll be right back. He said something about going to the bar for a six-pack and some cigarettes."

Ashley's eyes widened. Turning quickly, she hurried out the door.

"Hey," the desk clerk called after her. "Any messages?"

Ashley disappeared in the dark.

"Crazy freaking woman," the college preppie mumbled. Pulling the magazine back out from underneath the counter, he picked up the telephone and dialed his baby's number.

———

Ashley hurried out of the hotel but stopped in the middle of the street. Mists of confusion washed over her face. Something was wrong. Out of place.

Missing.

"The green Cougar," she whispered to herself.

The stranger's car was gone. While she stood inside talking to the clerk he went for a ride.

"Keenan." Her voice inflated with dread.

Racing to her car she started the engine and skidded around a corner, down the road.

17

Goldilocks Rocks

Getting in the car and driving up the road, Ashley pulled into the Olympian Drive-In. She left Keenan at AJ Samson's house, earlier in the evening. Pulling out her phone, she placed a call. AJ's grandmother answered the phone.

"They were here awhile ago but they're gone now," she said. "Probably sneaked out the bedroom window," AJ's grandmother said angrily on the other end of the line. "Your son Keenan was with him, so no doubt they're together."

Ashley turned three shades of pale. Her worst fears were suddenly confirmed; the boys were missing.

"There's nothing to worry about," AJ's grandmother said. "They'll come home soon enough. You know kids. It isn't the first time AJ sneaked out after dark. They're troublemakers." She paused. "Hello, Miss Braddock, are you there?"

———

Ashley hung up the phone. Gunning the car's engine, she sailed down the road and veered right on Center Avenue. Pulling in her driveway she quickly exited the vehicle.

The evening was secretive. The air, dormant and thick. A dog chained to a wooden coop in the neighbor's yard gave a lonesome moan. Ashley looked around. She feared that she might find the man at the American Hotel awaiting her arrival. However, there was no trace of him.

Rushing up the sidewalk she peered through a window on

the side of the house. The place looked dark. Unmoving. She jiggled the handle on the front door. It was still locked, thank God. Fumbling with her keys she opened the door and stepped inside. The rooms were shadowy. Dark. The refrigerator hummed and the clock ticked on the wall. Everything appeared normal.

"Keenan?"

No response.

Ashley walked in the front room. She reached to pull the drapes closed but stopped cold. A cavity of despair caved in on her chest. She didn't see it before. The green Cougar. It was parked up the street. The car's dull hood glinted off a streetlamp.

"Harry Grimm," she whispered breathlessly.

Ashley eyes shifted over the dark panels of the room.

"Don't let your head go ballistic," she told herself. *"Keep calm. Check if Keenan is in the house. Then dial 911."*

A faint breeze fanned the back of her neck. She whirled around. The living-room window was wedged open. Summer curtains flapped tiredly in the breeze.

Ashley pushed back a mat of hair that fell in her face. She studied the unmoving shadows of the darkened room. In the house. The bastard was in the house! She reached for the phone to call the police but stopped short. If Harry Grimm heard her dialing the cops and he had her son, he might panic. Do something desperate.

"Think Ashley. Think." Her mind clicked into high gear.

Hurrying into the kitchen she pulled a steak knife out of a drawer. Gripping it tight, her hand shook fiercely. She walked to the bottom of the staircase. Every creak of a floorboard detonated in her ears. Taking a deep breath, she began to climb.

———

Ashley turned left at the top of the hall. She suspiciously eyed the dark corners of the corridor.

"Easy Goldilocks," she told herself. *"You left the window open this morning while you were cleaning. Nobody is here."*

Walking down the hallway she stopped at the door of Keenan's room. Peeking inside, nothing moved.

"Keenan?" she whispered.

Ashley looked closer and sighed. Buried in a faint light of the moon that brushed through the window, Keenan rustled under blankets. His shallow breath haunted the paneled walls.

Ashley crept into the room. She tucked the covers tight around the kid. Her fingers traced the outline of the sheets. It took less than a second to realize her mistake. The person under the covers appeared far too large to be her son.

"Ok Goldilocks, who's sleeping in this bed?" a voice in her head asked.

A hand shot out from under the blankets and grabbed her throat. Ashley raised the knife. The perpetrator seized her wrist and twisted it. Gasping, she dropped the weapon.

"I told you we'd meet again." Harry Grimm smiled greenly. "Enough talk." His grin faded. He tightened his fingers around her throat. "Where's the boy?"

The question caught her off guard. Her eyes shifted around the room. Keenan must have never come home.

"I don't know," she answered.

"Stop lying," he said. Picking up the knife he raised it to her throat. "I can make the kid an orphan in zero point two seconds."

"I already told you," Ashley said. "I don't know where he is."

The cold blade of Grimm's knife probed her neck. "You want to die?"

Grabbing his arm boldly Ashley locked her teeth into his wrist and crunched down hard. Grimm moaned. He dropped the knife.

Ashley raced out of the room and down the hall. Her assailant was already in pursuit, moving in fast for the kill.

She ran into the bathroom, slammed the door and bolted it. For a minute she put her hands over her ears and tried to stifle the sound of her own mounting terror.

Things grew quiet on the other side of the door. Too quiet. Maybe she scared him off. Frightened him away. A loud knock altered that train of thought.

Knock knock.

"Go away!" she shouted. "The police are coming."

Knock knock.

"Who are you?"

"It isn't Gaspe's Pizza," a muffled voice toyed from the opposite side of the door. "Open up."

Ashley rummaged through the medicine cabinet. She tossed everything on the floor in search of a means of defense. Outside of a dull disposable razor and a hairbrush, there were no viable means of defense.

Knock knock.

"Get out of here." Her trembling voice sounded less than brave. "I have a knife," she lied.

A delicate moment of silence and then the blast of a gun. The doorknob shattered. The door rolled open on creaking hinges.

The intruder stepped in. Holding the gun up, he blew on the smoking barrel. Grinning from ear to ear he coolly said, "But I have a gun."

18

Night Riders

Harry Grimm shoved Ashley into the driver's seat of the green Cougar and tossed her the keys. "You drive," he said. "I always did support that women's lib shit."

Ashley's hands trembled. Her frightened eyes looked into his cold ones. "What do you want from me?"

"Easy missy." He shoved a gun in her ribs. The icy touch of the cold barrel sent tremors over her skin. "I do the talking. That way." He pointed towards North Street.

"Calm down Braddock," Ashley told herself. *"Think straight. Don't submit to hysteria. Barricade the door shut. Stay focused. If you don't, you'll be dead."*

Ashley's thoughts drifted back to Keenan. How did he figure into the plan? If the boy was in the house and heard an intruder he might have fled. But where to? If nothing else Grimm still hadn't found him.

The girl looked out the window at the Mount Pisgah Hotel. A man with straggly hair and a wrangler jacket stood under a neon beer light. Leaning coolly against a beat-up Chevy he made small talk with a bleached blonde woman in tight jeans. Her halter top that punctuated her every delicious curve.

"If you're looking for help from him, forget it," Grimm said. "He's preoccupied with the idea of getting laid. Yup, guys like that are pretty damn egotistical. He won't remember the color of her panties ten minutes after he screws her brains out."

Tears misted up in Ashley's eyes. Her fingers gripped the steering wheel with white knuckled fists.

Harry Grimm asked, "So where's the kid's father?"

Ashley didn't answer.

"After all we've been through, you're giving me the silent treatment?"

"He's gone," she answered flatly.

"Gone where?"

Ashley went silent again.

"I think I get it," said Grimm. "You got pregnant and probably just out of high school You wanted the baby, but the father wanted his freedom. Men are pigs, right?" Grimm said indifferently.

"Why are you doing this?" Ashley asked. "What do you want from my son?"

"That's not important right now." He pointed. "Turn here."

Ashley veered right on Pine Street. Out of the corner of her eye she saw three small figures running across Sam Miller's baseball field. They were headed towards the woods. Taking a second look they disappeared.

The streets grew blacker with every passing moment. Like evil children playing in dark alleys under streetlamps, her rising fears chased each other in the shadows of her own worried mind. Danger sat only inches from her and on the same car seat.

Grimm pointed. "Turn up the backstreet. Behind the old Elementary School."

Ashley turned. The car's headlights bounced off ruts in the road.

Grimm's haughty eyes studied her naked leg, just below the hem of her dress. Keeping the gun tight against her hip, he reached over and probed her knee with damp fingers. Ashley shivered at the touch.

"Pull over," he ordered.

Ashley parked the car next to a dilapidated building surrounded by a grey fence. A faded sign had been crookedly nailed on the front door that read BLUEBERRY HILL, a name given by some of the local youths who cleaned the place up and turned it into a clubhouse. The structure was once used as an embalming facility for a funeral parlor. By the brutal look in her captor's eyes, the place would be re-opening for business before the night ended.

Ashley said shakily, "If it's money you want…"

"Money?" Harry Grimm laughed. "No, no money. Don't want your V either." He lifted her skirt with the barrel of his gun and examined her panties.

Ashley flinched.

Grimm's cold eyes bore down her. "I'm guessing a woman like you did some whoring around, right? I know the type. Loose women." An icy edge of hate dripped from his tongue. "If there's one thing I can't stomach it's a slut. My mother warned me about women like that. She called them molls. She said a moll would even screw a monkey for a dollar and a half."

Ashley searched for a light of mercy in the tunnels of her captor's darkened eyes but found none. In the end, escaping alive would be doubtful and unscathed, impossible.

The sound of an approaching engine rumbled up the road. Inside a shabby convertible a bunch of tanked up teenagers peeled their tires.

Grimm held the gun on Ashley's gut. He pulled her across the seat and pressed his hand over her mouth. The convertible sped by and out of sight. Ashley drew back in revulsion. She wiped at her face as if a nest of maggots festered on her lips.

Opening the door, Harry Grimm jumped out of the car. "Get out," he ordered. "Don't make any sudden moves. Stay quiet and you might stay alive."

Swallowing hard, Ashley slowly exited the vehicle.

———

Even with a full moon flying brightly overhead, the night was impenetrable. In the distance the sound of a locomotive whistle echoed in the valley, the clatter of railroad cars fading into the vista. On the opposite side of the road a path went up the mountainside. It was once used to haul coal deposits by miners in trolley cars and led into the heart of the forest.

"What are we doing here?" Ashley steadied her voice.

"Relax," Grimm told her and lit a cigarette.

"Don't rape me," she implored him.

"Rape you?" Grimm seemed astonished. "What kind of scum do you think I am? Rape you?" He lifted his arm and gave her a firm backhand, hard enough to knock the girl to her knees. "My mother raised me proper." He grabbed her by the hair and yanked her head back. "I like a clean woman. In fact, I used to know someone like that. Man. That bitch sparkled like a diamond. Sound like anyone you know? She used to wear this beautiful gold necklace. I kept it as a trophy after I killed her. Then it disappeared. I guess things don't last forever, right?" He grinned.

Blackness charted across Ashley's heart. Her worst fears were confirmed. It was no accident that Keenan found her sister's necklace in the yard. The executioner had put it there. Now he was coming for her.

"You killed my sister," Ashley said.

"Don't sweat it," Grimm advised. "Goddamn you're a feisty woman. Your sister was the same way. What was her name, Lisa? She didn't die easy," he said. "It took a bit of doing."

Rage suddenly washed over Ashley. Turning towards Grimm she lunged forward, fingernails aimed at his eyes.

Grimm whirled around and hit the side of Ashley's cheek with the butt of his gun. She fell to the ground. A trickle of blood dripped from her nose.

"Another trick like that and you'll become expendable," he reminded. "Rest assured missy. This isn't about rape, getting laid, or dead family members." He peered into the bleak forest. Dragging hard on a cigarette, he exhaled slowly. "You believe in monsters?"

Ashley didn't answer. Nor did she hear the question. Her sister lay dead in a graveyard. The killer stood in the wings, ready to strike again.

Harry Grimm threw the spent butt of his cigarette in the dirt and tramped it out next to Ashley's face. Leaning over he studied the girl with careful intent.

"You probably think I'm a real bad ass," he said. "So I killed your sister. Sue me." He shrugged. "Maybe you even think I murdered that girl on the mountain, but you know something? You're wrong. Dead wrong. The person that killed her is one crazy bastard. He got a natural hatred for anything that breathes. Nope," he said again. "This isn't about anything as simple as a sexual assault." He stood up straight and peered into the dark of the forest. "This is about hunting and you just happen to be the bait."

19

Meeting under the Stars

It was near midnight when Keenan Braddock made his way down to the old castle in the woods, flashlight in hand. AJ and Becca already arrived. Sitting on a rock ledge, a candle flickered and winked in their somber faces.

"I never realized how creepy this place was at night," AJ said.

Becca pulled anxiously at her pigtails. "What are we doing here?"

AJ answered, "Tugger didn't come home last night."

"I know. The police were around. He never does that," Becca said. "Something must be wrong."

AJ turned his head towards Keenan. "Go ahead. Tell her."

Keenan stuffed his hands in his pockets and kicked a rock. "I had a dream."

Becca tilted her head questioningly.

"It was about Tugger," said Keenan. "That thing that we saw in the cemetery. It has him. I'm sure of it."

Hesitating, Becca asked, "What if this crazy story is true? The police wouldn't believe us. What could we do about it?"

Keenan bent down on his knees and stared into the darkness. "I know where to find him."

"Where?" Becca blinked.

Keenan paused. "Pisgah Mountain."

Becca stopped twiddling her pigtail and stared. "That's where they found the murdered girl."

A hush fell over all of them. The haunting wind rustled in the trees.

"It sounds insane." AJ bent his sprained wrist and winced. After a minute he slapped his knee and stood up. "I'm not sure if I believe in dreams that come true or not but I'm always up for a good adventure. Besides, we can't leave Tugger out there. Count me and Taff in." He reached down and scratched his dog behind the ears.

Becca stared with eyes filled with dread. Finally, she stood up and nodded her head. "Then we go."

———

The small band of misfits walked along wordlessly in single file towards a path that led to Pisgah Mountain. Perhaps it was just fear pricking their skin, but mutterings of impending danger coupled with Keenan's foreboding dreams whispered like demons in their ears.

Keenan looked up at the starry sky and shivered. The journey they were about to embark on had all the twisted shadows of a knife's blade falling behind a curtain; the hand of doom could crash down on them all at any instant.

20

Brave Strangers

"Everybody ditch it!" AJ fell down in the dewy grass of Sam Miller's baseball field. Headlights from a car fleetingly passed over them and then faded down the road. AJ stuck his head up and gawked around. "All clear." He crawled off his knees and began running across the field.

Becca and Keenan hurried along behind him towards the brooding underbelly of Pisgah Mountain. AJ's dog Taff led the charge as they crossed a thin reedy path at the foot of the woods. A thousand crickets sang in the night air.

"Tugger is out there," Keenan said. "I can feel him."

Becca slipped an arm around her friend. "Don't worry," she said. "We'll find him."

AJ flicked on his flashlight. "Stay together. If you see something move, shout."

"That killer who murdered the girl on the mountain could be slinking around," Becca shuddered. "What if he finds us first?"

A devilish grin played across AJ's lips. Digging into his trousers he pulled out a surprise. "This is what we do." He eyed the shiny barrel of a .38 revolver.

"You brought a gun!" Becca drew back in fright, her knees knocking just a bit.

"I hooked it from my grandparent's house."

"You really think it'll come to that?"

"Who knows?" AJ snapped a twig off a birch tree and stuck it in his mouth. "At least if trouble knocks we'll be ready." He stuck the gun back in his trousers, shook his head smartly and squinted like a gunslinger looking into the sights of the sun. "Okay then." He took a deep breath. "Let's kick some ass."

———

Sticking their sneakers in the dirt they began the long hard climb up the mountainside. Traveling wordlessly, Keenan led the group by way of a sixth sense.

Hampered by a bad leg, Becca struggled to keep pace with AJ. His faithful dog Taff plodded alongside of them. More than once he reached down and rubbed the animal's head as if it were a magic lamp. With any luck it would help bring them all back home safely when the adventure finally ended.

Something in the forest made AJ abruptly stop.

"What is it?" Becca whispered.

"Up ahead on that ridge," he said. "I thought I saw something move." He spun around with the gun. Becca and Keenan ducked.

"Take it easy with that thing." Becca said. "You could kill someone."

AJ took his hand off the trigger and hoisted himself over the rotted trunk of a tree. "Relax," he said. "The safety is on."

Keenan's eyes shifted over the landscape. Struggling to see, he pointed into the misty darkness that led to a ridge cut into the mountain's highest cliff.

"That way, I think," he said.

The stars shined but were mostly hid behind the towering forest. Ripe with clusters of fat leaves, the trees rustled in the warm wind. AJ gasped when he thought he saw a large figure crouching in the shadows. He pointed his flashlight at it and exhaled.

"It's just a big rock. Scared you, didn't it?" He wiped a runner of sweat off his brow.

"Shush." Keenan stalled cold in the dirt. "Turn off your flashlight," he whispered.

The forest turned dead silent. Cryptic as the cold breath of a killer, the only noise heard was the wind whispering in the leaves of trees. Still the most menacing sound of impending danger did not come from the murky bowels of the forest but unmistakably from one of their own.

Taff began to growl.

———

The dog's eyes cemented into the darkness. A suppressed growl intent on warding off unwelcome guests emerged from deep within the animal's throat.

"Easy Taff." AJ trembled and held the dog's collar.

"Over there!" Becca pointed towards a backdrop of massive pines. "Something moved behind those trees."

"Are you sure?" AJ whirled around.

"It's just up ahead. Near the top of that ridge." Becca's unblinking eyes fixed on a shadow that crept silently from tree to tree. Noiseless as a black cat, it quietly moved closer.

"Maybe it's an animal," whispered AJ.

"That's no animal," Keenan leaned forward and peered into the darkness from behind a fallen tree trunk. His face burned with a distant and dream-like glow. Something out there was probing his thoughts. Opening them like the lid on a soup can and invading every secret crawlspace of his entranced mind.

And Taff growled louder.

21

Taff

Whatever foe stalked them moved steadily closer. Stagnant fissures of moonlight cast an eerie glow over the creeping shadow that meshed itself in the forest.

"Get down." Becca tugged AJ's shirt. "It'll see us."

AJ's sneakers were stuck firmly in the dirt. He leaned up on a broken log and peered into the woods, heart wedged in both fear and anger. "What did you do with Tugger, you slinking wretch!" He picked up a rock and hurled it.

Gape-mouthed, Becca stared at him. "Are you crazy? You'll give us away!"

Keenan's eyes widened. He backed up a step. The darkman no longer remained content to study the young heroes from a distance. Game time was over. Bursting out of a nest of tightly hemmed branches he rushed forward. A determined predator, he headed straight towards the children.

"Run!" Becca sounded off.

AJ stepped backwards and tripped over his own feet. He fell down hard on his knees but managed to keep his fingers locked on Taff's collar. The dog growled fiercely and tried to break free of the boy's grip. Twice the animal lurched forward with such strength that it nearly dragged AJ in the dirt.

Keenan refused to move at all. Near dumbstruck, the boy played captive audience to the heavy footsteps tramping the leaves and rushing towards him. Still Keenan wouldn't relinquish his position. His embattled face hung in a life and death struggle as if any wink of broken concentration would leave him defenseless.

"Shoot it. Hurry!" Becca pulled at AJ's arm.

"Easy Taff." AJ loosened his grip on the dog's collar and removed the safety on the weapon. That action would prove costly. In fact, it would haunt him until the end of his days. In that critical moment as fate would have it, his fingers accidentally slipped out from underneath Taff's collar.

—

"Taff!" AJ shouted. He leaned forward and dug his fingers in moist soil.

"Shoot it!" Keenan implored his friend.

"I can't." AJ's voice rattled with fear. "Taff is out there. I might hit her."

In the distance, paws thumped over bramble and weedy growth. Taff raced towards the intruder. Several times the dog veered off course, swerving around trees and dense brush. Aimed and targeted, the animal approached enemy lines. Battle was imminent.

—

The darkman stopped cold. He watched the young heroes hiding in the woods. They were brave but terrified. Gloom hung over their hearts surely as the black clouds of a rising summer storm.

There were also other threats, one of which approached from another corner of the forest. A dog raced towards him. The darkman grew stunned at its speed and aggression.

He pulled out a knife tucked underneath his belt but it was too late. The dog leapt in the air. With sudden fury its lean jaws sunk into the tender flesh of his shoulder.

The darkman stumbled backwards. He flexed a damp muscle and pushed the animal away. A thin reed of gory flesh like a shaving of uncooked bacon remained clenched in the dog's teeth.

Ramping up for another assault, the animal struck again with full force, this time digging even deeper.

The darkman let out a loathsome groan. He stumbled but quickly regained his balance. Fighting for control, finally he got a firm grip on the animal's limbs.

———

"Go get him Taff!" AJ waved a fist in the air and cheered the animal on. "Bloody his nose up and give him the worst of it!"

However, the worst came all too quickly and like so many heroes in the heat of battle, not according to plan. A sudden snap followed by a loud squeal cut through AJ's heart like an arrow dipped in blood. Everything went abruptly silent. In the near distance and silhouetted in moonlight, the dark figure stood in the woods and boldly glared at them.

"Taff?" Panic washed over AJ's voice. Rising to his feet he tried running to the dog's rescue. Becca and Keenan wrestled him back to the ground.

"You can't go out there," whispered Becca. "It'll see us." She gently rested AJ's head on her shoulder. Swallowing hard, she steadied her faltering courage.

AJ's tears fell against Becca's neck. Frightened and alone, Taff's mournful cries haunted the open trenches of darkness.

"It's moving." Keenan's head jerked. He looked around with eyes bright as searchlights. "Over there." He pointed.

Swift as fire in a windstorm, the darkman took flight. He hurtled himself through the woods and headed straight for them.

"Shoot it!" Becca shouted.

Tears stinging his eyes, AJ stood up and raised the weapon and tried to get off a shot. The darkman batted the kid away like a spiritless puppet. The gun flew from his hand. AJ tumbled down a rock hill and came to a sudden halt against the withered stump of a tree. Groaning, he clutched at his ribs.

Becca tried scrambling away but escape proved impossible.

Black as night and probing her every move, the darkman glared at her with soulless eyes.

Searching for a morsel of empathy in her adversary's presence, Becca backed up and stared. However, any rivers of compassion that might have once existed were now a waterless desert.

Grabbing the girl by the arms he pulled her off the ground and studied her closely. He pulled at her arms like a cruel child intent on shredding the wings of a fly. The young girl's inflexible bones were less than an instant away from snapping at the joints.

"No!" someone suddenly cried out.

So strong and spirited was the voice that the dark visitant dropped Becca almost as if receiving a stern command. Painted with brutality, his beastly eyes glared at the young hero standing in front of him.

It was Keenan.

+

22

The Enemy Within

Terrorized but unscathed, Becca curled up in the weeds. Scattered in surrounding corners of enemy lines, she watched in silent awe as an unspeakable evil faced off against one of their own.

The intruder stood there, lips trembling with fury. Keenan's eyes misted over in an impenetrable gaze. Like David and Goliath caged in walls of iron, both contestants refused to give up their perspective positions. Concentration between the contenders was limitless.

"Brat!" the darkman hissed.

Keenan clenched his fists. He stared with unwavering eyes. For an instant he grew woozy. His knees buckled. The darkman crept inside his head, prying the lid of his thoughts open. Keenan felt himself spiraling towards a head-on collision. When the fusion of minds ultimately happened, it had the force of a freight train hitting a steel wall. Keenan jolted backward on impact.

———

Keenan floated. The cold sea of the darkman's thoughts circled all around him; ravens in a graveyard.

He found himself in a dark place. Emotions of war ran rampant and any hint of peace that may have once existed had long ago faded into rumor. Much like a rotted corpse in the dead of winter, an arctic chill of hate had settled in for the duration.

"Don't fight me," warned the darkman. "You'll only die harder."

Still the boy refused to mount a retreat. His eyes were sharp. Targeted. Nailed to his foe tighter than the lid of a coffin. The naked wind moaned in the trees, almost as if the elements themselves were making a hasty retreat from battle.

The darkman took a step towards the boy.

"Get back!" Keenan shouted in a commanding tone. His expression grew so intense that even his friends covered up in fear.

Driven backward by the slap of an invisible hand, the darkman reversed his stride, wobbled and fell to one knee. Letting out a ferocious cry he quickly got back up and charged forward.

Keenan stiffened and refused to back down. But even the mysterious powers that rested in the boy's foreboding mind couldn't halt the attacker's fierce assault.

"Run!" Becca tugged at Keenan's arm.

However, Keenan remained immobilized. His dogged vision played host to a brutal enemy. Only inches before the hand of doom fell AJ grabbed the gun off the ground, bolted forward and pushed Keenan out of the way.

"Take this!" he shouted.

AJ fired the gun. A succession of bullets ricocheted off rocks and reverberated in the night. His finger continued clicking the trigger long after the gun chamber had been emptied.

23

Shot In The Dark

Harry Grimm and Ashley Braddock stood near the bottom of the mountain. Shots echoed in the valley. The woman's heart skipped a beat at the sound of the blast.

"We got company." Grimm's face stiffened. He fingered the trigger on his weapon. Leaning into the car he pulled out a spotlight wired into a cigarette lighter. Flicking it, he shined it into the woods. "Come on my friend. Show yourself!"

Ashley looked at her captor. His eyes studied the mountainside as if to remove them the trees might come to life, reach out and swallow him up.

She considered making a run for it. However, fear overrode the attempt to escape. Furthermore, she wouldn't get far. Grimm had a gun. He wasn't afraid to use it. If she tried to run, he'd shoot her. Leave her bleeding remains buried in forest leaves; dry bones for homeless dogs to gnaw on.

Staving off dread, Ashley stood up. She took a step backward. That plan didn't go far. Her captor whirled around and seized her by the back of the neck. He locked the barrel of the gun underneath her chin.

"What's wrong? Don't you want to stay for the show?" Grimm tightened his grip. After a moment of consideration, he said, "Scream."

"What?"

"You heard me. Scream. Loud. Wake the fucking dead." He jammed the gun tighter under Ashley's jaw.

Ashley looked at Grimm, her eyes wet and pleading. "Please."

She issued a last request. "Don't hurt my son."

Grimm yanked her head back hard. "I said scream!"

Opening her mouth, she let out a wrenching cry. Her shrill voice carried through the air like a shot in the dark, shattering every corner of nightfall.

———

Harry Grimm scanned the dark timbers. Picking up the spotlight, he shined it on a winding trolley path that led up the mountainside. Within minutes they heard footsteps.

An open gate of excitement emerged on Grimm's face. Locking an arm around Ashley, he held her in front of him like a human shield.

"That's right pal," Grimm said. "Remember me? I brought you a present." He held Ashley tight, his fingers ripping at her hair. "I got a Moll. Come on down. We'll party like the old days."

Ashley's heart beat faster. She peered into the woods. In the distance the sparkle of green eyes flickered. Someone headed straight for them.

"Tell me something sweetheart," Grimm said in her ear. "What do you see?"

"What?"

"Tell me what you see!" He grabbed her face and held it.

Ashley stared in the dark. Illuminated by the spotlight's glow, a small boy emerged from the woods. He hurried down the darkened path; a storybook character who just vaulted off the page of a novel.

"It's a boy," she told him.

"Really?" Harry Grimm mused. "All I see is monsters," he said. He raised his weapon and took aim.

"For God's sake!" Ashley struggled to loosen the grip of her captor. "Stop!"

However, Harry Grimm had little concern with lost and troubled children. Nor did he appear curious about why a young teenager might be running around in the woods after midnight.

Grimm's only interest was murder. A malicious grin on his face, he angled the weapon to a precise degree. The thug was determined to get off a clean shot; one that would finish the job.

"A little closer." He targeted the boy racing down the path as if he were a clay duck.

"No!" Ashley cried.

Twisting around, she rammed a knee in Grimm's groin. He buckled over. The gun flew from his hand. It skidded across the road. Ashley grabbed it. Rolling on the ground she quickly got back on her feet. A crimson rush of fear and rage flooded her cheeks.

"Don't move!" she warned.

Windless horror crossed Grimm's face. His eyes froze on the dark figure emerging from the forest path. "Shoot, damn-it!" he shouted.

"He's just a boy," Ashley said.

"That's no boy. You're only seeing what he wants you to see!"

Ashley leaned over. She grabbed the spotlight. Shining it on the wooded path, her heart suddenly crackled with dread. Something was wrong. Terribly wrong. What appeared to be a young boy only moments ago now transformed into a portrait of trepidation. The person rising out of the darkness grew tall. Stocky. A moat of sweat and a long scar cannibalized his face. Spatters of blood on his neck and shirt showed that he had already faced a battle.

Harry Grimm quickly got up. He grabbed the gun from Ashley's hand.

"Eat this." He pulled the trigger at point blank range.

The darkman buckled as a bullet grazed his arm. Impact was close enough that a sprinkle of blood drizzled on Ashley's blouse. He quickly veered left and hurried back into a wall of trees that lined the mountainside.

"Giving up so easy?" Grimm shouted. "Chicken shit!" He fired three more shots. "What's wrong?" He grabbed Ashley by the throat. "You want me to kill her for you?"

Catching her captor off guard, Ashley elbowed Grimm in the

ribs. She wiggled free and dashed across the road. Vaulting over a shabby grey picket fence, she fell to the ground with a thud. Grimm whirled around. He fired off another shot. The bullet splintered a wooden fencepost, inches from her head. Quickly crawling behind the sparse cover of some garbage cans, she crouched down. Stagnant as petrified wood, she held still and silent.

Harry Grimm stopped cold. In the near distance police sirens wailed and zoomed up the Main Street.

"I'll be back," he whispered. "I'll do you the same way I did your sister." He turned the gun from one side to another. Finally, the barrel settled in on the garbage cans. "Bang bang, your dead."

Ashley braced for impact as she waited for a bullet to burst through the metal exterior of the trashcan and burrow itself in her racing heart. Instead the thug twirled the weapon in his fingers and hastily moved off. Jumping in the green Cougar, he revved the engine and peeled out. The tailpipe of his car bounced off a rut in the road as he disappeared around a bend in the alley. Seconds later two police cruisers barreled up the road.

24

Fallen

"What happened?" Becca blinked in the darkness. "Keenan?" She looked at her friend.

Shivering at the joints Keenan stared into the night. His vision remained fixed on the somber forest that only moments ago played host to a brutal enemy.

Becca shook his shoulders. "Keeenan. Snap out of it!"

Color suddenly rushed into the kid's cheeks. "Where are we? What…" He stopped short. Recalling the encounter with the rival in the woods, he plunked down in the dirt and rubbed his fingers through his hair. Turning his head, he asked, "Are you okay AJ?"

AJ climbed up a rock embankment and pawed at his ribs. "That thing in the woods really caught me good but I'm still alive." Looking around he said, "Taff?"

A weak sound haunted the forest. It was barely audible. Somewhere in the darkness, AJ's dog whimpered. Its cries grew fainter with each passing instance.

AJ crawled forward on his hands and knees but Becca latched on to his arm.

"Don't make a move," she said. "That thing still might be out there."

AJ's lips trembled. He stared into the gloom. A shadow of tears fell across his eyes. He listened to the mournful sounds in the forest as his mind drifted back in time.

———

It happened on a winter night. Edna and Marko Samson were returning home from a skiing trip in the Poconos. The car hit an icy patch. It spun out of control. Smashing through a guardrail, it landed in a ditch down an embankment. There were no survivors.

After the accident AJ went to live with his grandparents. He fell into a shell of emotional isolation and welded the lid shut. The boy reasoned that he could never love anyone again. It just hurt too damn much.

Eventually AJ started talking. Things were okay just as long as the conversation didn't get too personal. Still he had an angry streak in him. Once he fired a rock through Spike Becker's front window on a dare. He got a spanking from his grandfather but as usual, he shrugged it off.

AJ shrugged everything off.

That all changed on the morning of his eleventh birthday. He woke up to find a puppy in a cardboard box sitting next to his bed. He wanted no part of the dog. He even told his grandma that he'd take it to Beasty's Pet Mill where they'd give it the gas like most unwanted mutts. Yup, AJ figured the furry little scrounger would bring him nothing but trouble. After all, it was love at first sight.

———

AJ's change of heart came on a warm open-windowed night. School had just let out for the summer. That's a great time for kids or at least it should be. Sitting alone in his bedroom, he listened to children laughing in the alley. They played shadow tag. He started thinking about things. Stupid things, like fishing down at the river or picnics at the lake with his parents. Those were good days and the memories always pinched his heart. Burying his head in a pillow, AJ began to cry.

Then wouldn't you know it? That little nuisance of a mutt plodded in. After three tries the pup hopped on the bed. It snuggled a wet nose next to AJ. Licked his face. From that day forward, they were the best of friends. Where you found one, you found the other.

AJ wasn't always the most open person when it came to spilling his guts. Still on the day when he fell in love with that dog he loosened up, and on a dark night in 1993 in a lonesome forest swollen with fear, he cracked altogether.

———

"Taff?" AJ rocked back and forth on his heels.

Up ahead in a patch of heavy brush something moaned. The sound tore at all of their emotions like old denim.

AJ looked at his friends. A tear fell down his cheek as he faced the terrible truth. "Please," he begged them. "I don't want Taff to die all alone."

Keenan swallowed a lump in his throat bigger than a box of marbles. "Let's go."

Trudging through wild vines, AJ shined his flashlight in the brush. A tremor dropped down the cliff of his spine when caught sight of something.

"Taff!"

Illuminated in the sunken glow of light, Taff curled up on her side in the bushes. The dog's defenseless eyes rolled up to look at her master.

AJ fell to the ground. He curled the dog's head up on his lap.

"You'll be okay Taff. I promise," the kid said with damp eyes. He stroked the animal behind the ears. Pulling a biscuit out that was stuffed in his pocket he stuck it in front of Taff's nose. "Now you eat this girl. Go on," he insisted. "You'll feel better. Eat it."

However, the dog had it bad. Taff couldn't move let alone eat. Shallow breaths rose and fell in short raspy gasps.

Leaning down, AJ put his head against the animal's face. His wounded eyes looked up at Becca and Keenan as he searched for an answer, any answer, that would spare his dog's life. Finally, AJ stood up and wagged a stern finger. "You get up now Taff, you hear me? Get up!" he ordered, hoping that will, and will alone, would lift the animal to its feet.

Even in certain misery Taff tried to obey. Bucking once or twice, she struggled but couldn't move. A long moan escaped the dog as it conceded the issue.

"That's okay girl." The corners of AJ's lips drooped into a half moon. He reached down and stroked the dog. "We'll rest here for a while. Then we'll go home."

But the damage was done. Taff was dying. And of course, there may be only one thing worse than death, that being the waiting. The watching. The inevitable finality. The awareness that there is no deed, no wish, no amount of money, no anything that can reverse death's lethal blow once it has struck.

Keenan bent down on his knees and pet Taff's head. "What do we do now?"

A shadow deeper than the night fell over AJ's face. He reached in his pocket and pulled something shiny out. "One bullet left," he said.

"No!" Becca cried, staying his hand. "You can't just shoot her."

"She's suffering." AJ set the dog's head down on a bed of leaves. He stood up and with trembling hands, loaded the bullet in the chamber. Taff lifted her head off the dirt. Her eyes never wandered far from her master.

"Don't look at me that way," AJ said sternly and wiped a tear from his eye. "It's for your own good. I always knew you'd come to be trouble. I knew it."

Still the dog refused to turn away. A lonely soldier boarding a train bound for some foreign field of death, Taff insisted on that last glimpse of the one she loved. The dog even managed, if ever so slightly, a wag of the tail.

AJ's heart burst in that moment. He threw the gun on the ground and fell to his knees. "I can't do it," he cried and folded his arms around the dog. "Please God." He raised his eyes up to the stars. "Please help my Taff."

And as if to receive an answer from the mysteries that rest in the heavens, the dog nuzzled itself against AJ's cheek. With one labored breath her eyes slowly closed and Taff slipped away.

———

The company sat quiet for a long time. AJ cried bitterly as he cradled the dog in his arms.

It was Keenan who finally broke the circle of silence. Crawling over to a small clearing, he picked up a rock and began digging a hole for their fallen friend. AJ and Becca soon joined him. Within the hour they had put Taff to rest in the bed of the forest. Pulling out some twine stuffed in his pocket, AJ tied two broken branches together to make a cross that he set at the foot of the grave.

After a while AJ's face turned from remorse to bitterness. He stared into the bleak darkness as the wind whispered in the trees.

"I'm going to get him for this," he swore. "I'm going to get him if it's the last thing I ever do."

Becca put an arm around her friend. "Tugger is still out there. I say we finish what we started." She turned to Keenan who nodded in agreement.

Gathering their courage and with a last look at their fallen friend, AJ, Becca and Keenan set off into the gloom. Their emotions smothered in fear and hearts standing in courage, they walked into the night to face the unknown.

Part Two

THE AGENCY

25

Sam Cage

At the same time as Keenan Braddock and his friends faced off against dangers that their hearts never imagined, Sam Cage jiggled a piece of ice in an empty glass of rum at Tiger's Alehouse, about thirty miles away.

Cage wasn't a barfly. On the few occasions that he drifted into Tiger's a bartender named Mackey who could charm the socks off the ladies (not to mention panties) usually stood behind the bar.

"You should take it easy on that stuff." Mackey pointed at a glass of Bacardi. "You're looking wrung out these days. Maybe you got some troubles. Want to talk about it?" The barkeep glanced at the clock. "It's almost closing time. Last call?"

Cage motioned for another round. A distant glaze hung in his eyes. Mackey tipped the bottle of rum and poured another double over melting ice.

With the exception of a petite Mexican senorita whose curves loitered against a pool table and waited for a late-night fiesta with the barkeep, the place was empty.

"I'll be okay." Cage took a sip of rum. A wrinkled sheet of stress ran across his forehead. "Maybe I'll crank the jukebox up and play that song that always breaks my heart. You know which one I'm talking about?"

Mackey tapped his fingers on the bar. He knew, of course. It was a song by Patsy Kline. Cage beat the hell out of it on the record machine every time he walked in the place. "I guess I can manage to sit through it once more. Besides, you're the only reason I keep the damned thing on the jukebox. My treat this time." He pulled a quarter out and tossed it to the Mexican girl. "Maria, toke up the music box. B5 is the magic number."

Maria flipped her hair saucily over her shoulder and stuck the quarter in the slot. In the dim lights of the quiet bar, Crazy began playing through the speakers.

It was the fourth time that night that Cage cranked up the tune. It reminded him of an old high-school sweetheart named Leona Smatters. He hadn't seen her in years but thought about her plenty. That came as no surprise. After all, it isn't every day that you come face to face with a ghost.

———

Life had been caving in on Sam Cage of late. The avalanche started about five months ago and the rockslide hadn't stopped ever since. He barely slept in weeks. Even when he did, he tossed on the sheets all night. Nightmares prodded him into the deep and often sleepless hours.

Looking up, Mackey fooled with the little Mexican dish over in the corner of the bar. He whispered something in her ear that made her giggle.

Cage's thoughts again drifted back to Leona Smatters. She died years ago and was buried six feet under. He still missed her terribly. Leona was the only girl he ever loved. By the way things were going these days, she would also be the last.

Cage took another swallow of rum. He wasn't a drinking hero, but tonight he'd drink. He'd drink to forget the horrors that roosted like ravens on the brittle wires of his tired mind.

The song on the jukebox ended.

"That's a wrap." The barkeep forced a smile. Walking over he pulled the plug on the Wurlitzer. The neon-colored lights blinked off. "The saloon is officially closed partner. I hate to scrap you out the door like this, Sam, but you understand." He glanced over at the spicy damsel who polished her face with a hand mirror in the muddy light. "You're not driving tonight, are you pal?"

"I'll be fine Mackey." Cage rubbed his temples. "My house is just up the street." He pulled a twenty out of his wallet and tossed it on the bar.

"Hey! That's a wad of green for someone who practically tossed you in the parking lot," the barkeep said.

Cage stood up. "No problem. Who knows when I'll see you again."

For that matter, Cage thought, who knew if he'd even be alive tomorrow.

Opening the door Cage walked out of the bar. He glanced around just in time to see the neon beer light flick off. Mackey and the young Mexican girl embraced in the shadows of the musty window as the barkeep reached out and pulled the shutters closed.

———

Outside the streets were empty. The only sound was Cage's shoes clicking against the sidewalk coupled with the pounding of an ever-growing migraine.

Turning the corner on Center Street, he stopped at the front door of his apartment. A slight wind mussed his hair on an otherwise warm May evening. Turning the key in the lock, he stepped inside the apartment. The rooms were dark. A mechanical drone from the refrigerator purred in the kitchen. A pendulum from a clock in the living-room struck 2:00 a.m.

Flicking on the hall light he climbed the stairs and went into the bedroom. Too tired to remove his clothes, he plopped down on the sheets and ran his hands over his eyes.

For an unguarded second the bloodless face of Leona Smatters' long dead corpse flashed in his mind. Hell, he hadn't even fallen asleep and the ghosts were already growling.

"Take it easy friend," he told himself. *"There's nothing out there. Maybe there'll be no nightmares tonight. With any luck the little bastard running the projector in your head will crash the film and the entire movie will be taken out of syndication."*

Still his thoughts were of little comfort. Even as he shut off the light and his eyes grew heavy, he could hear the tape rewind in his head.

Soon he'd be dreaming. Transported back in time. Five months back in time. That was the night that life crossed over into the red zone. It threatened to blow up in his face ever since.

As Sam Cage's eyes blinked shut, the house lights fell. The projector flicked on and illuminated the big screen of his interior mind.

It was ShowTime.

26

Jonas Blackheart takes Manhattan

Sporting pork chop sideburns and humming an Elvis tune, Jonas Blackheart stood beside the cashier at Harvey's Quick Mart, a Manhattan convenience store.

On the morning of the incident Blackheart wore faded blue jeans, a button-down plaid shirt with the tails hanging out and penny loafers. Hell, he even had a plastic pen protector in his shirt pocket. The only thing really noticeable about him that tended to be out of the ordinary was the sawed-off shotgun in his hands, poised to strike.

Jonas was a big man, the kind you didn't want to come up against in a dark alley. After quitting college, he tried making an honest living doing menial jobs. They paid him piss poor wages with even more piss poor health benefits. Meeting the rent was impossible.

Despite it all, Jonas stayed on the right side of the law. But lately his mind had become a little unhinged. He began to discover other financial opportunities such as robbing all night liquor stores and gas stations. With as little overhead as a carton of shotgun shells, he could roll in the door, demand money at gunpoint and then disappear as mysteriously as he arrived. Yup, it's called easy pickings.

The real problem began when he started hearing voices. That's never a good sign.

Finally, one morning he woke up and something snapped. He decided he had enough of the entire goddamn capitalistic system. Before leaving his house for work that morning, he pulled out a shotgun stuffed underneath his bed and tossed it in the backseat of his car. Instead of heading to the job he took a detour that landed him at the First National Bank. Wearing a dirty green woolen beanie on his head, he walked in and threatened to kill everyone unless they gave him all the money. Afterwards the crazy son-of-a-bitch stopped at Harvey's Quick Mart for coffee and cigarettes. A Congo line of police cruisers longer than the escort on OJ Simpson's white Bronco followed him into Harvey's parking lot. Jonas quickly got out of the car and ducked inside the store.

"Ladies and gentlemen," Jonas announced and cocked his shotgun. "Welcome to Harvey's Quick Mart. I'm hoping to have your full attention today." He pulled the trigger and blew a hole in the ceiling.

Over by the bread aisle, a frightened women and a little boy holding a chocolate ice cream cone crouched down on the floor. A teenager with a nose ring and a weepy girlfriend stood next to the coffee island. There were also a couple of big galoots, one standing by a lottery machine and wearing a construction hat. Behind the counter by the cash register a young man held his hands over his head.

Outside the building, police cruisers with blaring lights pulled into the parking lot. Cops ducked behind vehicles with guns pointed at the door. It was gonna be a real good day in hell.

———

"Hey man, are you the manager?" Jonas asked the guy behind the register and glanced at his nametag. "Roy is it?"

Roy nodded fearfully.

"How about a pack of smokes Roy? Make it menthol lights." Jonas threw a five spot on the counter.

Roy shivered so hard his teeth chattered. He pulled the cigarettes out of a rack and handed them over. Jonas glanced at the NO SMOKING sign in the window. Giggling, he flicked a lighter and lit up.

"I'm gonna level with you Roy." Jonas puffed hard all the while keeping a firm grip on his shotgun. "Nobody needs to get hurt here. I mean you're just trying to do some shitty minimum wage job, right?"

Stiff as a rock, Roy stared at him with big eyes.

"The thing is you got to understand my position Roy." He blew smoke in the air and looked around the room. "I got cops up my ass and hostages all over the place. These bastards would love to cut my throat right about now. Some of them might even crack under the pressure. Think of the logistics Roy," he said. "If one of these people loses it, I'm gonna have to shoot them. That means people would get killed. Think about it. That'd be on your watch. You don't need that kind of drama, you know what I'm saying? These people need to be convinced to do the right thing," he said. "That's where you come in Roy. I'm counting on you, my man. Get my drift?"

Roy shook his head. "Yes." He stuttered. "I mean yes sir."

"That's the spirit!" Jonas puffed hard on his cigarette.

"You want the money from the register?" Roy finally asked.

"No money Roy. Trust me," he said. "I just robbed the First National. I got enough of the green stuff to drink margaritas on the beach in the Caribbean for the millennium. What I need from you, Roy, is to convince these people to stay calm and not do anything stupid. You think you can handle that?"

Roy nodded.

"Listen up!" Jonas shouted and waved his gun. The woman with a little boy held her kid tight. The construction workers in the corner of the room who looked like they just stepped out of a Village People video clamped their fists tight. "As you probably surmised, we've got ourselves a situation," Jonas said and put his arm around the store manager. "Roy here has agreed to help me convince all of you to remain composed. We don't need any heroes, right Roy?"

"Yes sir." Roy gulped nervously. "Everyone just do as you're told. We'll get through this."

One of the construction workers took a slow step forward.

Jonas looked over at him and cocked the shotgun. "Excuse me, asshole? Are you listening to the instructions or should I paint the place red?"

The construction worker slowly backed off.

"Give that guy a banana!" Jonas shouted. "He's a team player, right?" He nudged Roy. "The problem is I'm still not convinced people are getting my message, including those police officers in the parking lot. My guess is that they need some positive reinforcement. What do you think Roy, any thoughts on that?"

Shivering in his shoes, Roy shrugged. "Whatever you say sir," he agreed.

"Cool beans. You're on my wavelength." He patted Roy on the shoulder. "The cops got a listening deficit. Sometimes those guys just need to be convinced. I'm guessing this is one of those times. You understand that, right Roy?"

Roy nodded.

Jonas grinned. "I'm glad we have an agreement."

Without hesitation Jonas put the shotgun underneath Roy's chin and pulled the trigger. The blast reverberated all through the building.

———

A spray of blood hit the convenience store window, right beside a 2 for 1 poster on an outdated hoagie rack. Screams of terror erupted in the building.

"Did you see that?" Behind a police cruiser Officer Brady stared through binoculars with a slack jaw. "The crazy bastard just shot the cashier!"

"What's he doing now?" his partner asked.

Brady squinted in the binoculars. The suspect grabbed a young woman who stood next to a boy with an ice cream cone in his hand. "He's got another one!" the cop jabbered on the radio. "It looks like he's headed towards the door. If you get a clean shot take him out."

———

Jonas Blackheart kept his shotgun tight against the woman's spine. Walking slowly behind her he opened the front door.

"Damn-it, it's the fuzz!" he shouted. "Looks like you're out of luck fellas. No free donuts and coffee for the men in blue today." Sniggering, he straightened up and jammed the gun tighter against the woman's back. "Now listen up," he told them. "We got ourselves a bad situation here. Roy the manager, God bless him, already got his head blown off trying to convince everyone to do the right thing. Don't even think about opening fire. I'll put a bullet through this woman's heart before you get off a single round." He stopped and said, "What's your name honey?"

The girl shivered. A tear rolled down her cheek.

"I said what's your fucking name?" He jammed the gun tighter against her.

"Melissa."

"Do you want to die Melissa?"

The girl shivered uncontrollably.

"I said do you want to die?" he shouted.

"No, please," she cried.

"You boys in blue here that?" Jonas shouted to the cops. "Melissa doesn't want to eat a bullet. That means I need a little cooperation, right?"

A policeman with a bullhorn leaned over the side of a car. "This is Officer Watkins. Take it easy," he advised. "Nobody needs to get hurt."

Jonas snorted. "It's a little late for that."

"I don't think I got your name," Officer Watkins said.

"Hey asshole," Jonas said. "I don't think I gave it to you. Besides, why would I tell you anything?"

"I'm just trying to help."

"What you're trying to do is get me to open this woman's skull with a shotgun shell," he said angrily.

"What do you want from us?" asked the cop.

"Call off the dogs and send the monkeys packing," Jonas insisted. "Leave a squad car. Make sure it has gas and guns. Lots of guns. I'll be taking hostages with me. I'll release them once I'm out of reach. If you follow me?" He tightened up the shotgun on the woman's back. "Things will get ugly, got it?"

Officer Watkins stopped to consider. "Whatever you want. We need you to show some good faith. Release some of the hostages."

Jonas sucked at his lip thoughtfully. After a minute he called to one of the construction workers standing over by the coffee island.

"Hey Mr. Wonderful. You with the pussy tattoos on his arm. It's your lucky day. Get out of my store and no shoplifting, damn-it."

The construction worker walked over. Hate scribbled his face. He stepped towards the door.

"Aren't you gonna say thank you?" asked Jonas.

It was in the construction worker's eyes. Given the chance he'd snap Blackheart's neck like a pencil. The guy glared as if tabulating an unpaid debt.

"See you in another life homeboy." Jonas winked.

Taking sudden aim, the shotgun discharged. The construction worker's cool demeanor became quickly rectified by a blast to the back of the head. Mr. Wonderful was dead before he ever hit the ground.

"Can you feel the love, brother?" He stared brutally from inside the door. "Now get your asses moving."

27

Magic

In sports it might be the last second interception or a baseball hit over the centerfield wall that wins the game. But there were no Joe DiMaggio's at Harvey's Quick Mart that day. There was, however, a sharpshooter with a rifle zoomed in on the suspect from the roof of a gas station across the road.

Sweat glistened on Scott Mohegan's forehead. The crazy bastard inside the convenience store just killed someone in cold blood. Holding the gun tight, Mohegan scoped the target. In the army he was one hell of a crack-shot. Man, he could take out an enemy at half a mile with a single bullet. This was trickier. The scumbag shielded himself with a woman. If he missed the mark, even by a hair, he'd take out the hostage.

"Come on," he whispered and zeroed in. "Just a little to the left."

Scott held his fire. Tried to stay cool. That didn't last long. A guy wearing a construction hat walked out of the store. He took a few steps in the parking lot and the suspect put a bullet in his head. All hell immediately broke loose. The women that the Perp used as a human shield screamed. Pulling away, she ducked down on the ground, out of the line of fire.

Seizing the moment, Scott Mohegan took a deep breath and pulled the trigger.

———

Jonas watched the construction worker fall flat on his face.

DOA before he ever hit the macadam. If the police doubted his veracity, those uncertainties were surely put to rest faster than a blood spill on a pavement.

The woman that Jonas held as a safeguard against rogue bullets shrieked when she saw the construction worker's head explode from the shotgun blast. Pulling free of her captor's grip she hit the ground and curled up in a fetal position. For one critical second Jonas Blackheart was an open target.

Plunk.

A bullet from Officer Scott Mohegan's rifle punched the side of Jonas Blackheart's leg. Moments later a second shot landed in his upper thigh.

"Put the gun down and raise your hands!" A cop yelled and ducked behind a police cruiser.

Jonas looked around. The police had him hemmed in. Those bastards were determined to get their free coffee and donuts at all costs.

"This is your last chance," a cop shouted again. "Are you gonna comply?"

Jonas delivered his answer by blowing a hole the size of a baseball in the side of a police car. In what could best be described as a good old-fashioned Swiss cheese assault, the cops opened fire. Bullets punched Jonas's arms and legs from all directions. He staggered backward. Instead of passive defeat Jonas regained his balance and glowed with heated contempt.

"You want some of me!" Smiling from ear to ear, he raised his shotgun in the air.

"Fire at will!" a cop shouted.

The boys in blue raised their weapons. However, a sudden intrusion redirected the violent mechanics of the famous final scene.

"Damn!" A rookie cop behind the corner of the building flinched. The gun flew out of his hands almost as if he grabbed a sizzling frying pan.

Two more officers behind police cruisers also yelped when their weapons turned fiery hot. Gape-mouthed, one of the cops stared at his hands as if they were possessed. He looked up just in time to see Jonas limping towards him, shotgun tucked under his arm.

"Freeze!" A loud voice thundered from somewhere above him.

Jonas scanned the perimeter. Glancing at the roof, he saw someone. A lone wolf, and clearly, a ram among the sheep.

———

For an instant a wave of heat rushed over Scott Mohegan. His hands sizzled. He almost dropped the rifle. Ignoring the pain, Mohegan squeezed the trigger. It was a direct hit to the side of the face. Not even a good plastic surgeon would be able to cover the shaving off his cheek.

Jonas jolted two steps backward on impact. The shotgun slid from his fingers. Staggering from left to right, he fell down on one knee, lingered there for a minute and then slithered to the ground.

———

Jonas Blackheart passed out. The fog lifting, edgy cops picked up their rifles and stared at them as if they were aliens.

"What the hell just happened?" Officer Watkins said. "My gun got hot as a bake oven."

Paramedics raced over. Police stormed the store. The construction worker and the store manager were pronounced dead at the scene. There was, however, one casualty still breathing.

An ambulance attendant pointed at the suspect. "We got a live one."

Officer Watkins craned his head around. "That's impossible."

"I'm telling you he got a pulse." The paramedic looked at the wounds on the suspect. "The guy took a lot of fire. He must be a freaking magician to be breathing."

Officer Watkin's face shattered like glass. He saw the routine before. If Blackheart lived, he'd get a court appointed lawyer. Cop an insanity plea. After hundreds of thousands of dollars in trial costs he'd get interred at some cushy mental facility, free college credits, a library card and three-square meals a day, all in the name of justice.

Watkins looked from left to right. Decidedly there were far too many witnesses to put the bastard out of his misery and save the American taxpayer the legal expense of a long trial.

"The guy is checking out fast," the paramedic announced. "If we don't get moving, he'll never make it to the hospital alive."

"Promise?" Officer Watkins asked. He looked down at the suspect. He felt compelled to put another chunk of lead in his skullcap. For an instant the suspect looked up at him with moose-mantel eyes. A second later they flicked shut again and everything turned dark.

28

Bulletproof

Sam Cage and Alan Stoner sat at a table drumming their fingers when the door opened. Jack Raison walked in the room.

Cage eyed Raison suspiciously. A bigwig at headquarters, Raison was a glorified gangster in a dapper black suit and tie. No doubt he made a few people disappear in the East River during his tenure at The Agency.

"Raison flicked a lighter and lit a cigarette. "Can you believe it? Jonas Blackheart is still alive. He even got shot in the head by the cops. I call that just plain freaky. The guy must be bulletproof."

Cage cleared his throat. "He's in a coma at Memorial Hospital. That isn't exactly dancing on Broadway."

Raison's eyes shifted towards Cage. He didn't like him. Nope. He didn't like him at all. Guys like him? They'd rather question orders than follow them. It was called bucking the system. Damn-it, when people began thinking for themselves the results always turned out the same; they became dangerous.

"You don't get it Cage," said Raison. "Do you have any idea how much money has been spent on this asshole?" Unable to contain himself he pounded a fist on the table. "We could purchase every condo in Key West and never scratch the surface."

Alan Stoner, headman at the facility, stood up and walked to the window. "Police are asking questions," he said. "They had Blackheart surrounded in the parking lot of a convenience store. Suddenly their guns got fiery hot, so hot they had to drop them on the ground. A couple of the police even checked in at county with third degree burns. If Blackheart gives them any information about what's been going on here, we'll all be doing time in Graterford."

Cage tapped a pencil on the tabletop. "I'm not sure there's anything we can do about it. Besides, Blackheart is in a coma. It isn't like the cops can question him."

Raison walked across the room. For a moment he looked so sickened that Cage thought he'd spit on him. "Are you stupid?" he asked knowingly. "What if Blackheart wakes up and starts talking? The son-of-a-bitch has more classified information at his disposal than a General at Normandy. Blackheart is a security risk. He has to disappear."

Cage tilted his head. "What do you mean disappear? Are you gonna kill him?"

"Figuratively speaking," said Raison. "We're going to extract him from the hospital. When we're done, as far as anyone knows, he'll be dead."

Cage looked at Raison and began to laugh.

"Is something funny?" he asked.

"More like hysterical." Cage settled down. "Blackheart is in a public hospital under heavy guard. You really think you can get him out of the place without getting arrested?"

"Trust me," Raison said. "He's going to be transferred."

"Transferred where?"

"Don't sweat the small stuff," Raison said. "You'll know when it happens. In the meantime, keep cool. Alan Stoner will be your contact point until we get through all the red tape."

Sam Cage looked at Stoner and crunched his fists. The guy was a cutthroat, not to mention an asshole. He'd pat you on the back with one hand and then stab you in the heart with a butcher knife, all in the same breath.

"I still don't see how you're gonna get him out of the hospital." Cage held an even tone.

"Leave it to the professionals." Raison snapped his fingers. Reaching in his shirt pocket he pulled out a pair of Raybans and put them on. "Just remember. We don't need any security breaches. I'd hate to see anyone buried in a box at the bottom of a marsh." His grin had all the charm of a copperhead ready to strike.

Alan Stoner nodded. "Don't worry. We got you covered. We're all on the same team." He glanced at Cage doubtfully. "When can we expect all this to go down?"

"You're already on the rollercoaster and hitting the highest hill. Hold your breath."

Reaching over, Raison doused a cigarette in Cage's coffee cup and walked out the door.

29

Dan Buzzard's Circus Story

It was 11:15 at night when Dan Buzzard jiggled the lock on his apartment door and opened it. Flicking on the light he went straight to the refrigerator, grabbed a cold one and flopped down on the couch. The last few days were the pits.

The trouble started at Ramrod's, a cheesy bar on the eastside of town. Some galoot with an attitude and tattoos pummeled him after he bought his girlfriend a drink. Man, he was just trying to find something warm and fuzzy for the night. When he walked outside her boyfriend caught him in the back alley. Not a good scene.

Dan ran down the street and hid in a Mercedes parked outside the Star Hotel until the coast was clear. The next thing he knew the cops arrived. They pulled him out of the vehicle and arrested him on a drunk and disorderly, not to mention attempted theft of a vehicle. It happened just that fast; he was thrown in the slammer.

As it turned out some dude named Jack Raison owned the Mercedes. The guy wore an expensive suit and looked like a real hard ass, but you know something? Even gorillas can have a heart. Maybe Raison just felt sorry for him but the crazy bastard actually posted bail.

"Thank you, sir," he told Raison outside the police station.

Raison smiled but suspicion cradled his face. "Tell me the truth." He crossed his arms. "Who are you working for? Did they hire you to loot my car? Those cruds from the CIA and FBI will stop at nothing to get their hands on classified information."

Dan stared blankly. What was the guy, a secret agent?

"Honest pal," he said. "I didn't mean anything. Some guy tried to rough me up. I jumped in your car to hide."

Doubt shadowed Raison's expression. Straightening his tie, the hard edges of his face softened a little. "Don't worry about it." He slapped him on the arm.

"Thanks man," Dan said. "Maybe I can make it up to you some day."

Raison pointed a finger as he walked away and said, "We'll be in touch real soon."

———

Dan flicked on the television and surfed the channels. Turning his head, he caught a glimpse of himself in the musty mirror. Not a pretty sight. As a kid he could have been a poster child for pimple commercials. Much like a fire-scarred building, the pockmarks never quite healed. That put a damper on his social life, particularly with the ladies.

The truth is that Dan Buzzard could have dropped off the face of the planet and not a soul would have noticed until they blew the whistle for the next shift down at the mill. Even that would have been to reprimand him for being late.

"It's just you and me tonight." Dan stared at his beer. Taking a last swallow, he scrunched up the can and tossed it in the trash.

Dan walked over to the refrigerator. He stopped for a moment and looked at a newspaper clipping tacked to the door with a magnet. The Times News did the article years ago, back when he was in high school. He and a group of students went to Washington on a field trip. During the outing by chance he shook hands with a Soviet entourage visiting the Pentagon. A photographer snapped a Polaroid. It ended up in the newspaper. It was one of the few instances in his meager life that Dan Buzzard felt like someone important.

Dan grabbed another beer out of the refrigerator. He sat down and flicked through the television channels again. A rerun of the

Honeymooners played on the tube. Ralph danced around like a man from space. He laughed his ass off every time he saw that rerun on the tube.

That's when the knock came at the door.

—

Dan glanced at the time. He never got visitors after 11:00 at night. He never got visitors period.

He set the beer can on the coffee table. "Who is it?"

"Dan Buzzard?"

"Yes?"

"This is the police."

"Say what?"

"There's trouble."

"Trouble?" Dan sat up straight. "What kind of trouble?"

"We need to ask you a few questions. Open the door."

Dan got off the couch. Turning the lock, he cracked the door open. Two shady characters in dark suits stood in the dim hall. One of them held out a wallet with a badge pinned in it.

"We have a few questions." One of the guys stared him down.

"Is this about the Mercedes?" asked Dan. "I already explained. I didn't steal it. I even spoke to the owner of the car, Jack Raison. Everything is cool."

"Don't make this hard on yourself."

Dan cracked the door open a little further. "What do you guys want?"

"We can't talk here. This is government business and all that crap. We'll fill you in at headquarters." The guy in the suit tapped his foot anxiously.

Dan again glanced at the men. They sure as hell didn't look like cops. The big one even wore sockless moccasins.

"I'd like some verification," Dan finally said. "Mind if I call the police station?"

Dan walked in the room and headed for the phone, mindful of

a pistol stuffed in the drawer of a corner table. Turning around he was surprised to see the men in suits traipsing behind him.

"Hey, this is a private residence. You can't just walk in here." Dan reached for the pistol.

"I wouldn't do that." One of the brutes jammed a gun into Dan's ribs. "Take it easy. Nobody has to get hurt."

Dan's face turned white with fear. "I didn't do anything wrong!" He raised his hands.

The other thug traipsed around the rooms. He stopped at the refrigerator in the kitchen and eyed the newspaper clipping of Dan shaking hands with a Soviet official.

"Very impressive," he said, not very seriously. "Foreign connections." Pulling the clipping off the refrigerator door, the thug shoved the article in his pocket.

Fear, hot as a blast furnace, surfaced in Dan Buzzard's face. He tried to run but never made it a step. Outside of a hard blow of a pistol on the nape of the neck, it was the last thing he remembered until he woke up gagged on the roadside with a Janis Joplin tune wailing through muffled speakers.

12:45 AM.

Nurse Russo turned sickly white and screamed when she saw the smoke. Snap quick, the fire appeared to be all through the hallways of Memorial Hospital.

"Help! We need help!" Her thin fist banged the intercom.

The smoke billowed out the second-floor window near the trauma unit.

"Evacuate!" Nurse Russo clucked like a chicken with an axed head. "Hurry!"

Patients, guided by terror-stricken hospital attendants, rolled down the hallway in wheelchairs towards an emergency exit. Sirens blared in the parking lot. A host of bold firefighters converged on the building. Within minutes the crisis had been abated.

"Some wise ass put a powder bomb in the ventilation system," the chief coughed and explained to the media.

Aside from Marlin Tanner, an elderly man with gallstones who suffered a mild heart attack, there were no casualties. However, in all the confusion, a patient named Jonas Blackheart had mysteriously disappeared from the trauma unit. The grounds were searched but almost as if his lethargic remains decided to yank out the IV's and take a midnight stroll, the patient disappeared without a trace.

———

Dan Buzzard woke up groggy. A gag was tied around his mouth. Reality quickly punched him in the face. He sat in the backseat of an automobile. The car had been parked on a downward slope. Trees were all around him. He struggled with thick cords of rope that bound his wrists.

"You moron, relax and stop jerking the car around." The thug in the front seat of the vehicle flicked his cigarette ash out the window and looked in the rearview. "In case you're wondering, I'm Harry Grimm. Pleased to meet you although I suspect it's gonna be a short-lived friendship." Tapping his fingers to an old Joplin tune on the radio, he checked his wristwatch. "Where the hell are they?" he complained bitterly to himself.

In the backseat, Dan's heart rattled in fear. The splintery rope cut into his wrists like rusted wire.

The thug again glanced in the rearview. "I told you to stop squirming. Those ropes are foolproof." He punched the dashboard. "Damn-it! Raker knows we're on a tight schedule, the little puke."

A radio in the front seat started to hum. "Harry, you there man?"

He picked up the receiver. "I've been sitting in the bush for over an hour. Where are you?"

"I just got the word from headquarters. The carnival is open. Start the ride."

"It's about goddamn time. Catch you at the pickup point." Harry set the receiver down and slid out of the car. Reaching in the backseat he removed Dan Buzzard's gag. "It's a beautiful night for a ride, right? Lots of stars are out. I'm telling you this will give you more thrills than a rollercoaster in Coney Island."

Dan's eyes amplified. He looked at the car's headlights that illuminated a steep bank down a mountainside. The vehicle lurched forward, not more than an inch.

"I hope you filled out those life insurance papers," Harry said.

Dan shivered. "You got to listen to me. There's been a mistake. I didn't do anything! You need to let me go."

"Sorry." Harry blew a smoke ring in the air. "I can't do that. The boys down at The Agency would stick a pair of tin snips up my ass if I didn't make you disappear. It's just business. You understand, right? Oops." He snapped his fingers. "I can't forget this." He pulled a watch out of his pocket and clipped it around Dan's wrist.

"You see my friend, you've got to recognize the gravity of the situation," Harry said. "Nobody screws with The Agency. That's what you did. You stole Jack Raison's car."

"I didn't steal it," Dan implored him.

"Whatever." He shrugged. "It's irrelevant. Down at The Agency we don't take chances. Suppose you worked for the other team? Suppose you were after hush-hush information." He said. "You wouldn't be the first person to get wasted for being a spy or in the wrong place at the wrong time. It happens."

The car lurched another inch forward.

"Please don't do this," Dan begged. "I'll scream!"

The thug shrugged. "Go ahead. There's no shame. Out here in the bush nobody is gonna here you anyway." He checked his wristwatch.

1:29 a.m.

"We could talk about this all night Dan but I'm afraid our time is up," he said. "If nothing else, sure as shit this ride is gonna clear up your complexion."

Reaching in the front seat, Harry released the emergency brake.

"No!" Dan frantically pulled at his restraints.

The car lurched ahead, slowly at first. Then it picked up speed, faster and faster. The horror-hooked eyes of Dan Buzzard were glued to the onrushing world in front of him as the car barreled down the embankment. Spiraling off a ledge, the wheels glided in midair for an instant before hitting the ground. The tailpipe sparked as it landed on rocks and then crashed through a guardrail. Racing down the mountainside, the vehicle raked against branches and underbrush. It came to a gut-wrenching stop against the neck of a tall tree.

Standing at the top of the incline Harry struggled to see the wreckage in the woods. For a minute he thought he heard Dan Buzzard moan. Just as well. In the killing business he liked to keep things natural as possible.

Pulling a small mechanism from his pocket, Harry Grimm took a final drag of his cigarette and flicked it against a rock. Listening for one more cry, he clicked a button. The car detonated and burst into flames.

Satisfied by the day's work Harry sprinted down a wooded path and landed on a highway that cut through the middle of the mountain. A vehicle came down the road. The driver slammed on the brakes and opened the passenger door.

Glancing once more at the burning wreckage, Harry jumped in and the car sped away down the highway.

Everything was right on schedule.

2:10 AM.

Paramedics and fire trucks arrived on the scene within minutes. Firing up the hoses they doused the flaming vehicle from all angles.

"No survivors," a gum chewing cop told the chief over a

handset. "Some poor bastard was hogtied in the backseat. He looks like a marshmallow that got caught in a bonfire. We're trying to ID him."

"No clues?" the chief asked.

"We found a wallet but it's burnt. There's also a wristwatch with an engraving." The cop wiped away dirt off the back of the watch. "The guy's name was Blackheart."

"What did you say?" The chief sounded surprised.

"Jonas Blackheart."

"I'll be damned."

"What?"

"It just came over the wire. That's the name of the comatose guy who went missing from Memorial Hospital tonight," the chief said.

Before the cop could say another word a station wagon, big as a hearse, barreled up the road and came to a screeching halt. A man got out of the vehicle waving a badge.

"Hold up!" he shouted.

The cop tilted his head. "Who the hell are you?"

"I'm on official business." He shoved his badge in the police officer's face. "I'm from the Center of Disease Control. We got a call from the higher ups. You see that corpse?" He pointed at the burnt car. "The person inside is carrying something and I'm not talking about a bad cough and the sniffles. I need the remains. Pronto."

"I can't just…"

"You want to be responsible for an epidemic?" he asked. "I'm not asking permission." He shoved a warrant in the cop's face. "If you got a problem, call your congressman."

The cop picked up his handset. "Chief, we got issues here. Some guy says he's from the CDC. He says the victim is contagious."

"We know all about it," the chief cut in. "The call just came down. Someone in DC got their hooks in this one. Do whatever he wants."

"Satisfied?" the CDC man asked and looked at the cop's badge. "Officer Smith is it? I'll see that mention is made." He snapped his fingers at the two goons with him that were dressed in hazmat suits. They jumped out of the station wagon and loaded the victim inside.

"That was easy. Just one more thing," he told the cop. "Screw with me again and I'll have your job, got it?"

The cop stared brutally.

Jumping back in the station wagon, the vehicle sped out of sight, almost mysteriously as it arrived.

24 Hours Later

The Agency headed up the investigation in regards to the crash on the mountainside. They concluded that the charred person in the car was indeed Jonas Blackheart who vanished from Memorial Hospital after someone threw a smoke bomb in the ventilation system.

A witness was bought and paid for of course. She claimed to have seen Jonas Blackheart in the area less than an hour earlier. She said that Blackheart was with someone who fit the description of Dan Buzzard, a man recently arrested for stealing a Mercedes. Buzzard was sought for questioning but disappeared without a trace. A search of his apartment uncovered not only an illegal gun stuffed in a drawer but also a wallet stuffed with twenties that belonged to Mr. Blackheart.

"We aren't ruling anything out," a representative of The Agency told the newspaper. "We have reason to believe that Buzzard may have been a sleeper cell working under the direction of a foreign government." He held up an old newspaper clipping that was tacked to Buzzard's refrigerator. The clipping showed Buzzard shaking hands with a Soviet diplomat. "Our best guess is that he fled the state. We'll find him. When we do, I'll personally pull the switch on the electric chair."

Coworkers were shocked at the news. They found it nearly impossible to believe that Dan Buzzard had the brains to be an international spy.

Regardless of what might be true, within 24 hours Jonas Blackheart had been successfully extracted from Memorial Hospital and his death faked, business as usual.

30

Table Number 2

It was a rainy morning, cold and damp. Jonas Blackheart arrived at the Allentown facility for processing. Presumed dead by the public he quietly took up residence on table number two of the Analysis Room. Unmoving and staring emptily at the ceiling, he could have been mistaken for a vegetable plant fermenting under a heat lamp.

Alan Stoner walked over to the table. He fingered Blackheart's skeletal flesh as if it were a rare dinosaur find. "Beautiful work," he told Jack Raison. "How the hell did you guys pull it off?"

Raison leaned coolly against the wall and crossed his arms. "We can't tell all of our secrets. Think of it as Houdini." He snapped his fingers. "We got the magic touch."

"This is crazy!" Sam Cage blurted out. "You can't just steal someone from a hospital."

"Relax," Raison advised and coughed in a hankie. Cage noticed a small spatter of blood in the tissue when he pulled it away. The guy was either sick or a drug addict. "Nobody suspects anything. I'd like you to meet someone." He looked towards the door.

A rough looking G-Man walked in. An irritable strand of hair hung in his eyes and a block of contempt chiseled his face. He looked about as compromising as a starved alligator in a swamp.

"This is Harry Grimm," Raison said. "He'll be heading up security."

A granite expression clung to Grimm's face like weedy vines on a wooden fence.

Cage again looked at Jonas Blackheart. He was sprawled out on table number two next to a cage of rats. "What's wrong with you people?" Cage spouted off.

"You're too damned sensitive Cage," said Raison. "In case you haven't noticed terrorism and third world countries are on the rise. The military needs something to counteract the bad element. Our boy here is gonna be famous. He's a nuclear warhead waiting to happen."

"He's a guinea pig?" Cage asked.

Raison crossed his arms. "I don't see what all the concern is."

"He's still a human being," said Cage.

Raison laughed. "He's in zombie land." He snapped his fingers in Blackheart's face. "The damage is already done. There's nothing we're gonna do to him to make it worse. Besides, he isn't the first asshole to get caught up in the system. The Agency makes people vanish all the time. You got to know that, right? Trust me. When people disappear in our business, they're not headed home to mommy for Sunday dinner."

Cage blinked. "What's your point?"

"Open your eyes Cage. Personally, I never had much faith in all that telekinetic bullshit. But when we found Blackheart that changed. He could move things without touching them. Other times he had the ability to make people see things that weren't there. Unfortunately, he started getting violent, even psychotic." Raison shrugged. "It was a minor drawback. Things happen. But if we can isolate what's going on with his chromosomes, no doubt there'll be more candidates in the stable."

"Candidates?" asked Cage.

"Homeless people, prostitutes, maybe even 5th Avenue tycoons who got the right stuff," Raison said. "It's just a matter of finding the right monkeys to experiment on."

Cage stared at Raison. He was right, of course. Jonas Blackheart was the new Area 51. A top secret and a rising star in military history. Once they got results with him, they'd want more. Much more. People would start vanishing. A new revolution would begin. An even more interesting question might be how the world would control an army of telekinetic and possibly psychotic superheroes.

"I want no part of this," Cage said.

Raison laughed. "Get serious. You can't quit. The only exit interviews these days involve a rock to weigh someone down at the bottom of a lake. Face it. Retirement isn't an option in the company. There is no out door."

Icy chills ran down Cage's spine. Jack Raison was right. The Agency invested a lot of money in the program. They wouldn't let him walk away carrying top secret information. He'd be dead by morning if he did.

"That's enough talk for one night." Raison walked towards the door. "Blackheart still has company value. Do your damnedest, dead or alive, to get it out of him."

Sticking his hands in his pockets, Raison gave Cage a suspicious glance then disappeared out the door.

31

A New Morning in America

It was daybreak when Sam Cage pulled into the parking lot for work at the Allentown facility, several weeks after Blackheart's arrival. A misty drizzle dripped in the air. He headed for the front door holding a takeout coffee from Starbucks.

Harry Grimm stood coolly at the entrance door. He puffed on a filterless cigarette and glared at Cage as he walked up the sidewalk.

"What's wrong?" Cage asked smartly. "You gonna give me a ticket for jaywalking?"

"Funny guy, aren't you?" Grimm took a long haul of his cigarette. Expelling a runner of smoke in the air he flicked the ashes at Cage's shoes. "Alan Stoner needs you downstairs."

"What does he want?"

"I'm just delivering a message cowboy." He fingered the pistol stuffed in his coat pocket.

Cage stared. Harry Grimm was crazy. A guy like that? One wrong move and he'd open fire.

Cage bowed his head and kept walking. His shoes clicked in the empty corridor. Approaching the Analysis Room, he hit a button on the wall and a door slid open. Inside, Alan Stoner sat at a desk thumbing through a file.

"You wanted to see me?" asked Cage.

Stoner tossed the file on the desk. "It's about our friend." He glanced at the table where Blackheart had been deposited. "We've had a few changes."

"What are you talking about?"

"He opened his eyes this morning."

Cage blinked. "Are you sure?"

"Do I look like a moron? He's awake. See for yourself."

Cage walked over to the table. Blackheart's frightened eyes darted around the room. Finally, they settled on the ceiling fan. A faint wind mussed his hair.

"How could he wake up?" Cage shined a pen light in his eyes. "He should be dead." He looked up at Stoner. "We need to get him to a hospital."

"Are you an idiot?" asked Stoner. "As far as anyone knows Blackheart is a corpse. Remember? We faked his death in a car crash. Unless he's Jesus rising from the grave, he can't check himself into Memorial Hospital to have his blood pressure taken."

Sam Cage bent down for a closer look. Blackheart looked disoriented. Groggy. He also appeared bigger than when he arrived at the facility. Stronger. If anything, he should have been wasting away.

"I know what you're thinking," said Stoner.

Cage gawked. He was thinking that he'd have liked to smash a tire iron over the guy's head.

"He's strong as a bull," Stoner said. "It's probably all the steroids we've been feeding him."

Cage looked close at Blackheart. "Can you hear me?"

Blackheart's eyes shifted but remained soulless.

"Don't waste your time," Stoner said. "He's living in a world of zombies."

Cage's face turned apple red. "This is crazy. He needs professional help."

"Are we gonna go through that again? Get with the program Cage. Look at him. He's a vegetable. We don't need to be doctors, just good gardeners. Maybe you think we're doing something immoral. You're wrong. Don't you realize what this is gonna mean to the world? It's a new morning in America. Everything we've ever known is about to change, compliments of our catatonic friend."

Blackheart shivered. A cold sweat beaded up on his forehead.

For an instant a rogue wave of heat swept the air. The last time Cage felt something like that was a July day in Las Vegas when he stepped out of the air conditioning at Caesars and into the desert sun.

Almost as if poked in the ribs, Blackheart's limp arms jumped. A minute later he began to thrash in his restraints. Across the room a stack of papers on a desk flew up in the air, wildly as autumn leaves in a windstorm.

"What the hell?" Cage looked around, confused.

Excitement glazed Stoner's eyes. "Are you seeing this?" He tapped the monitor on the side of Blackheart's bed. "His rates are off the grid. He's responding to the treatments."

Across the room a pile of books flew off a shelf, one of which hit Cage from behind.

"Quick!" Stoner grabbed a syringe off the table. "He'll wreck the place. We need to sedate him."

Cage stared in wonder.

"Are you listening?" Stoner shouted. "Cage!"

Shaking himself out of the trance, Cage grabbed Blackheart's arms and held them down. Stoner rolled up his sleeve and injected him. Almost immediately Blackheart fell into a more relaxed state of terror. Just behind them a medical journal suspended six feet in the air hung there for a second and then dropped to the floor.

Breathing hard, Cage looked at Stoner with hexed eyes. "What in God's name have you created here?"

Alan Stoner grinned. "Something wonderful."

32

Occupied Territories

Minutes?

Years?

Jonas Blackheart drifted. Everything hurt as if his bones were shattered. His throat felt parched as dried wood in an open fire. Struggling to lift his eyelids, finally he did. A cool wind rushed in on him like frost on a windowpane. Things were cloudy but he could see the shapes of men in long white coats standing around him. Perhaps he died. That might explain things. The men in white coats might be angels or more likely devils in disguise.

Looking around, Jonas grew uncertain as to his whereabouts. One thing remained clear. If he still resided in the body he once called home, someone had overthrown the neighborhood and set the house on fire. A nameless presence lurked in the murky pools of his contaminated mind. It hid there like a thief in the dark.

"Who's there?" asked Jonas.

For a minute he heard a muted whisper, frosty as cold breath on an icy winter's morning. Then everything went silent again.

Jonas tried to sit up but couldn't move. Something, perhaps restraints, held his arms down. He also couldn't recall much of his life. Memories were fleeting as clouds in a summer storm. Nevertheless, something bad must have happened to him.

He again sensed a hostile force. Something watched him.

"Who's there? Show yourself."

Wet laughter echoed across the murky chambers of his mind. A cold chill pressed in on his spine. Whatever lurked in the darkness, it was fierce. Militant.

Unstoppable.

"What are you?" asked Jonas.

A silent pause, then, *"You mean you really don't know? I'm the dark side."*

A cannonball of adrenaline shot through Jonas. His heart raced uncontrollably. It had been confirmed. A trespasser entered the grounds and permeated his mind.

Jonas grew scared. Frightened as hell. He again tried to stand and run but something, perhaps the men in the white coats, held him down. He felt the pinch of a needle prick his arm. Then everything grew hazy. The world turned to shadows. He began to drift. In the cool and dark confines of his cataleptic life, everything turned black.

The weeks passed.

33

When Lightning Strikes

Alan Stoner yawned and glanced at the clock. The hands just hit 4:30 a.m. That in itself was enough to piss him off.

Stoner had been rolling into work in the middle of the night for weeks. Sometimes he didn't go home at all. Most of his research got done over black coffee and caffeine pills.

The late and secretive hours were unavoidable. Sam Cage, recipient of the moral shithead award, would go ballistic if he knew what really had been going on. Over the last weeks he gave Blackheart enough drugs to tranquilize a buffalo. If Cage found out he'd run to the authorities and quack like a duck with his balls stuck in a dresser drawer.

At times Blackheart regained consciousness. His metabolic rates skyrocketed off the charts, particularly when he got spooked. All breakables were removed from the room. Whatever wasn't nailed down ended up smashed against the walls. Yup, that crazy son-of-a-bitch was making history and didn't even know it.

"I know you can hear me," Stoner whispered in Blackheart's ear. "Move the glass."

Stoner turned his head. He stared at a water glass sitting on a table. Nothing happened.

On the other side of the room, Harry Grimm leaned against a wall. "You really think he knows what you're saying, huh?"

"He hears," Stoner answered. "He just isn't listening."

At times Blackheart responded to commands. He'd make books topple over. Doors open. Like a good mutt he complied with the house rules. But even dogs have a defiant streak. They forget who the boss is and need their nose rubbed in piss. That's what happened to Jonas Blackheart over the last few days. He became noncompliant. He started pissing on the rug.

Harry Grimm took a drag of his cigarette. "He still looks like a burnt-out junkie from the '60s to me." He flicked his ashes on the floor.

"He's just being difficult." Stoner grabbed Blackheart by the chin. "You hear that? Things can get ugly. I'd hate to see that happen," he said. "I'm less than a heartbeat away from sticking a lightning rod up your ass." He looked at the table. "Move the glass."

Blackheart's eyes shifted fearfully in bruised sockets. Still nothing.

"I guess we'll have to do things the hard way." Standing up, Stoner walked towards the door and looked at Grimm.

Harry Grimm stared back with impenetrable eyes. "Give me an hour," he said. "He'll be dancing."

———

"We're finally alone," Grimm said. "You wouldn't get fresh with me, right?" He smiled greenly and slapped back a strand of greasy hair that hung in his face.

Jonas's eyes shifted wearily around the room. He watched Grimm traipse the floor.

"You see pal, this is nothing personal," he said. "You just got caught in the loop. It happens. Translated in English it's simple; you're screwed." He flicked the ashes of his cigarette in Blackheart's face and leaned against the side rail of table number two. "I'll tell you how this is gonna play out. Cooperate and everything will be cool beans. We might even get a little shuteye tonight. But if you buck the system?" Grimm shook his head. "I hate to even think about it."

Grimm walked over to a table against the wall and picked up a taser gun. Clicking the trigger, it made a loud crack and blue spark. A burning smell like sulfur from an old stoker singed the air.

"I got a confession." Grimm walked towards the table. "I wasn't an altar boy growing up. Maybe you already gathered that. Then again nobody who gets involved in this business ever is. Look at the trouble it brought you," he said. "Before my father deserted me for some whore in San Juan, he caught me playing with matches in the cellar. The bastard held my hands over a hot oven. I swear that sometimes I can still hear the blisters sizzling." He stared at his hands and grimaced. "I'll tell you this much. I didn't play with matches anymore. The old man taught me a lesson. I might have even grown up to be one of the good guys if he wouldn't have taken off. Mom was a Christian soul but she couldn't control me. In the end that's what life is all about," he said. "Controlling things." He looked at Blackheart and sniffed. "You look parched." Picking up a glass of water he threw it in Blackheart's face. "That's refreshing."

Jonas's eyes were bolted on Grimm.

"I got another confession. I'm afraid of lightning," Grimm continued. "Do you believe that brother? Fire clippers used to send me hiding under a bed. Probably not the best attribute for a pyromaniac. I had a friend named George Bemus. We called him Beetle because he had this half assed shaggy haircut. One night he was outside when a storm hit. It was thundering and lightning. He got nailed by a bolt of the hot stuff. I'm telling you that sonofabitch was stuck like ticky tape to the front lawn when they found him. I didn't really care." He shrugged indifferently. "The guy was a real asshole.

"The point is that lightning is a powerful force." Holding the taser up, he clicked the trigger again. A blue flame shot out of the tip. "Before I'm done here, you'll respect it too."

Pressing the trigger again he held the device against Jonas's cheek. There was a loud sizzling sound, like steaks in a barbecue pit. The stink of burnt flesh filtered in the air.

Jonas groaned. His wrists twisted in their restraints.

"That had to hurt," Grimm said. "You know growing up I had a dog named Spike. Kicking his ass was the only way I could get him to perform tricks. That's all we're doing here," he said. "Call it obedience school. Move that stupid glass, even an inch, and class will be cancelled for the day, got it?"

Jonas stared at the glass on the table. He concentrated. Struggled to move it. The attempt was futile. No matter how he tried, it wouldn't budge.

Shaking his head in frustration, Grimm stared at his prey and held up the taser. "It looks like it's gonna be a long night."

34

Missing Persons

Sam Cage flicked on the intercom. "Stoner!" he yelled.

Turning around he looked at Jonas Blackheart on table number two. A gruesome wound had been cut across his cheek. It had all the charm of a drainage ditch expelling green antifreeze.

Suddenly the door opened. Alan Stoner walked in.

"What are you doing in here?" Hands on hips, he tapped his foot impatiently.

Cage turned his attention back to Blackheart. A roadwork of angry contusions crisscrossed his sunken face. "What happened?"

"Hard to tell," said Stoner. "Maybe an intern cleaned him up and caught a few rough spots with a razor."

"Are you trying to be funny?" Cage clenched his fists. "Those aren't shaving cuts."

Stoner stuck his hands in his pockets and walked to the window. "Think of this as Gitmo. We're just doing a little water boarding. It isn't always margaritas and roses when it comes to extracting information," he reminded.

"Quit with the theatrics. What information?"

"I think you know the answer to that."

"I'm calling headquarters," said Cage.

Stoner sat down and folded his hands around his knee. "Do you really think you're innocent in all of this?" he mused. "You were here on the day we wheeled Blackheart in. You even helped strap him to the table. Face it Cage. If the authorities arrest me, you'll be the second man in line on the firing squad." Stoner glanced at a manila folder that Cage held in his hand.

"What's that?"

Cage tossed the folder on the table. "I've been reading up on our friend. There's an entire file dedicated to him. It seems Jonas Blackheart started working for The Agency a long time ago. He entered a volunteer program called Harbor Point. Jack Raison was in charge of the operation."

"What about it?" Stoner put his hands on his hips.

"I thought you could answer that."

"So maybe he was one of their stooges pissing in a cup to make a few extra bucks in college. That's none of our business."

"It's not gonna stop here, is it?" Cage said. "Blackheart is just the start of things. There's more abductions and kidnappings to come."

"Don't be so goddamn ignorant," Stoner said. "Grow some balls. Progress doesn't come cheap. Do you have any idea what this research is going to do to the world? We're gonna shake the planet up like a box of marbles. Everything is about to change Cage." Standing up, he gathered some papers and walked towards the door. "The military is counting on us to deliver the goods. We aren't going to let them down."

Cage glared hatefully.

"Get some rest," Stoner said. "You'll see things differently in the morning. In the meantime, watch it. You're becoming a security threat. I'd hate like hell for something to happen to you."

———

Later that night, Cage punched the pillow for the third time as he turned restlessly on twisted bed sheets.

It was true. Blackheart was a despot. At the same time, he was also a victim. The magic little injections pumped in him made PCP look like a butterscotch lollipop on a lazy Sunday afternoon. Blackheart went crazy from it. Criminal or not, the idea of him strapped down on a table next to the rats kept Cage's thoughts tacked to a bed of nails.

Cage rubbed his temples and lay in bed staring at the ceiling. He saw no clear passage of light. Calling the police would be futile. Even worse, it'd prove deadly. The Agency had experience in the art of disposing of turncoats both quickly and quietly, all means necessary.

Thinking it over, other than the final moments spent in Leona Smatter's arms, he never felt so helpless.

Cage reached over. He grabbed a piece of purple yarn off the night table. Tying it in a loop he slipped it on his finger. After all the many years, looking at it still made him feel young and indestructible. Most of all it made him feel in love.

Staring at the yarn, sometimes he wondered what would have happened if Leona lived. When he closed his eyes, he still swore he could smell her perfume.

"Midnight perfume," he whispered as his head melted on the pillow.

With memories of Leona floating in his head and a scrap of purple yarn tied around his finger, Sam Cage drifted off into the land of dreams.

35

The Ballad of Leona and Sam

Falling in love when you're a teenager is breathless. You didn't need champagne or dinner at a fancy club in New York City. When you're eighteen, a favorite song on the radio in a dusty Chevy and a beautiful woman made you feel invincible.

That's how Sam Cage viewed things on that warm spring night at Beltsville Lake. He lingered on the boat dock with his friend Carl, one of the last great hippies to grace the planet.

"Man, can you believe it?" Carl flipped his long hair over his shoulder and jiggled a cold one in his hand. "It's almost graduation dude." His feet dangled off the dock as he stared in the water. "What do we do now?"

"What do you mean?" Sam picked up a rock and tossed it in the lake. Ripples of starlight danced on the water.

"Don't you get it man?" Carl sighed. "There's no more skipping school or clowning around in gym class. Everything changes the minute you graduate, right?"

Carl wasn't brilliant but he knew stuff. In the years that followed they'd turn back the pages to the carefree days of their youth and the times they loved best. But not today. Today they drove in undiscovered country. Graduation had arrived; a time to say goodbye to old friends. Some would go off to college. Others would pick up the gauntlet of life and work in factories and stores. The only thing certain was this; lives would change.

"Think of it as an adventure," said Sam. He craned his head around for the third time to look at a girl on a bench by the boathouse. She had long dark hair. Stars shimmered in her emerald-green eyes that seemed to brighten every dark corner of the world. Man, a girl like that? If she ever wept the entire world would want to comfort her.

"That's Leona Smatters. I had a thing for her ever since grammar school," Cage said.

"That's the worst kept secret since Eileen Klump took the entire senior football team underneath the bleachers at halftime." Carl tossed a rock in the water. "Rumor has it she doesn't have a date for the prom."

"Really?" Cage's eyes brightened.

"I saw her looking over here. She got hot eggs for you."

"Eggs?" Cage blinked. "What do you mean eggs?"

"Dude, are you blind?" Carl scrunched up a beer can and tossed it in a trash barrel. "She wants you bad. All you need to do is ask her for a date. Would I lie?"

You're damn right he would, but just the same Sam stood up and trudged over to Leona. The lack of confidence mustered over his face made him look like a man walking to the gallows.

"Hi Leona." Cold sweat dampened Sam's neck.

Leona smiled.

For a minute Sam stood there stupid, unable to speak. When he finally did the words came out like the sputter of a busted muffler.

"Excuse me?" Leona stared at him with those big eyes. "Did you say something Sam?"

"The prom." He shifted from foot to foot.

"What?"

"You know."

Leona stared.

"I thought you might like to go," Sam said and exhaled.

There now. After twelve years he finally found the courage to ask the girl on a date. Even if he got shot down in flames, he made the big audition on Hollywood Boulevard.

After a slight pause Leona lifted her eyes, smiled and said, "Yes."

———

In a tuxedo and sweating bullets, Sam Cage waddled up to the front door of Leona's house. Holding a bent corsage and a pack of breath mints, he wiped a strand of hair into place as he rang the doorbell.

The outside light flicked on. The door opened. A man with a blue button down and faded jeans stood in the doorway. He looked at Sam with careful scrutiny over a pair of black glasses.

"You must be Sam," he said.

"Yes sir," he answered. "Is Leona here?"

The man's eyes narrowed. "What makes you think you can saunter up to the door and take my daughter out, hmm?"

Sam fidgeted and gulped.

The man at the door laughed and slapped Sam on the shoulder. "Just ribbing you kid. Come on in."

———

Sam stood inside the doorway when Leona walked down the steps. She wore a sleeveless gold satin dress that could have dragged every ounce of moonlight with her wherever she walked. Throw a cloud under that girl's feet; she was an angel.

"You kids don't be too late," her father said as they exited the house.

Sam nearly tripped over his feet when they got to the car. Leona reached over and touched his arm. "There's no reason to be nervous Sam."

"I'm not nervous," he said and dabbed at sweat on his forehead with a tissue.

Leona held up her wrist. "Do you like this?"

Sam sniffed. The scent resembled lilacs drifting in a windy field.

"It's called Midnight Perfume," said Leona. "Isn't it romantic?"

She sighed. "I wore it just for you."

Sam smiled. It was funny. Damn funny. He and Leona hadn't even made it to the dance and he was already waltzing under the stars. Looking at her, the formation of the world changed in less than a second. She was beautiful. Even his hands sweat like an African rainforest. In truth he got so nervous that he swore he'd be completely and utterly sick.

It was wonderful.

———

Clusters of balloons dabbed the ceiling and a glittering column sat in front of a red carpet. White rope rails sat at the entranceway to the prom hall. Flowers were wrapped and braided around chairs, twisted in colored light strings of Gossamer. A huge island sunset mural flanked the back wall of the place and sparkling star centerpieces adorned the tables.

On stage a local band called Becky and the Beasts played good old fashioned rock and roll. Some of the cool cats in the class put on Malibu sunglasses and danced to the smoky beat.

Sam walked over to the punch table and filled two glasses. His hands shook a little. He still couldn't believe that Leona Smatters agreed to be his date.

"Hey out there in prom land." The singer blew on the microphone. "Grab your partners. We got something smooth and soft." The drummer counted four and the sax player cranked up an old Eddie and the Cruisers song.

Maurice Biggs, star running back for the football team, sauntered through the crowd like Prince Charles. He just got signed to Alabama on a scholarship. Guys like that made all the women swoon. Walking over to Leona, he eyed her from head to toe.

"Dance?" he asked.

Leona smiled. "Sorry." She took Sam's hand. "My dance card is filled." The girl dragged Sam out on the floor.

Sam turned beet red. His dancing was coordinated as flailing spaghetti arms attempting to control the hostile disconnect of his limbs. Even during a slow dance, he looked as if he were doing the Macarena in reverse on a wobbly foot.

"Don't be nervous," Leona whispered in his ear.

Draping her arms around Sam's neck, her head melted into his shoulder. Her hair smelled like fresh strawberries mixed with the lilac scent of Midnight Perfume. When they finally kissed, nobody else in the world existed.

———

Sam and Leona drove up to the lake after the prom. Pulling a blanket out of the trunk of the car they sat on the beach and watched the shooting stars.

"Can I ask you something?" Leona looked in his eyes.

Sam nodded.

"Have you ever made love to someone?"

Sam's cheeks turned crimson. "What do you mean?"

"I've never done it." The girl sighed. "The first time should be special, don't you think?"

Sam shook his head and shyly answered, "I've never done it either."

Leona smiled. Leaning over she tucked her head on his shoulder. "Sometimes it feels as if I've known you forever Sam Cage. Does that sound crazy?"

Sam pulled Leona closer. It didn't sound crazy at all. Sometimes things just happened that way. People never have to say a word. You know all about them with just one look.

"When I make love, I want it to be with someone that I care about. Someone like you Sam," she said and for a minute her smile collapsed. "That's what makes this sad."

Sam stared blankly. "What do you mean?"

"I have to go away for the summer," she said. "My family has relations in San Diego. I'll be leaving right after graduation."

Sam's heart sunk like a chunk of iron in a lake.

"There's something I'd like to ask you," she said.

"What is it?"

"Would you wait for me?" She smiled and suddenly the stars lit up. In the background from his car radio, an old Patsy Kline song played. Yup, life was crazy alright.

"For as long as it takes." He pulled her close.

———

A few weeks later Leona Smatters boarded a plane at Philadelphia International. Her tears fell on Sam's neck as they embraced at the gate.

"Here," she said. "Take this stupid thing." She pulled a purple piece of yarn off that she kept tied around her finger. "My mother worked in a sewing machine factory. She gave this to me one day when I was a little girl. Call it a keepsake. I want you to have it now. I want you to remember me every time you look at it." She put it in the palm of his hand. Sam closed his fingers around it. "We'll write every day," she told him. Standing on her heels, she kissed him and walked into the tunnel that led to the plane.

It happened just that quick. A long kiss goodbye and the plane lifted off the runway. Sam watched it disappear into the clouds. The scent of Midnight perfume lingered on his shirt collar.

For the most part life happened just the way Leona said. They called each other and counted the days until they'd see each other again.

To pass time and make a little extra money for college, Leona got a part-time job at Big Scott's convenience store.

The weeks slowly went by. Sam marked off the days on a calendar. Before long summer came to an end. It was time to restart his life. Leona was coming home.

———

"Wednesday!" Leona told Sam on the phone. "I can't wait to

see you again."

Leona hung up the cell phone. It was the last shift at Big Scott's before she packed up her life and went back to Pennsylvania.

A smile strung across her face, Leona punched out of her job and headed home. Sadly, fate had other plans than a 747 headed back to the northeast. At the same time when she crossed the street on 5th and Main, a drunk driver barreled down the street. He slammed on the brakes but it was too late. Leona never saw the car coming. Two hours after arriving at the hospital she was pronounced dead.

The news crushed Sam. He was a man apart and didn't know how to put himself back together. Often at night he'd sit on the beach where he and Leona first kissed, staring at the stars. Sometimes he swore that he could still feel her body against his and smell the scent of Midnight perfume on his shirt collar. At times they'd talk about that magic moment when they'd finally make love; a memory that would last forever.

Sam Cage would not have that conversation again with Leona Smatters for another twenty odd years, long after she was dead and rotting away in some backwoods cemetery in northeastern Pennsylvania.

36

Life after Midnight

Cage woke up sweating. He was dreaming again. Stark visions of Leona Smatters danced in his head. Long before the alarm clock sounded, he sat at the kitchen table, staring at blank walls and long dead ghosts. Finally, he grabbed his car keys and headed out the door.

The highway was dark. Empty. When he pulled into the parking lot at work the only person around was the security guard.

"Morning Doctor Cage." The guard, Bill Ranger, greeted him. "You're early today."

"Insomnia," answered Cage. He pulled out his pass and handed it to the security guard. "I should invest in some sleeping pills." He looked around. "All quiet?"

"Nobody here besides me and the rats," he said. Punching in a clearance code the security doors slid open.

Nodding, Cage walked down the hall.

———

Air conditioning vents hummed. The halls were stone quiet. His footsteps echoed against the dim lit walls of the vacant chamber. He was alone.

"No," Cage grimly reminded himself. "Not alone. A dead man named Jonas Blackheart rotted away on table number two, just down the hall and to the left."

Turning a corner, he punched a button on the wall. The door of the Analysis Room opened and his knees momentarily turned to rubber.

Sam Cage walked over to the table. Blackheart had gone through more changes. He continued to grow, perhaps by inches. The miserable scab on his face also hadn't healed. Spattered with dried gore and thick as a soda straw, it ran the length of his cheek. Cage shuddered and pulled the curtain shut that surrounded the table.

A sultry and underlying heat seemed to hang in the air. Rubbing his hands over his face, he grew faint and shuffled against the wall. Lack of sleep and nightmares had drained him. Still he sensed something else was amiss. He looked around but the only movement appeared to be a steady green blip on Jonas Blackheart's monitor.

"Spooked," he mumbled and shook the ghosts off his shoulders.

Cage turned to leave but abruptly stopped. He sniffed twice. A familiar scent lingered in the room. The fragrance was sweet and mixed with a slight trace of sweat. When he finally recalled where he last smelled it, the memory hit him like a wooden baseball bat.

Whirling around, Cage stared at the closed curtain circling table number two. He sniffed again. The scent was nostalgic. Unmistakable.

"Midnight perfume," he whispered breathlessly.

———

The green blip on Blackheart's monitor pulsed faster. A noticeable temperature shift singed the air, almost as if someone turned on a blast furnace. An instant later he heard someone whisper.

"Sam?" a thin voice called.

Cage stiffened. His eyes remained fixed on the closed curtain surrounding the table.

"Sam?" The voice called again. It was frail. Delicate.

Cage's heart raced. He took a step closer. A restless shadow stirred from behind the drapes. Listening close, everything grew quiet. Maybe he was hearing things. It wouldn't be the first time. Lack of sleep had that effect. It's called hallucinations. No sir, nobody here but us bogeymen.

"I'm here Sam," a voice sounded off again.

And there it was. The confirmation of a ghost. It jumped out with all the surprise of a kid riding a bike on the Philadelphia Expressway during rush hour.

Hairs bristled on the back of Cage's neck. He circled the closed curtain; a weary hunter who stumbled across a sleeping bear in the woods.

"Sam." The voice said. Soft. Pathetic. Deadly.

Cage bit down on his lip. He could almost hear the smug game show host jabbering in a microphone.

"Take a look at what's behind curtain number two Sam Cage. Sure as hell it won't be a new BMW or a trip to Acapulco."

Grabbing the curtain, Cage abruptly yanked it open. His jaw dropped and knees buckled at the joints.

"Leona?"

37

Things that come back

Instead of Jonas Blackheart, Cage saw the vision of a young girl in her late teens with long dark hair deposited on table number two. Mascara smudged her cheek. She wore a shredded gold prom dress and hell if there wasn't even a spot of ketchup on the sleeve from dinner. The gown itself had been pulled down over her shoulder, far enough to expose a single white breast, all the while a faint scent of Midnight perfume funneled through the facility's ventilation system.

"It's me Sam. It's your Leona."

Cage staggered backwards on rubbery legs. He grabbed the bed railing for leverage.

"You're not Leona." Cage eyed the imposter.

She looked at him through half lidded eyes. "You're wrong Sam. Dead wrong. Remember that night on the beach all those years ago?"

Cage said nothing. Still he did remember. It was the night of the prom. He fell in love with the girl as they sat under the stars.

"You wanted to make love to me on the beach, didn't you? I wanted that too. I swear I wanted it so bad I could taste it." She licked her lips.

Cage stared. One thing was certain. The person on table number two had become one hell of an impersonator. The ghostly replica of the woman he once loved magnetized his every emotion. She was a perfect facsimile, right down to the mole under her jaw and certainly molded from the dark recesses of his memory.

"What's wrong Sam?" Her face riddled in confusion. "Don't

you want to make love to me? You must like to screw," she said. "Everyone likes screwing." Her tongue rolled over the moist edge of her lip.

"You're dead," Cage said flatly.

"I came back," she disagreed. Her thin wrists twisted in the restraints. "Sometimes people do that. They come back from the other side."

"You're dead!" Cage shouted angrily and pounded his fist on the bed railing.

She blinked back a tear. "Is that any way to talk to me? Don't you understand Sam? Things are on the other side. Bad things. I told them if they didn't let me come back that I'd fade away to nothing."

Cage tilted his head. "Who did you tell?"

"They're not people Sam." She shuddered. "They're more like shadows. You can't see them. Can't touch them. Still they're out there. They feed on people. Not the body Sam. They feed on the soul." She shivered. "Please. Don't send me back there."

Despite being an illusion, the sight of the helpless girl jolted Cage. Distant memories of Leona sailed down the rusted pipes of his heart. A landslide of hesitation crashed in all around him. Balling up his fists and tightening his resolve, he quickly moved out of the way of the avalanche.

"Where's Jonas Blackheart?" Cage asked sternly.

"He's dead," she said. "I took his place Sam. I took his place so we could always be together."

"We can never be together," Cage said. "You're just an delusion. You're not real!" he shouted.

The smile on the girl's face wilted and the sweet scent of Midnight perfume turned rancid in his nostrils. Wobbling to his feet Cage tried to clear his head. He again looked at the girl. It couldn't be Leona. The book had a perfect cover but the pages didn't fit. The only real resemblance she bore to Leona Smatters was that much like her final days on the planet when she got run down by a drunk driver in the streets, all of this was destined to have an unhappy ending.

"The restraints hurt Sam." Struggling, she turned her bruised wrists in metallic fetters. "Please don't send me back," she begged. "It's so cold there. It's so very cold and dead. Nothing breathes." For a second her face sagged like a prune drying in the sun but then plumped back up again.

A streak of hate sliced the imposter's face. "How can you treat me this way?"

Cage stumbled over to the intercom and hit a button. "Is anyone out there? I need security. Hurry!"

"Do you really want me to die so bad?" she asked. "Then go ahead Sam. Kill me." She sniffed but then laughed sinisterly. "Don't worry. You'll pay. I'll take care of things when I get back on the other side. Remember Aunt Sadie? She's over there, did you know that Sam?"

"Shut up."

"Poor little Sadie, so sweet and innocent."

"I said shut up!"

"I got friends over there. They're mean. Dirty. Criminal." She lifted her head off a pillow, the cords of her neck thick as telephone wire. "Poor poor Sadie," she said. "When I'm done she'll be tied to her bed with a conga line waiting their turn!"

Fierce anger painted on Cage's face. He lunged forward with closed fists but suddenly stopped. The monster on table number two tried to rattle him. Shake him up.

Cage took a breath. He walked over to a cabinet. Pulling out a syringe, he filled it with BDZ. The sedative could take down a bear.

"This won't hurt." He rolled Jonas Blackheart's sleeve up. Without warning he stuck his arm with the needle.

Cage exhaled. An iron weight of anxiety lifted off his shoulder. Whatever link connected him with Blackheart had been momentarily broken.

Looking down at table number two he saw a vulgar image emerge out of the ashes of what only seconds ago had been his long-lost lover.

Cage glanced at the clock. If he could keep Blackheart sedated, he might be able to get him out of the building and back to a hospital before Alan Stoner arrived at work.

"Jonas, can you hear me?" Cage searched his face. "We're getting out of here. Do you understand?" He cautiously loosened the restraints from his wrists.

Jonas Blackheart groggily got to his feet. Putting an arm around his waist, Cage led him out the door and down the hallway.

———

The corridor was empty, nobody in sight. That didn't solve the problem. A guard would be on duty at the main entrance. Even if they managed to get to the front door the question remained; how do they get by security?

Blackheart mumbled incoherently as they hurried through the hall.

"Snap it up." Cage prodded him to move faster.

Suddenly Cage heard other voices in the corridor. Thinking fast, he nudged Blackheart into an entryway that led to the boiler room. They hunched down behind some lockers.

"Don't say a word," Cage whispered.

Footsteps raced up the hall.

"Quick!" Alan Stoner shouted. "Seal the exits. We can't let him out of the building." His voice faded down the corridor.

Perspiration dripped from Cage's brow. His heart banged loud as a drum. He was in deep. One wrong move and the game would be over.

The Agency didn't take kindly to conspirators. If they found out what he did they'd soak his head in gasoline and light it up. Still no matter how he jiggled the numbers escape didn't seem possible. The facility had been designed to eliminate security risks, not add to them.

Cage peered into the hall. The walkway was vacant. They'd need to move fast.

"We're almost there." Cage tugged at Blackheart's arm. However, this time Blackheart stood stock-still.

"Sam," a soft voice called.

Cage froze. There it was again; the shadow of a ghost and the scent of Midnight perfume. It rose in the air like a spirit in the night.

Sam turned to see a vision of Leona Smatters standing alongside of him. Illusion or not, he couldn't help but to want to keep her right there beside him forever.

That was Cage's last thought before an elbow swung around and crashed in on his head, knocking him unconscious on the floor.

38

Code 3

Bill Ranger bit into a liverwurst sandwich just as the alarm sounded. The guard stood there dumbly, the sandwich hanging out of his mouth. It had been the first time in three years that a Code 3 had been issued. He had no idea why nor was he privy to what went on down in the tunnels. Outside of a few hotshot scientists and a brute named Harry Grimm, the area was off limits.

"Morning sir," he sometimes greeted Grimm when he entered the facility. "How is everything today?"

Grimm's face hardened into concrete. He'd stop, stare, and blow cigarette smoke in the guard's face. "Mind your own business." Grimm poked him in the chest and sauntered down the hall.

Ranger wouldn't take that kind of crap from anyone, but that guy? He'd blow a six-inch hole in someone's head for looking at him sideways.

The shrill alarm continued to sound.

"Rats?" He blinked and scratched his head.

The other day a shipment of mice got delivered to the facility. He wondered if some of them got lose. That had to be it. The little bastards were scurrying around down in the tunnels and driving all the resident scientists ape-shit.

Pondering the mysteries, Ranger reached across the desk and flipped a red switch. A loud clunk sounded out as the security doors locked.

"That does it." He slapped his hands together at a job well done. Verbatim the company handbook, during a Code 3 alert, all entrances and exits shall be locked until the crisis is averted.

Ranger was about to take another bite of his sandwich when a yellow light flicked on the intercom. "Are you up there?"

The security guard swallowed a hunk of liverwurst and flicked the button. "Yes sir?"

"Is the gate locked?"

"Well…"

"Is the goddamn gate locked!" Stoner shouted so loud the speaker nearly fractured.

"Yes but…"

"Don't talk moron," Stoner said. "Just listen. Keep things secure. Nobody gets in or out of the building. Are we clear?"

"Yes," Ranger said. "But what if…"

"Nobody!" Stoner roared. "Not even the president has clearance without my say so, got it?" The intercom blinked back off.

Staring at the receiver, Ranger shrugged and sat down on a chair. "Might as well relax." Sniffing indifferently, he poured a cup of coffee from his thermos.

Again, he wondered what crisis might be unfolding in the building's lower levels. Sometimes he almost wished some of the action would surface. A big night at the office for him usually consisted of staring at blank monitors and paging through old car and driver magazines. Man, what he'd do for a little excitement in his life.

Taking a sip of coffee, Ranger stopped short and stared down the corridor. Someone was coming.

———

Sam Cage lifted his head off the boiler room floor. Groaning from where he got clubbed, he rubbed the back of his neck and opened his eyes. Alan Stoner stood in front of him.

"You're bleeding," Stoner pulled out a handkerchief and tossed it to Cage.

Memories of the escape flooded Cage's mind like a coastal

wave. "Blackheart hit me," he said groggily. "I think he's gone."

Out in the corridor, Harry Grimm barreled down the hall. Gun in hand, he systematically did a room to room search.

Cage pushed himself up on bruised elbows and rattled the dust from his head. He needed to think fast. If Stoner suspected that he helped Blackheart get away, he'd disappear quicker than a prop in a magic act.

"Wait for me in my office," Stoner told him. "We'll talk more when we're out of the alert."

Cage said nothing. He could see the glow of suspicion in Stoner's eyes. He considered running. It wouldn't do much good of course. Security would stop him before he ever stepped off the curb of the property.

Wobbling to his feet, Cage headed towards Stoner's office. Whether Jonas Blackheart got recaptured was irrelevant. The Agency had a notorious reputation for quick trials. If they deemed Cage guilty of aiding Blackheart in his escape, there'd be no stay of execution. In fact, as far as Cage was concerned, the switch had already been pulled.

39

Dead Man Walking

The coffee cup dropped from Ranger's hand when he saw the man lumbering up the corridor. His eyes widened as if staring down a ghost. It was all over the news a few weeks back. He still remembered the story. The guy's name was Jonas Blackheart. He shot some people at a convenience store. The police gunned him down. Afterwards he disappeared out of a hospital and then supposedly died in a car crash out on 903. Ranger of course had a different vantage point. If the bastard was dead, he turned into a walking zombie.

Sleepless black sacks festered under Blackheart's eyes. He looked so cold and lifeless you'd have sworn someone kept him hogtied in a meat locker.

"Hold it right there," Ranger yelled and pointed a finger.

Blackheart ignored him. Reaching the security desk, he staggered against the wall. "Open the gate," he ordered.

Ranger reached for his gun but Blackheart grabbed his arm. Cracking his hand against the steel desk the security guard dropped the weapon. "I said open up!"

"I can't do that." Ranger swallowed hard. "We're under a Code 3 alert."

"Do you want to die?" Blackheart reached around and grabbed Ranger by the throat. "Open it."

Sweat beaded off Ranger's face. Blackheart wasn't just desperate; he looked deranged. You could see it in his eyes. They were hollow. Unforgiving. Damp greasy hair hung in his face. A fat scar zigzagged down the side of his cheek.

"Last chance." He squeezed Ranger's throat.

Gagging, Ranger reached across the desk and reluctantly punched a code in on a panel. The security door at the main entrance opened. Releasing his grip, Blackheart bolted out the door. Ranger, down on one knee, gasped for air.

———

"Shit!" Harry Grimm glanced in a hall monitor near the conference room.

Jonas Blackheart stood at the front desk. His arm was wrapped around the security guard's throat.

Grimm pulled out his gun and raced up the hall. Before he ever turned the corner leading to the main entrance, he opened fire. Hot bullets ricocheted off walls and ceilings. Ranger hit the floor to avoid a spray of metal.

"Where is he?" Grimm shouted.

Ranger peeked out from under a desk. "I don't know."

Grimm slammed a fist on the exit door and pointed an accusing finger. "You're lying." Kicking the desk, Grimm fired off another shot that landed in an air duct. Bending down under the desk he put his gun to Ranger's throat. "Listen asshole, I don't have time for games. Did you leave anyone out of the building?"

"No, I mean…"

"Answer. I'll open a hole in your head the size of a tangerine!"

"He threatened to kill me," Ranger blurted out.

"I'll kill you!" Grimm shouted.

"It was that guy on television that killed those people at a convenience store," Ranger said. "Jonas Blackheart. I swear it was him!"

Harry Grimm looked up to see Alan Stoner approaching the front desk. "Bad news," he told Stoner. "The rat is out of the cage. Our friend here opened the damn door." He jammed the gun tighter against Ranger's throat. Icy chills congealed on the security guard's shivering bones.

"You let him out?" Stoner's eyes narrowed.

"Say goodbye," Grimm jostled the trigger of his gun.

"Wait," Stoner said. "Don't kill him yet." He looked at the exit door and then glared at Ranger. "I have other plans for our friend."

40

A Sleepless Night Summer Night (Revisited)

"I still can't figure out how he got loose." Harry Grimm tightened his fists. "Blackheart was tied up in restraints. He had to have help."

Alan Stoner sat quietly in the corner of the room. He drummed his fingers on the table and glanced at Cage whose face was dabbed with suspicion.

Cage fidgeted and rubbed at the bruise on his head. Stoner suspected him. Even worse. If the Agency thought he had a hand in Blackheart's escape he'd be dead by morning. He glanced at the clock. It was 4:00 a.m. and raining buckets. A heavy clap of thunder boomed outside. Somewhere out there, Blackheart wandered the night.

"Blackheart is crazy but even a guy like that has an agenda," Grimm said. "Where do you suppose he'll go?"

"Does it matter?" Cage shifted nervously in his seat. "He's psychotic. Has anyone called headquarters or told Jack Raison? Nobody heard from him since this entire thing started."

"Raison is out of the loop right now," Stoner answered.

"Out of the loop?"

"Some kind of sickness. He'll be out on leave for a while."

"What about the police?" Cage asked.

Harry Grimm glared. "What the hell is wrong with you? Cops are the one thing we don't need. You were one of the last people to see Blackheart." He eyed Cage suspiciously. "What's your take on what happened?"

"I already told you." Cage stuck to his guns. "I don't know anything. He hit me from behind."

On the other side of the room Alan Stoner stood up. Turning around he looked out the darkened window. Thunder ripped the night. An evening shower broke from the clouds.

"No sense pointing fingers. We'll deal with that later." He glanced at Cage. A crayon of distrust scribbled his face.

Cage wiped sweat off his neck. The more he tried to stay dry, the more he dripped with admissions of guilt.

"There's nothing left to do but wait." Stoner tapped his fingers on the windowsill. After a minute he turned around. "There's a small town north of here. It's called Jim Thorpe, named after some Indian athlete. It might be a good place to start looking."

Cage tilted his head. "What makes you think Blackheart would head in that direction?"

Alan Stoner's eyes bolted on Cage and then turned back to the rain spattered window. "I guess it's irrelevant. Sure as hell we'll know when he turns up. In the meantime, we wait for him to make a mistake. Then we make our move."

Part Three

The 7th JACKAL

41

An Unexpected Visitor

Wind rustled in the trees on Pisgah Mountain. AJ Samson kneeled down on the ground and clutched at loose soil. Along with dirt and leaves, tears covered his dog's final resting place.

Lifting his head, AJ peered into the woods and wiped his nose with a dirty sleeve. "That thing killed my dog. I'm gonna get him for that. I swear I'm gonna get him."

Becca put an arm around AJ. Standing beside them, Keenan's eyes remained cemented in the darkness, watchful and alert.

"We've got to keep moving," Keenan warned. "Whatever is out there can't be far."

Becca stared into an impenetrable darkness that was only outweighed by her rising dread. "Maybe we should go home. We could tell the police what happened."

"What about Tugger?" asked Keenan. "He's in trouble. There isn't much time."

Getting off his knees, AJ stood up. His eyes scanned the forest. "Do what you want," he told his friends. "I'm not turning back."

Determination swam in AJ's eyes. He began climbing the mountainside. Refusing to abandon their friend, Becca and Keenan followed along like candles flickering in the wind. Decayed leaves and broken branches crunched under their feet as they scaled the hills.

Keenan sniffed as he walked. The fragrance of wild flowers dabbed the air as did the hint of sweet apples and pine. Still, there was something else. An ill odor; the stink of something rotting and cold as death itself.

———

A sunken breeze whispered in tree branches. A canopy of leaves grew so thick that even if the sun shined, little light could have seeped through and would have been reduced to a flickering shadow. A distant echo of far-off thunder sounded. A storm passed somewhere in the ancient ruins of a forgotten world. With each step taken up the mountainside their sneakers sunk deeper into the damp soil.

"I think we're being watched." Becca looked at the trees.

"It's just your imagination," AJ said hopefully.

"I don't think so." Keenan stiffened. He stared into the gloom. "Douse your flashlights."

"What is it?" asked AJ.

"Something's out there. Just over that ridge." He pointed. "It's coming towards us."

The forest had all the makings of a black cloak shrouded in mystery. Still they could see the dark figure moving under passing traces of moonlight.

Keenan whispered. "Stay quiet and don't move."

Rigid and inflexible, AJ's fists balled at his sides. Disregarding the danger, he stood up and glared fearlessly into the gloom.

"AJ!" Becca gasped. "Get down before it sees us."

But AJ refused to move. Shaking with anger and wet with tears, his embattled eyes were cemented to the oncoming threat.

"You killed my dog, you stinking wretch!" AJ shouted.

The darkman stopped cold. His impenetrable gaze hung tight

as a noose around their necks. He moved slowly forward. Suddenly he broke into a full sprint and headed directly towards them.

"Run!" Becca grabbed AJ's arm.

However, running was futile and escape, impossible. The darkman's arrival would be measured in seconds rather than minutes.

Keenan pawed at the forest floor and searched for something to use as a defense. He gasped when he looked up to find the adversary nearly on him. Suddenly the darkman veered left. He disappeared behind a mound of rocks and weeds.

"Where did he go?" Becca's teeth chattered like broken bones. She flicked on the flashlight and shined it around the trees. The light landed on the brute's face. His jaws snapped; a shark preparing to gobble a meal intact rather than pick it apart piece by piece. Pipelines of terror shot through the girl. The darkman leapt over a log straight towards her.

AJ jumped in front of Becca and raised his fists. Taken off guard, the attacker backed up but quickly lunged forward again. Swinging wildly, he swatted AJ and Becca out of the way. Turning, he glared at Keenan. Contempt painted his face. Moments from a certain kill, a large hand reached out and pushed Keenan out of the way.

———

The sudden blast of a shotgun reverberated in the night.

"Take that!" someone shouted and fired again.

The darkman quickly reversed direction. Tramping over weeds and bushes he retreated back up the mountainside.

"No stomach for a fight!" the stranger hollered. He looked around at the small soldiers. "Are you kids okay?"

AJ stood up and dusted himself off. Becca flicked on her flashlight and shined it in the face of the unexpected visitor.

The stranger had a salt and pepper beard. His brown eyes glinted like polished pennies in the sun. Given his red cheeks and lines webbing his eyes, he was the survivor of many years and any number of whiskey bottles. Grimy with holes at the knees, his tattered denims were a size too big and bunched up around a pair of mud-spattered clodhoppers.

AJ stared and slapped a mosquito off his neck. Finally, he asked, "Who are you?"

"I should be asking you that question," the stranger answered.

Becca looked around fearfully. "What is that thing?"

The stranger sucked at his lips. "It isn't the first time I've seen him and probably won't be the last. He's been prowling around these woods for days."

Peering into the night, Keenan probed the forest lawn. "I think he's gone for now."

"Maybe." The stranger pulled at his beard stubble. "Just the same, I think you better follow me. Whatever that devil is it's likely he isn't far off." He pointed the barrel of his gun as if to insist. "That way."

42

Wild Bill Finch

"In here." The stranger pushed open the door of a shack buried in the woods. Striking a match, he lit a kerosene lantern. The wick flickered and danced off the wooden walls. Holding the lantern up, his grayish beard looked like a hastily made bird's nest against a face smudged with grime.

"Who are you?" asked Becca.

"The name is Willie Finch," he said. "You can call me Wild Bill." Walking over to the stove he picked up a dirty spoon and a frying pan from the griddle. Scooping out a gob of brown muck that clung to the bottom of the pan, he savored the foodstuff in his mouth for a moment then swallowed and belched. "You kids hungry?" He set the pan down in front of AJ.

Sitting cross-legged on the floor, AJ sniffed and crinkled his nose. Burnt black beans stuck fast to the bottom of the pan. Flies hungrily buzzed around the outdated cuisine.

"I'll pass," AJ reached down and fingered his bruised ribs.

"Looks like you got sucker punched," said Wild Bill.

"It's just a scratch but it hurts."

"Ha!" Wild Bill slapped the kitchen table. "Trust me. You don't know what pain is." He walked over to a contraption sitting in the middle of the room. It was constructed from ash buckets and rubber hoses. Pushing a handle, he poured a concoction into a grimy cup and drank it down.

On the other side of the room, Keenan Braddock stared out the window into darkness. Satisfied that any immediate threat of

159

danger had passed, he turned around. "What are you doing out here all alone in the woods?" he asked.

Wild Bill plopped down on a milkcrate. "That's a long story." He took a swig of whiskey. "Years ago I worked at the steel mills in Bethlehem. Life was good back then. Saturday nights were spent drunk and fooling with the local floosies," he said. "Then one day an army recruiter in a snazzy uniform turned up on my doorstep. He did a lot of fast talking. Said I should think about enlisting in the army. He even told me I'd get free room and board. Best of all, everyone knows soldiers in uniforms get all the women. People sometimes called them WAC's. Yup, I was gonna get me a WAC.

"Well guess what?" he complained. "After boot camp my unit got ordered to board a plane and stand a post on some shit island in the south pacific. Half the time the bastards sent us on maneuvers. We slept in a jungle under green tarps. We'd get bit up by mosquitoes all night and the food didn't taste much better than morning puke. And all those WAC's everyone told me about?" Irritation crusted his face. "The only thing that came even close to a beautiful woman was a village whore named Niamey who doubled as a tattoo artist. I remember that sonofabitch." He pursed his lips bitterly. "One night we were getting a little frisky in a tent. I pulled off my fatigues and she hit me with a shovel. She stole all my money, not to mention my shoes. I had to crawl back to my unit butt naked."

AJ Samson stared dumbly and scratched his head. "What does any of this have to do with that thing in the woods?" he asked.

Wild Bill pointed a crooked finger. "I'll tell you what it has to do with it you little smart ass. Back then we were all just milksops that should have been home telling lies to our girlfriends about how much we loved them. Instead we were over on some shit island playing with guns and sleeping under tarps with rain dripping off our noses. When I finally got back home I had enough of people. I picked up my belongings and moved to the mountains. I've been here ever since."

AJ and Becca stared in bewilderment.

"Enough talk." Wild Bill set his whiskey down. "Now give it to me straight. What are you kids doing out here in the middle of the night?"

Keenan's face glowed with empty silence. Finally, he stepped forward. "Our friend is missing. We think that thing in the woods has him."

Wild Bill scratched his chin thoughtfully. "If that's true then the lid on your friend's coffin is probably already nailed shut. I know a killer when I see one."

"I don't think so." Keenan insisted. "He's still alive."

"How do you know?"

"I just know. I can feel it."

Wild Bill said, "Dead or alive, I'm telling you something." He pointed outside. "That thing out there? He's not just angry. He's hungry. I've seen him before."

Becca leaned forward. "Do you know what it is?"

Wild Bill stood up. He walked over to the window and peered into the dark. A suspicious glow overshadowed his face as if they were being watched. After a minute he turned back around, pulled out a kitchen chair and sat down.

———

"When I was in the military, I had a friend named Spider Lugosi," Wild Bill said. "His family had more money than there is mud on a pack of hogs. They could have paid the army off or got some uppity ass in the pentagon to give him a discharge. But a kid like that? He wanted to stick it out. Play superhero," he said. "Spider figured that once he got out of the service he'd become a doctor and make a fortune cutting corns off toes.

"Ha!" Wild Bill laughed and slapped a knee. "People like that don't have the stomach for combat let alone being a medical doctor. Even a paper cut made Spider squeamish."

Wild Bill took another slug of whiskey. "We had this crazy bastard named Raker Biggs in our outfit. One night he decided to play a prank on Spider. Raker stole some raw hamburger and a quart of applesauce from the mess tent. Afterwards he dressed down to his skivvies and sprawled out on his bunk. Some of Raker's buddies, myself included, dumped the foodstuff all over him. Then we stood in a circle around Raker, holding knives and forks.

"Raker started howling, "Help me! I'm being eaten alive!"

"Spider slept close by. He told Raker that he was just having a nightmare and to shut the hell up before he wakes the entire camp. Finally, Spider turned on a lamp. He saw all of us standing around Raker pretending to spoon out his innards. One crazy bastard actually put on a chef's hat and sprinkled a salt shaker.

"Spider screamed and ran out the door," Wild Bill said. "He disappeared in the darkness. Nobody ever heard from him again. I always figured he just starved to death in the jungle." He swished hooch around in his mouth and then swallowed hard. Leaning forward he said, "At least that's what I thought all these years until last night."

———

"It was early evening," Wild Bill said. "I sat here drinking hooch and whittling a stick. Then I heard something outside and opened the door to take a look around. Sure enough, someone with green eyes peered at me from behind a trash barrel. I thought it was a pesky bear. The thing is, something looked familiar about those eyes.

"Who's out there?" I shouted.

"Nobody answered. Still you could imagine the surprise when I saw Spider Lugosi staring back at me. He didn't look as if he aged a day since our stint in the army.

"Spider, is that you boy?" I called.

"Grunting miserably, he kept digging in the trash barrel. I ran back in the house and bolted myself in. The next thing I heard, someone knocked at the door. I figured it might be Spider's ghost coming back to haunt me for that prank we played on him back on that shit island in the south pacific all those years ago.

"Spider, you old coot!" I shouted. "Get the hell back to the dead where you belong or I'll put a buckshot up your ass, if'n ghosts even have asses!" I fired off a round to put the fear of God in him." Wild Bill pointed at a hole in the ceiling. "Spider took off like a frightened raccoon. Still there was something strange," he said. "I turned around and caught a glimpse of him in the moonlight. He didn't look like Spider any longer. He was more bullish, even hefty with a little deformity in his loins."

Becca stiffened. "That's him!"

Wild Bill sighed and got to his feet. Stepping over to the window, his eyes were two search lights combing the darkness. "It'll be daybreak in a few hours." Opening a closet drawer, he pulled out some musty blankets and tossed them on the floor. "My guess is that thing out there is a vampire; he does his best hunting at night. He could come back. Wherever your friend is tonight, he'll have to fend for himself." Pulling a chair over to the window he sat down with the shotgun in his lap. "Get some sleep. I'll take the first watch."

43

Premonitions

Somewhere in the middle of the night, Keenan Braddock sat up quickly. He looked around in confusion. Wild Bill slumped down in a chair beside the window, snoring soundly. His shotgun and a slanted mug of moonshine were still in his hands. Directly in front of him AJ Samson sat cross-legged on the floor, staring at him.

Keenan pushed himself up on bruised elbows. "What's wrong?"

"You were having a nightmare," AJ whispered.

Keenan hesitated. "I think something bad happened to Tugger."

"Where do you suppose he is?"

"I'm not sure but if we don't find him soon, we'll never see him again."

"We'll find him." AJ tapped his friend's shoulder.

"There was something else," Keenan said.

"What?"

"I was at a funeral."

AJ paused and swallowed hard. "Is one of us going to die?"

Keenan remained silent.

AJ sat up straight. He touched his side and grimaced. "That thing in the woods really clipped me." He lifted his shirt. A cherry color bruise garnished his side, just above the ribs.

A veil of sorrow covered Keenan's face. "Does it hurt much?" he asked.

"Don't worry." AJ kept his head up and lip firm. "It'll be a cold day in the devil's sandbox before this slows me down."

Fingering the wound again he flinched. "The bruise burns a little, almost as if someone poured salt in it. I'd imagine it'll take some time to heal."

A thin coat of tears glistened Keenan's eyes. Finally, he said, "Sometimes it's the old wounds that never heal."

44

Tugger Rhodes' Big Escape

Crickets chirped and the wind blew in the trees as Tugger Rhodes peered into the gloom.

The nightmare started after sneaking out of his house to meet AJ and his friends. On his way home, a stranger abducted and dragged him off into the forest. After tying his hands around a tree with a piece of rope, his captor then disappeared. Tugger had been sawing the rope against a tree trunk ever since until it finally snapped.

Staring into canyons of darkness, he had no idea how to get back home or which direction to take. One thing was certain. When the darkman returned he needed to be gone.

Tugger started to walk. The smell of damp earth and decomposing leaves made the atmosphere feel thick and stuffy. At times the moon broke through a canopy of trees; it bleached the stones on the mountainside. For the most part night pressed in on him from all sides, darker than a coffin covered with dirt.

"Hang on," he told himself. "You'll get out of this."

To the left of him water permeated the inky blanket of night. A stream was close by. If nothing else the sound of running water might help cover the noise of twigs snapping and stones being kicked as he trudged along.

A noise up ahead made him flinch. He wondered if it might be a bear or a wolf. A loud grunt that sounded nearly human made his heart stop cold. If his captor realized he escaped, he'd be searching for him. If he got caught again, he sensed that there would be no stay of execution.

Directionless or not, rather than be captured the boy decided to take flight. Trudging through the forest, he came across a creek and splashed through it to the other side. However, the far side of the stream provided little means of escape. A large wall of rocks that led to the mountain's summit cutoff any hope of refuge. Climbing wouldn't be easy but considering the consequences, standing still would prove deadly.

Somewhere in the near distance the clatter of footsteps tromped over leaves and broken branches. The hunter grew close.

Tugger put a firm foot on a rock and tried climbing the embankment. If nothing else he might be able to avoid capture by hiding in one of the crevices of rock until daybreak. With any luck he could then find his way back home.

———

The jagged rocks felt sharp against Tugger's skin. He hardly noticed it with the adrenaline pumping. Still fear struck him like an anvil. He was afraid of heights. The slightest glance downward left his limbs flailing in the wind. Some of the rocks were slippery. Twice his feet slid off the megalith. Grasping at an overhanging cliff he hung tight in midair. His foot eventually caught solid ground and he sighed in relief. Focus was key and without he'd be dead.

Breathing heavy, the boy found another open fissure and managed to pull himself up the rugged terrain a little further.

More than once his eyes drifted down to the foot of the gully. Any wrong move and he'd crash to the bottom of the ravine. Pebbles of stones fell off a ledge as his fingers struggled to grasp something solid.

Tugger looked up at the peak of a cliff above him. Only a few more yards and he'd be at the top.

"Another good push," he encouraged himself.

Lifting up his leg he searched for a foothold. Finding one, he inched his way upward another step or two.

"Yes!" he cried, sensing that he just might make it.

However, that same elation was short-lived. He glanced down at the bottom of the gully and saw a pair of green eyes staring up at him.

45

The Ledge

"Is that you AJ?" Tugger called out.

Nobody answered but clearly something had taken up residence at the foot of the embankment. In a ghostly glow of moonlight, a shadowy figure scaled the rugged boulders and steep rocks. It moved at a deliberate pace, directly towards him.

"Get out of here!" Tugger picked up a rock and hurled it.

The darkman stopped on the ledge. Looking up, he stared at Tugger with eyes sunk in deep cavities of unmeasured hate.

"Help!" Tugger cried, flapping his arms in the wind.

Quiet laughter seeped from the darkman's throat. "It's no use. Your friends have abandoned you." Grabbing the ridge of a rock, he hoisted himself closer.

"I'm warning you. Stay away." Tugger clutched at the stone wall.

"Why don't you come down here?" he asked. "This is no place for a boy. Things walk in these woods at night. Bad things. Dead things. Crawl down. Let me help you."

A worm of fear wriggled in the Tugger's young guts. "I'll be managing just fine, thank you very much," he answered. "My friends will be along soon enough. You go on now." He shushed him away. "Go back to the dead or wherever it is you came from."

A wire of uncertainty crossed the darkman's face. He anticipated terror but got what amounted to a good scolding by a thirteen-year-old boy.

"Don't be stupid," he whispered. "You're trapped like a corpse nailed in a crate. Don't move. I'll come and help you or at least make the end quick." The darkman latched on to another cleft in the rock and took a step up.

Tugger's heart raced. "Stay away!" he shouted.

Stinking like rotted meat, the darkman glared with fiery red eyes. "What's wrong, are you afraid to die? You should be," he assured him. "It's cold over there in the dead lands. Zombies are everywhere. I think they'd be fond of a lad like you. They'd tear you up. Slaughter you like a spring lamb."

"What do you want from me?" Tugger asked.

The darkman paused. "I want you to die."

Tugger shivered. He looked from one direction to the next, hoping that some unsung champion would ride out of the darkness and save him. Still, nothing moved besides the wind against the leaves of trees.

"You might as well give up." Tugger held firm. "I'm not coming down."

The skinless edge of the darkman's top lip turned up fiercely. "Brat!" He glared and pulled himself up another mark.

Tugger gasped. He tried to move. However, the darkness made it nearly impossible to see any stable ridges in the rocks to use for footing. Nightfall, on the other hand, didn't change the pace of his adversary. Gravel spilling off the mountainside under the weight of his shoes, he climbed closer.

A great chasm of blackness coupled with the threat of a treacherous enemy overshadowed Tugger's heart. Looking around, he spotted a breach in the wall. The fissure looked deep. Perhaps even deep enough to crawl inside.

Stretching his legs, he got a foothold in the crevice and pulled himself over to the breach in the rocks. Directly beneath him the enemy's eyes glittered madly in the moonlight. Reaching up he grabbed Tugger's ankle.

"Ah!" Tugger howled and wriggled free.

"Don't fight me," he said in a gravelly voice. "It'll only make things worse."

Bending down, Tugger wriggled into the opening in the rocks

and looked at the hollow insides of the deep chasm. He couldn't see bottom. When he looked up, he gasped when he saw his captor's ghostly face staring back at him.

"It's time to die." He raised a fist.

Tugger screamed. His foot slipped off the ledge. Seconds later, he found himself tumbling down into the darkness.

———

The darkman lurched forward and tried to latch on to Tugger's arm before he made a getaway but the kid was too quick. He disappeared through a breach in the rocks. Given the size of the opening, pursuit proved impossible. The boy had escaped.

"Wicked scum!" He angrily pounded a fist off the rocks.

Aside from the moaning wind, he found himself alone in the wilderness. The darkman tried to recall his past, and although memory failed him, surely something bad happened. At times familiar people flashed in and out of his mind like lost and floating ghosts.

Peering down at the rocks far beneath him, for an instant he had a compulsion to jump.

"Killing yourself won't resolve anything," a rogue voice sounded out. For a minute he thought that the boy in the hole talked to him but realized the voice came from inside his head.

"Who's there?" he called out.

No answer.

"Talk to me!" he shouted. "Who am I?"

"You really don't know?" the voice said. *"Your name is Jonas. Jonas Blackheart. You were a real gunslinger sport, remember?"*

The darkman closed his eyes. He fought to remember the past. He recalled being in a convenience store. There was a gunfight. He blacked out and almost died.

"Almost died?" The voice hissed. *"You were rotting away in a coma. That's worse than death."*

The darkman coughed. A rope of phlegm dribbled down the

corners of his lips. His head hurt as if it were smashed with a hammer. "Who are you?" he asked.

"You really haven't figured it out? I'm the dark half," the voice buzzed in his head. *"I'm that quiet woman at the end of the block who wakes up in the middle of the night and sticks a butcher knife in her husband's throat. I'm that momentary madness in a shy teenager's life, the one who walks into a store and blows the cashier's head off with a shotgun for a ten dollar bill and a pack of cigarettes. I'm the dark side, the corpse in the corner of the cemetery, the uncivilized half that people try and keep buried. You shoveled me out."*

The darkman didn't see the need for a psychological profile. Even with a faded memory, he had enough sense to know that he wasn't the most stable brick in the wall. Some people were born mad. Others achieved madness and still others had madness thrust upon them. He suspected he had a little of each.

Still his past, at best, was murky. As a kid he remembered being self-doubting. Oversensitive. Then again, what kid wasn't a little insecure? Nope. Most of his life had been normal. Still something happened to make an invisible monster take shape and rise out of the ashes. It slowly took control of his thoughts. Ate them up like cancer. Celebrated killers like Lizzie Borden would have been proud of the transformation.

——

If memory served him correct, he hadn't been lucky when it came to making money. Broken down apartment buildings and fast food diners were a way of life. Sometimes he picked up a few bucks working at car washes and grocery stores during his college days. He also slept under a bridge or two in his life. Welcome to capitalism personified.

One day while paging through a newspaper he found an ad for work at a place called Harbor Point. It was a governmental program. They were doing research on volunteers who wanted to make an extra buck. He fit the bill.

Harbor Point insisted that all candidates sign wavers in the event of mental or physical damage during the research phase of the program. The job itself seemed easy enough. He was required to drink a daily dosage of something that tasted about as appetizing as sour milk. The concoction made him woozy. Sometimes outright sick. Afterwards he'd take a battery of tests. Most of it was geared towards clairvoyance aptitude. There were also those embarrassing moments when he was asked to masturbate or pee in a plastic cup. In the end he knew very little about the modus operandi but it didn't matter. He needed the money.

One thing was certain. If the government was trying to engineer a telepath or a mind reader, he didn't feel the power. He did, however, begin to have other side effects. At times he grew abnormally tense. Sometimes he suffered a mounting urgency for violence. He also didn't sleep much. A few hours a night at best. Mostly he flipped through channels on the television until sunrise.

Still, once upon a time normality had been part of his life. He even recalled having a girlfriend. She attended the University of Pittsburgh. Man, she had one hell of a chassis on her. He got so angry when he found out that she was sleeping with someone else that he broke into her dorm, tore all her posters off the walls and threw her books out the window. Later that week he saw her boyfriend, Mr. Cool Toes, walking down the street. He spun his tires, pulled out of an alley, and snapped the guy's ankles like pencils. He didn't intend to harm anyone. He just wanted to put the fear of God in the guy.

The point is he never would have done something like that a few months back, but after he joined Harbor Point? Things were different. His mind changed. The thing is, before the week ended? He was uncertain whether he ran the guy down with his car or if it had all been just a dream.

At times he didn't recognize if things were real. He even remembered going into the supermarket and having a conversation with his mother, and she died fifteen years ago. Call it schizophrenia.

"Excuse me," the guy across the hall in 4B of his old apartment building had told the landlord after he threw his television out the window in a fit of rage for playing it too loud. "I think your tenant is going insane."

That was an understatement. Once he contemplated suicide. In the end he never had the guts to swallow a bullet or a bottle of pills. Still, he slowly went crazy. Even worse. He started to hear voices in his head.

———

"Are you listening, Jonas?" A voice inside his head pulled him out of the daydream. He was surprised to find himself standing on the ledge. *"Don't fight me."*

"Leave me alone!" Jonas shouted, wind in his face.

"I'm not the enemy."

"Then who is?"

"I think you know the answer to that."

Jonas turned his head. He stared into the black chasm where Tugger disappeared.

"You should have killed the boy when you had the chance," the voice said. *"Now things got complicated. Soon his friends will come. They'll try and save him, but that's okay too, and as it turns out, necessary. There's a ram among the sheep. One of them is named Keenan. You've see him in your dreams at times, haunting you. He needs to die. It's the only way you'll ever find any peace."*

Jonas looked blankly in the darkness. "I don't understand. Why kill him?"

"Don't talk stupid. He can read your mind. He knows your thoughts. In the end, he'll kill us both if we don't kill him first. Now," the voice said. *"Go after the boy that got away."*

"I can't fit through the opening in the rocks," he said.

"It's a cave, you moron," the voice said angrily. *"There has to be another way in."*

"I can't kill him in cold blood," Jonas insisted.

"Then I will," the voice insisted, resolving the issue.

Jonas blinked tiredly. Soon he'd fall asleep. That scared the hell out of him. Whenever he blacked out his thoughts dissolved like acid. He got swallowed inside nightmares.

And then it happened; the darkman woke up.

"Go ahead," the voice told him. *"Get some sleep. Leave the details to me."*

Jonas sat down tiredly on a rock. Unable to keep his eyes open, he fell into a restless sleep and shifted into a land of dark dreams.

46

A Visit with Jack Raison

Some miles south of Jim Thorpe in Bethlehem PA there was a knock on a door and a porch light flicked on.

"Are you a goddamn moron!" someone shouted and opened up. "It's the middle of the night." A man in a green bathrobe and grayish slippers pointed a handgun. He looked closely and blinked. "Sam Cage? What the hell are you doing here?"

Cage looked at the two Dobermans that flanked each side of Jack Raison. Their teeth were white and fully bared. Clearly a gun wasn't his only means of self-preservation.

"It's urgent that we talk." Cage's trench coat dripped from a drizzly rain.

Raison tilted his head and eyed him suspiciously. "I'm guessing you're not selling subscriptions to The Post." He lowered his gun. The Dobermans perked up almost as if compensating for the lack of security. Raison coughed hard. "In case you haven't noticed I haven't worked for the company in weeks. You might say I'm on a permanent vacation. Ha!" He wiped at his nose with a tissue. "In our business you'd think I could at least end up with a bullet to the head, something quick and painless. Nope. Instead I contracted a rare blood disease. Trust me on this one. Leukemia sucks."

Cage stood in the rain and stared. "I came a long way. Nobody knows I'm here. I only need a few minutes."

Raison eyed Cage carefully. "If you're working under the radar against The Agency you've got less breathing time on the planet than I do. Those bastards down at headquarters will have you boxed and buried before sunup."

Hands in pockets, Cage held firm. "I know the consequences. This is important."

Jack Raison paused and then suddenly laughed. "Okay Sam Cage. I'm doomed from a blood disease. You're walking the gallows on death row." He opened the door wide. "Step inside. I'd suggest that you don't make any sudden moves." He glanced down at his enormous pets. "Come and have a seat. We'll speak as one dead man to another."

———

"Drink?" Raison hobbled over to the bar and pulled out a bottle of the wet stuff. "This is fifty-year-old scotch. It'll wake your ass up. Not to mention it makes a great chaser for morphine." He pulled a pill out of the pocket of his bathrobe, popped it in his mouth and followed up with a stiff drink. Pouring another glass, he handed it to Cage and sat down on a recliner. "I got to tell you Cage. I don't get many visitors. It's kind of treat for me. Besides, it isn't every day that I get to talk to a corpse."

Cage reminded, "I'm still breathing."

Raison raised his glass and took another swallow. "The question is for how long?"

Even in muddy light, Raison's face sagged with nested lines, a trademark of too much liquor and cigarettes.

Sam Cage fidgeted. He gripped the arms of the chair as if he had gorilla glue on his hands. He knew Jack Raison. The guy was a piranha. Extortion. Murder. You name it. Clearly, he went downhill over the last few weeks. That didn't matter. He was still dangerous.

Looking down, the Dobermans continued to draw a circle around their master. No doubt about it. On Raison's command he'd be dinner inside of a minute.

"It happened about a year ago," Raison said. "I got diagnosed with leukemia. Fought like hell to beat it. Doctors told me to make the best of my time, something I had very little of. What you got to understand is this. In the end it always wins."

"Given the information I had, I figured I'd end up with a cinderblock tied around my neck and dragging the bottom of the East River," he continued. "That's the way The Agency usually does business when people cease to be useful. They disappear. Nope," he said. "The company put me on temporary status. In short, all that means is that some scumbag G-Man knocks on my door once a week and interrogates me. The boys down at headquarters want to know if I'm withholding any information before I go down to the worms."

Sam Cage leaned forward in his chair. "Are you?"

"Am I what?"

"Withholding information."

Jack Raison's eyes narrowed. "Don't try any of that smart shit on me," he said. One of the Dobermans growled in agreement. Taking a sip of his drink, he looked and said, "So how about it Cage? What are you really doing here?"

———

"What do you know about Jonas Blackheart?" asked Cage.

"What's to know?" Raison asked. "The Agency has him tied up in their little chamber of horrors, right?"

"Not anymore."

Raison stopped and stared. "He escaped?"

Cage paused. "There was an accident. He's on the loose. Nobody knows where."

A spark of excitement flickered in Raison's eyes. "So, someone finally got one up on The Agency." He grinned with amusement. "What does any of that got to do with me?"

"When Blackheart arrived at the facility, I read some of his old files," Cage said.

"He's a killer," Raison assured him.

"Only since we got our hands on him," Cage countered. "Before that he didn't even get a parking ticket. Back then he joined Harbor Point, a volunteer program you headed up on the other side of the state. I need to know what happened there."

Raison whistled. "Wow. You're a regular goddamn Dick Tracey. But I wouldn't get too smart," he warned. "Men with guns and Dobermans always have the upper hand." Taking another sip of his drink he leaned back in his easy chair. "To answer your question, Harbor Point was one of the company's satellite buildings. We did research on telekinesis, not to mention some other hocus pocus bullshit. Jonas Blackheart was one of our prodigies."

Cage tilted his head and leaned forward. "What do you mean?"

"It started with a hotshot scientist in the Swiss Alps. His name was Nester Hyde. He claimed he had a drug that promoted heightened states of awareness and opened untapped areas of the mind. Terrorism was on the rise. The military wanted a new super weapon to combat extremists. We needed volunteers to test the stuff."

Cage shifted uncomfortably. "Jonas Blackheart?"

"Blackheart was one of the monkeys, the last of seven candidates," Raison said.

"What happened to the first six?"

Raison paused. "There were side effects."

"Side effects?"

"The drug didn't work on everyone," he said. "The other candidates were about as psychic as a two-dollar gypsy in a boardwalk tent. We would have let them go. The problem was that they developed dementia and psychosis. They would have killed someone if they got loose on the streets," he said. "Eventually we needed to dispose of them."

Cage's eyes widened. "You killed them?"

"Not me, dumb ass. The Agency took them out."

"Blackheart killed people. Why didn't they get rid of him?" asked Cage.

"That's easy," Raison answered. "Blackheart responded to the treatment. The crazy bastard actually became telepathic. He was dangerous. Sort of the human version of a jackal. But we needed him alive. Unlike his cohorts he had the gift. The Agency could overlook murder if it got them the desired results."

Cage stared at Jack Raison. He tried not to get pushy. On the other hand, none of it seemed to matter to Raison. Now that death knocked on the doorstep, he was perfectly willing to spout off about top secret information that he had no business talking about.

"So, Blackheart is the only one left alive of the seven volunteers?" asked Cage.

"Yes and no." Raison hesitated. He picked up his drink, sipped it, and then set it back down on the table. "Harbor Point was a research facility. It also posed as a gynecology center. One day this woman walked in. She was naïve as hell." He crossed his legs and folded his hands. "We sedated her during a checkup. The next thing you know, bingo. She woke up pregnant and didn't know a goddamn thing."

Cage tilted his head. "What are you saying?"

"It's called artificial insemination," Raison said. "All that pissing and masturbating in cups that we had Blackheart doing during his stint at Harbor Point finally paid off."

Cage gripped the arms of the chair. "Blackheart has an offspring?"

The Dobermans ears perked up and they growled.

"Take it easy." He patted the dogs on the head. "These bastards sense tension. One wrong move and they'll tear your throat out," he said. "To answer your question, the kid's name is Keenan Braddock. He lives in a town about thirty miles north. If you want to locate Blackheart, find his son. My guess is that he's looking for him. There's no telling what he'll do if he finds the boy."

Cage said, "I don't understand. Even if Blackheart found out that he has a son, why would he kill him?"

"Why wouldn't he?" Raison countered. "Blackheart is narcissistic psychotic. Take a lesson from serial killers like Gacy. To him murder was a kind of love. Dalhmer ate his victims. That's how I see Blackheart," Raison said. "He's out of his mind."

"That's crazy," Cage said.

Raison smirked and jiggled the ice in his drink. "I'll tell you something crazier. You can bet your ass the company is just getting started. Give them time. They'll capitalize on their investments. Homeless people. Illegal aliens. Anyone who can evaporate from society without a trace. The Agency plans on building an army."

Cage stared. Of course, Raison was right. Before this was over others would disappear. Superheroes with psychic gifts would emerge, perhaps mentally unstable and almost certainly deadly.

Abruptly standing up, the Dobermans stiffened.

"Thank you," Cage said. "Can I count on you to keep a low profile on our conversation?"

Raison grinned like a shark. "You can't count on a sonofabitch like me for anything," he said. "You think you can take on the company? I'll make a deal with you Cage. You've got 24 hours before I report you. Do your dirtiest. Just keep this in mind. The Agency never loses. When things go nuclear, you'll be in Hiroshima."

Cage walked to the door. The Dobermans accompanied him with jaws dripping and wet.

"Goddamn-it heel!" Raison yelled and coughed up a storm. "Remember what I said Cage. You got 24 hours. After that the end comes quickly."

Nodding, Cage walked out the door and disappeared into the stormy darkness.

47

Interrogations

Alan Stoner glared at the man on table number two.

Joe Ranger's eyes darted around the room. His wrists twisted in their restraints. The last thing he remembered was standing at the front desk. The facility had been under a Code 3 alert. That's when he saw Jonas Blackheart headed up the ramp. Blackheart escaped. Now everyone was out to crucify him.

"Nobody is trying to blame you for anything." Stoner's fists were clenched so tight that his fingernails dug into the palms of his hands. "I just need to know if Blackheart said anything on his way out the door."

"I swear he didn't." Ranger trembled. "I couldn't stop him. He threatened me."

Harry Grimm paced the floor. Suddenly he stopped and whirled around. "The shithead is lying."

Stoner said to Ranger, "Nobody wants to hurt you. In fact, I'm sympathetic to your situation. Blackheart was a bad egg. I get that. He'd kill you faster than you could spit. Still I need to be certain. You can understand that, right? Think hard. Damn hard." He circled the table like a vulture. "Blackheart must have said something about where he was going."

"Nothing," Ranger insisted, his wrists twisting in irons. Fear swam in his eyes as if a gang of famished piranhas were eating him up from the inside. "He would have killed me if I didn't open the door."

Harry Grimm kicked the back wall. He looked mad enough to piss on a sleeping bear in the woods. "Can't you see he's just telling you what you want to hear? Give me a few minutes alone with him," he said. "If there's a story, trust me, he'll talk."

Stoner tapped his fingers impatiently on a table. "I'm a fair man Ranger. The last thing I want is for anything to happen to you, but this guy?" He glanced at Grimm. "He's a bastard. If you don't cooperate who knows what he'll do. You get what I'm saying, right?"

Ranger's eyes shifted from one enemy to the next. Dread avalanched down his face.

"This is pointless," Grimm said. He pulled out his gun and stuck it in Ranger's eye. "Three seconds. Start talking."

Ranger's face was a mass of electrical wires on overload. He looked ready to implode.

Grimm aimed his gun. Alan Stoner put his hand on the weapon and lowered it.

"Hold your fire," Stoner said. "There's better targets." He glanced at the security guard. "I'll finish up here. Right now, we got other problems."

"Like what?" Grimm asked.

Stoner walked towards the door. "Follow me."

———

Harry Grimm stepped into Stoner's office. Ignoring a NO SMOKING sign Grimm pulled out a cigarette and lit up.

Fists closed, Stoner put his hands on his hips. "We got trouble."

"That's an understatement." Grimm blew a smoke ring in the air.

Stoner stared at Grimm with thin dry lips. He didn't like the guy. Strictly speaking, he was a company trained thug whose prime directive hinged on killing. It didn't matter. Allies were scarce these days. In fact, they were nonexistent.

"I'll need to trust you," Stoner said.

Grimm raised a curious eyebrow.

"You need to go back to Jim Thorpe."

Stone-faced, Grimm stared at his associate. "Is that so?" He leaned coolly against the wall nearest the exit door. "I'll tell you what I think. I talked to headquarters this morning. It seems they're not up to snuff on our friendly neighborhood telekinetic killer roaming the streets. They think Jonas Blackheart is still locked up. They also have no idea about the progress that has been made. After Jack Raison vacated his post, everything turned to shit. You didn't file any reports. It's almost as if you've been hiding something."

Stoner stood up. "I resent that."

"You also resemble it," Grimm reminded. "It's no secret what happens to people who hide things from the company, right?"

Stoner turned ghostly pale.

"Relax," Grimm said. "I didn't blow the whistle, at least not yet." He walked over to a candy dish and unraveled the foil off a mint. "Toffee?"

A bead of sweat gathered on Stoner's forehead. "I did nothing wrong."

"You're starting to sound like a parrot." Grimm laughed. "I've seen it all Stoner. Murder. Blackmail. You name it. I even smuggled machine guns to Iranian radicals in exchange for a spy who turned informant. Trust me. He won't be telling secrets anymore. It's tough talking with your tongue sliced off." The G-Man's eyes narrowed. "The moral of the story is, don't screw with me."

Stoner sat still and unmoving on his chair. "What's your point?"

Grimm walked over to the window. "The Agency thinks they control everything. Hell, I wouldn't even be surprised if they were the second shooter on the grassy knoll during the Kennedy assassination. They're only real downfall is substandard personnel working in the company. Murderers and extortionists aren't always the most loyal employees." He stuffed his hands in his pockets and put a foot up on a chair. "Then there's you."

Alan Stoner glanced at a desk in the corner of the room.

"Excuse me." Grimm snapped his fingers. "Am I boring you?" he asked. "I know there's a gun in that desk drawer. Don't even think about it. I'll rip out your throat before you get two steps." He took another drag of his cigarette and left out an exaggerated plume of smoke. "You've got a lot of secrets Stoner, especially where The Agency is concerned. I should commend you. It takes a real professional to blindside the company and avoid a bullet to the skull."

"I heard enough." Stoner stood up. "I'm leaving."

Grimm smiled and kicked a chair out from underneath the table. "You're going nowhere," he said. "Sit down."

———

Harry Grimm pulled a burlap sack from his pocket. Uncorking it he took a swallow.

On the other side of the room a puddle of sweat mopped Stoner's brow. Holding a pencil in his fingers, it snapped under the weight of the pressure.

"You're crazy," Stoner announced.

"Am I?"

"You really think I'm stupid enough to take on The Agency?"

Grimm smirked. "I think guys like you would do anything for money and power. Face facts Stoner. You're not exactly Mother Teresa. You got balls the size of oranges."

A shadow of contempt passed over Stoner's eyes. Perhaps the G-Man had more brains than he gave him credit for. He was right of course. Undesirables would be eager to contribute to his offshore bank account by purchasing the formula. Within days The Agency would put a contract on his head. That wouldn't matter. He'd have already changed his identity. Moved on. Fruity cocktails on an island in the tropics sounded better all the time.

There was still the little matter of Jonas Blackheart. The authorities signed his death papers. Now he rose from the dead. If the police identified him, the trail would lead straight to his doorstep. Instead of a beach house in Maui he'd be sharing a toilet and toothpaste with some brute in the state pen.

Staring at Grimm, man, he'd just love to knock that shit-eating grin off his face. But he needed to be careful. Grimm was a tripwire. He'd detonate if someone stepped on his toes. Then again that didn't matter either. He only needed him for one more job. After that the bastard would have an accident, like getting tied to railroad track on freight day.

Alan Stoner stared through steepled fingers. "You're perceptive. I'll give you that. Tell me. What is it you want from me?"

Grimm flicked ashes on the floor. "A million in cash would be good for starters.

Stoner paused and laughed. "Where would I get that kind of money?"

Grimm's lips stretched across his face like a morning worm. "It's called funding. All it takes is a little coercing. I'm sure all the fat asses down at the Treasury Department would be more than happy to accommodate you."

"That's blackmail," Stoner told him.

"Damn straight," Grimm agreed. "You crossed the line Stoner. You'd be dead in less than a heartbeat if The Agency found out what you did. They will unless you comply, get it?"

Stoner stared but said nothing.

"Also, there's still the problem of Sam Cage," Grimm continued. "He'll spill his guts to the authorities before this is over."

Stoner tapped his foot hard and fast on the floor. "Forget Cage," he said. "I'll take care of him. It's everything else that I'm worried about."

"Like what?" Grimm asked.

"Jonas Blackheart is on the loose," said Stoner. "Sooner or later the cops will catch him. When they do, they'll find out who he is. The authorities will arrest us. Blackheart needs to disappear. Kill him. Burn the evidence."

Grimm tapped his gun handle. "That's a snap." He clicked his fingers. "Of course, it'll cost another hundred grand or so."

"Don't worry. You'll get what's coming." Stoner stared. The bastard grated on his nerves. "Just one thing." He pulled a picture out of his pocket. "I need you to find this person."

Grimm stared at the photo. "You going into the kidnapping business?"

"His name is Keenan Braddock."

"I know who he is," Grimm said. "I tried to abduct him a few months back and ended up wasting his aunt. You want me to kill him?"

"Negative," Stoner said. "I need him alive. My guess is that Blackheart is looking for him. Find one and you'll find them both."

Harry Grimm's smug expression hung over the room like a stink bomb. Picking at his teeth he appeared no more moved over the idea of murder than leaving a dollar tip at a diner after drinking a cup of coffee.

"Leave the targets to me," he said. "Just a friendly reminder. Don't cross me Stoner. If you do, I'll hunt you down and mess up the office décor with blood."

Pointing his finger like the loaded trigger of a gun, Grimm exited the room.

48

Sam Cage takes a Walk

It was late evening when Henry Cage pulled his car into Wong's Chinese Pagoda. The parking lot was empty. Busboys and waitresses were cleaning up. The business was located within a two-block radius of the facility. It was no secret that the Agency had the complex rigged to blow in the event of a hostile incursion. For all Cage knew the blast might take out an entire city block. He could see the headlines in the newspaper.

TWELVE PEOPLE TRAPPED IN EXPLOSION
SMOTHER TO DEATH IN $4.00 PLATES OF CHICKEN
CHOW MEIN, WONGS SPECIAL OF THE DAY.

Cage's insomnia started earlier last evening. He paced the floor in the middle of the night. His mind kept filtering back to a crazy service technician who turned up a few weeks prior to run a safety check on all the computers.

According to him, a loophole in the security system could ultimately blow the entire Allentown facility off the face of the map. He jabbered on tirelessly about this stupid blue wire.

"Some crazy asshole snips the blue wire. BANG!"

"It can't be that easy," said Cage.

"Are you calling me a liar?"

"You're serious," Cage said in disbelief. "You mean that's really all it would take?" The eerie sensation of traipsing around a minefield overcame Cage. "It couldn't be that easy. The Agency would never overlook a detail like that."

"How many times do I have to say it? The blue wire. Snip." The tech man clapped his hands. "Bang! The whole place would go up like a rocket," he insisted. "It wouldn't matter. The company would just get funding and rake more tax dollars off the American taxpayer to rebuild the place. What do those scumbags care if my kid needs braces?"

It was ludicrous to think that The Agency could overlook a detail like that. Still brilliance had quirks. Some of the greatest scientific minds in the world couldn't tie their shoes.

"That would mean that anyone could blow up the place. The Agency has more sense than that, don't they?" Cage asked. "Everyone here would be killed. Innocent people would die. What about all that?"

"How do you think I feel?" The tech man looked bitter. He stuck a lime green lollipop in his mouth. "My tax rebate is riding on this piece of shit," he concluded. He packed up his toolbox and abruptly left.

That was the crazy service technician's words just a few weeks ago. Cage had been replaying that tape in his head ever since.

———

Cage giggled. For a moment he questioned whether he might be cracking up. He again thought about the disturbing conversation he had with the service technician some weeks ago.

"The blue wire. Snip. Bang," Cage muttered.

If what the crazy tech man said was true, the Allentown facility had a glitch in the system.

It came as no secret to anyone that company took precautions to guard against undesirables breaking into the facility and getting their hands-on classified information. When they made the Allentown facility, they installed an insurance policy. It came in the form of enough plastic explosives built into the interior walls to blast the entire structure into eternity.

"The building is rigged with detonation wire." The tech man

told him and pointed at a wall. "It burns at 3,600 feet per second. If a crisis happened, The Agency would handle it the same way they handle everything else. They'd make the place disappear. Everything would be fried hamburger faster than you could bite the skin off an apple," he told him.

The explosives were wired into a detonation station near the downstairs entrance of the facility. The dayshift supervisor at the Detonation Booth was a real hard ass named Isaac France. He was your typical company stooge. He'd blow a hole in anyone's skull that walked within twenty feet of the perimeter.

The same couldn't be said of Johnny Hammers, the G-Man assigned to the detonation booth. Hammers was tough but had a soft spot. Unlike his peers, he'd smile and shake hands before killing you. If needed, he'd have no problem adhering to the sign that hung on the front door that read:

ABSOLUTELY NO ADMITTANCE
VIOLATORS WILL BE SHOT

It was a constant reminder to even the highest brass that The Agency would not tolerate mistakes, intruders, or for that matter even a pizza delivery man from getting too close to the place.

Hammers stood in the security booth, face cold as ice. He sported the typical macho attitude. As far as he was concerned people were inanimate objects. They could breakdown and force him to dismantle them, piece by piece.

Unfortunately, something else happened to Hammers as the weeks passed. He became afflicted with the worst thing that could ever happen to a person in his position of control. Hammers grew comfortable with his surroundings. His cold exterior thawed. He started to become human. If headquarters would have been aware of the complication, they would have curled up in a fetal ball and wretched at the thought of one of their own mutating into something less than a killing machine.

"Morning," Hammers mumbled one day when Cage walked

by. The greeting caught in the G-Man's throat as if it were hooked on a zipper.

Cage drew back in surprise that Hammers said anything and nearly dropped his coffee cup. Hammers never spoke. Still there he was acknowledging people as something more than inorganic matter. Periodically he even risked a crude version of a smile and raising the inflexible corners of his lips.

One morning Johnny Hammers broke protocol altogether. He unbolted the security door after Cage expressed interest as to what was inside.

"Is this aloud?" asked Cage.

Hammers shrugged his shoulders. After considering for a minute, he opened the door.

Hammers didn't have the gift of being a conversationalist. At times his bottom lip quivered when he spoke, almost as if friendliness had been a foreign language that he never quite learned how to master. Sometimes he appeared shy. Except that he'd cut someone's heart out and stuff it in a meat grinder if they crossed him, he was one hell of a nice guy.

Cage knew that Johnny Hammers trusted him, an unlikely trait for any Agency hit man. That too would change before the day ended.

———

Cage called Ashley Braddock to warn her that she and her son were in danger. With luck she'd leave town before Jonas Blackheart found them. No matter what ensued, he wouldn't be able to help the woman. He had his own demons to wrestle.

Draping an elbow out the car window, Cage sat in front of Wong's. The evening was a bake oven. A disk jockey jabbered on the radio about the heat wave.

"We got another scorcher," the DJ said. "By sunup there'll be buns burning in bikinis. We're liable to all be dead from the heat by the afternoon."

No doubt about it. The DJ had a gift, but if it was up to Cage, the blast furnace would get stoked and burning long before sunrise.

Cage flicked off the radio. He reached in the glove compartment and pulled out a stick of gum, then exited the vehicle. Just across the highway and over the ridge of a grassy field, he could see the dark outline of the facility under a stark moon. Cage loosened his tie. Man, the DJ really hit the nail. The heat was stifling. That guy had to be a prophet.

Cage started walking. He liked that, walking that is. One of his greatest fears had been that one day he might lose the use of his legs. He'd be unable to enjoy that simple pleasure in life.

Looking up and down the highway, he crossed the road and stepped into a meadow of freshly cut grass. He headed straight for the facility. A warm wind played with his hair. He reached down and touched the purple yarn tied around his finger, a memento once given to him by Leona Smatters. Smiling, Cage looked up at the stars. He'd make this a good walk. A memorable one. Almost certainly his last.

49

Stepping Over the Blue Wire

It didn't take long to reach the back wall of the facility. Cage kept low. Staying unnoticed meant staying alive.

Cage almost laughed when he thought about the DJ again. He was probably spouting off right now. "It's gonna be a real blast for all you zombies hanging around the Agency parking lot," he'd say. "Crank up the pyrotechnics!"

The grounds were blanketed with electronic eyes. Still, there were blind spots. Cage became aware of them when the security guard at the front desk pointed it out.

"You can't see a thing around the corners of the building. Someone could walk in with a bazooka and nobody would know." The security guard, Joe Ranger, knocked a knuckle on the monitor.

Aside from inadequate cameras, a wooded backdrop of trees made for good camouflage if he needed to run.

Cage wiped a puddle of sweat off his neck. Tension strung itself across his forehead like taut cords of piano wire. If he had any say in it, he'd Lucky 13 the whole damn place before the night ended.

"If the detonation sequence becomes active, start running. Don't stop until you hit the Jersey shore," the crazy service technician told him on a routine check of the computers. "Headquarters calls it the Lucky 13. Snip and bang." He clapped his hands and spilled out information that he had no business discussing. He was your typical blowhard who didn't know when to keep his mouth shut. If headquarters would have known that he regularly spouted off about classified information they would have tied him to a whale and had him dragged out to sea.

———

One day Johnny Hammers left to check on something, leaving the tech man alone in the blast station. Cage happened to walk by. The tech man immediately started jabbering about classified information.

"Aren't you telling me restricted information?" asked Cage.

The tech man sniffed indifferently and pointed at a switch. "That's' a delay mechanism. Once the building's explosives are armed, there's thirteen minutes to clear the facility before she blows. Ha! Leave it to the company to pick a goddamn number like thirteen, right?" He pinged the switch with his finger. "Once the countdown reaches three minutes there's no way to shut it down. She'll go up in smoke faster than a nuclear strike."

No secret there. He had it right about the thirteen-minute countdown. If the detonation timer started, only two ways existed to shut it down. One was to have the G-Men assigned to the station call headquarters and override the system. The other was for Cage and Stoner, the leading men on the project, to both type a security code into the computer.

The alternate, and unofficial method of destruction, was a bit more complicated. By cutting the blue wire inside the mainframe, something that nobody was supposed to know about, someone could make the place instantaneously self-destruct.

"I got to laugh," the crazy tech man told Cage while Hammers was out of the room. Pulling a panel off the backside of the mainframe computer, he shined a flashlight in an open grate. "Take a look at this." Ignoring the rules, he motioned for Cage to step closer.

The unit housed a mass of tangled cables. It was designed to ensure that all strategically placed explosives would detonate and the entire building would disappear off the face of the planet in the event of an emergency. Among the tangle of cables sat an ominous blue wire.

"Look at that bastard in there." He reached in and slapped it around with his hand. "Headquarters might as well rent a billboard sign on Airport Road and announce it to every low-life in the state. I can just see it." He sniggered and said, "FOR A REAL BLAST, CALL 1-900-BLU-WIRE".

Cage scratched his chin and stared. "It's hard to believe that anyone would overlook something like that."

The crazy tech man curled his lips distastefully. "You guys think you're so smart, don't you?" He walked out of the room and then walked right back in again. "That stupid little blue wire controls all the communication between Central Control and this facility. If someone snips it the bigwigs down at headquarters would be blind as rats in a cellar filled with mousetraps. They couldn't disengage the explosives. The place would go up faster than a hot roman candle."

Cage's blank eyes stared at the wire guts. "You want me to buy this story? I'm no electrician but I doubt something like that would go overlooked."

"Are you an idiot?" The tech man asked. "Headquarters always planned on fixing the problem. Then funding fell by the wayside. Sure," he said. "Eventually the Treasury Department filched more money off the American taxpayer." He pulled out his check-stub and waved it under Cage's nose. "But you know something tough guy?" He poked Cage in the chest. "They never remedied the problem. By that time the company was dabbling in other dirt. They needed to use the money to fund new projects."

Cage shook his head. "That's ludicrous." He pointed at the electrical wires. "Thousands of volts run through those cables. If anyone cut a wire they'd fry like an egg."

"I get it." The irritable tech man shook his head. "You think you're smarter than me, right? Assholes are born every day." He walked across the room. "Take a look over here."

———

The tech man opened a breaker box filled with switches and pointed. "You know what happens if I hit this one?"

"For all I know it turns off the vending machine in the cafeteria," said Cage.

"Really?" the tech man mocked. "If you're gonna be a smart ass then screw it." Waving his hand, he walked across the room and then stormed right back again. "The walls of this entire building are lined with C4. If there were an electrical fire the place would be toast in minutes."

"What's your point?" asked Cage.

The tech man tapped one of the switches with his knuckle. "This is a master switch. It shuts down all the power for ten minutes. That's how long someone has to get things back under control before the power turns on."

"I don't understand," Cage said.

"What are you, stupid?" the tech man mocked. "Think about it. What if someone cut the blue wire during those ten minutes? When the system came back on it would detect that it had been tampered with. It would automatically begin the thirteen-minute destruct sequence.

"The computer would send a signal to Central Control asking them if they wanted to abort. The problem is that they couldn't comply. The only way to terminate the bomb is by transmitting over that shitty little blue wire. Since the wire had been cut, headquarters couldn't do a thing to stop it." He clapped his hands together gingerly. "I'd like to see their faces when they tried to terminate the bomb. I'd really like to see that. They'd be running around like a pack of starved rats in a minefield trying to figure out what went wrong."

Cage scratched his chin and stared at the tech man. Frighteningly enough, he almost made sense. "How do I know you're telling the truth?" he asked.

"Are you calling me a liar?" The tech man balled up his fists defiantly. For an instant Cage thought things might come to blows.

"Just keep talking hotshot. I guess you'll never know for sure unless you got the stones to Lucky 13 the place." Picking up his toolbox, he walked boldly out the door but this time didn't return.

Cage yelled after him, "Wait! What makes you think I won't report this to headquarters?"

The tech man craned his head around and laughed. "Go ahead. I might get snuffed but you'll end up chum feeding the sharks." He stuck a lollipop in his mouth and swished it around. "You know how The Agency does business. If they think we're on to their secret, they'll kill both of us." Thrusting out a defiant jaw he stormed out of the corridor.

———

As Sam Cage walked through a lush green field towards the Allentown facility, he considered what the crazy tech man had told him. In the end he never filed a report with headquarters regarding the incident. After all, the tech man had been right. The company prided itself on safeguarding classified information. If they got wind that he knew the truth he'd be taking a leave of absence in a wooden crate, six feet under.

Cage kept walking.

50

Ruff Chiquita

Sam Cage walked towards the building. If everything went according to plan, the horizon would be filled with black smoke long before dawn.

Plodding through a cluster of trees near the edge of the compound, he emerged at the rear wall of the facility. The building was painted in drab grey colors and had no windows. It resembled a warehouse for used automobile parts rather than a multimillion-dollar government installation.

Cage looked up at a security monitor bolted to the roof. Circling on a metal post like a black crow, it searched the grounds. Breathing hard, he hurried across the lawn. He waited for the security system to let out a shrill alarm but everything remained quiet. Cage wiped a runner of sweat off his forehead. So far, he beat the odds.

Hanging tight against the exterior wall, his ankles flet rubbery. Any morsel of bravery that once existed now parachuted out from underneath his legs. He wanted to run. Hightail it back to the 443 Diner. Maybe grab a cup of coffee. Think things over.

"Don't get squeamish old buddy," he told himself. "You're on the ten-yard line. Drive the score home."

Cage peeked around a stone corner. The sidewalk that led to the front entrance of the building was empty. Outside of a bird that chirped on a wire, nobody was in sight. On the interstate, traffic remained slow but steady. He could almost hear the DJ talking in the back of his mind.

"Grab the steaks and throw them on the grill. "There's gonna be one hell of a monster bonfire in The Agency parking lot down on Airport Road."

Cage brushed back his hair. He tried to pull things together. No sense losing his cool. It certainly wouldn't help him pull off the rabbit trick.

"Composure and confidence. That's key," he told himself and straightened his tie.

Cage walked forward. He thought he heard footsteps behind him only to discover that it was his own shoes clicking against the sidewalk.

"Breathe Sam. Damn-it breathe." He gripped his chest. "What a waste of time it would be if he went down from a coronary before he even hit the front door. He needed to settle down. Count to thirteen. Lucky thirteen, that is."

———

Colin Fibbs paged through an issue of Ruff Chiquita lying on the desk when Sam Cage walk through the front door. On any other day Fibbs might have seen Cage coming. But today he was a little out of sorts. That's putting it mild. Plain and simple, he was pissed.

A few hours ago, he got a call from the brass. They wanted him to work a double shift. One of the guards, Joe Ranger, took an unexpected leave of absence. You know where that left Fibbs? Shit out of luck, that's where. If the place would have been a union shop, he would have told them to kiss off.

Staring at a centerfold of a brunette whose caboose could cause a ten-car pileup on the Jersey turnpike, his face was little more than a staring eye. The guard dropped the magazine and kicked it under the desk at Cage's approach. Guilt dripped off both men's expressions.

"Good evening Doctor Cage." Fibbs glanced at the clock and scratched his head. "It's the middle of the night."

Cage's heart pounded. He had to stay cool. Composed. If only he could stop sweating. "I couldn't sleep." His voice sounded shaky. Uncertain. "Figured I might as well come to work and get a few things done." He looked around. "Where's Joe Ranger? Isn't he working the nightshift?"

A moat of irritation filled Fibbs' face. "He took a leave of absence. Some kind of emergency." He paused. "Doctor Stoner has been here all night. You want me to buzz you in and tell him you're here?"

"No," Cage said, a bit too quickly. "I'll see Stoner myself."

Fibbs scratched his head again. Stoner insisted that he be notified if anyone turned up at the front door. If he disobeyed orders, he'd have his head on a flagpole.

"It'll only take a minute." He reached for the intercom.

"Wait," Cage said firmly and pointed. "What's that?"

Fibbs glanced underneath the desk. "Nothing."

"Pick it up."

Fibbs gulped. He reached down and scooped up the magazine. A centerfold of a well-endowed brunette unraveled on the desktop.

"How convenient," said Cage.

Fibbs stared blankly.

"How can you get your job done when you're staring at this trash?" Cage said, hands trembling.

However, if Cage was scared, Fibbs appeared terrified. His face twitched with worriment, almost as if hooked on the line of a stubborn fisherman. "It won't happen again sir. I got some problems at home. A nagging wife and that kind of crap." He distributed blame accordingly. "I can't afford to lose my job."

Cage stared. "Forget it. I won't file a report this time. Just don't let it happen again, got it?"

"Yes sir."

"One more thing. Don't bother Doctor Stoner. Are we clear?"

"But…"

"Are we clear?"

"Sparkling."

Cage scanned the perimeter. "Is anyone else here?"

"Johnny Hammers," Fibbs said. "The other guy, Harry Grimm, left hours ago. He looked like he was in a hurry."

Cage glanced at the magazine again. "You're a good man Fibbs. We'd hate to lose you. Let's keep this episode to ourselves."

Expelling a silent sigh of relief, Cage turned the corner and headed straight for Johnny Hammers.

51

Johnny Hammers

The hall was lit in neon and deathly quiet. A bold sign hung in the entranceway read:

RESTRICTED AREA
KEEP OUT

Inside the blast station, Johnny Hammers fiddled with some switches on a control panel. He nodded when Sam Cage approached.

Cage smiled but heard a clacking noise. His teeth were chattering. Alarms sounded off in his head.

"Stay calm and look natural," he told himself.

Stripes of perspiration streaked Cage's cheek. He wiped at his face with a sleeve. Clearing his throat, he knocked on the window of the blast station.

Johnny Hammers walked over and unbolted the door. He looked at Cage's watery complexion.

"You sick or something?" he asked.

Cage momentarily froze. Johnny Hammers towered over him. Hours of pumping iron at the local health spa left him ribbed with finely chiseled muscles. The guy could be a pussycat to his friends. Still underneath that mountain of flesh stood a born killer. Like any wild animal that gets cornered, he'd attack and turn deadly if threatened.

Cage coughed. "I woke up hugging the toilet. Touch of the

flu."

"You should take the day off," Hammers suggested. "I could call Stoner and…"

"No," Cage cut in. "I already spoke to him. No sense hanging around at home. I'd only end up on the couch watching reruns on the late show.

A glimmer of suspicion swam in Hammers's eyes. Cage looked down in horror to discover that his hands were still shaking.

Thinking about it, trying to overpower the G-Man wouldn't be in his best interest. Hammers would pound him into eternity in a fist fight. Still he'd have to do something if he wanted to finish what he started. Hammers kept a pistol in a desk drawer in the corner of the room. Getting his hands on it was imperative.

"You look faint," Hammers told him.

That was an understatement. Cage wiped more sweat off his forehead. "Maybe I just need to catch my breath." He glanced at the chair next to the desk. Hobbling over, he sat down.

Cage shivered. If Johnny Hammers wouldn't have turned around at that precise moment to pour coffee, he might have been mistaken for a man having a seizure.

Turning, Cage glanced at the breaker box on the wall. He remembered what the crazy tech man said. If he flicked the red switch the power in the compound would turn off for ten minutes. That's how long he'd have to cut the blue wire.

"Snip, bang," he muttered to himself.

Hammers turned around. "You say something?"

"Just mumbling to myself," he told him.

Hammers turned his attention back to the coffee and poured some in a cup. Cage reasoned that there'd be no miracles falling from the sky. Trembling fiercely, he quietly opened the desk drawer where Hammers kept his pistol. His palms sweating, he picked up the weapon.

"You should see a doctor," Hammers reiterated. "If they don't cure you, at least you'll get some good meds."

Hammers turned around. Any hint of a smile quickly wilted

like dry weeds when Cage pressed the cold barrel of the gun against his neck.

———

"Are you serious?" Hammers looked amused rather than fearful.

Cage said nothing. The cold barrel of the gun remained bolted on Hammers's thick neck. The G-Man's smile shifted to uncertainty.

"Sorry Johnny. This is business." Cage kept his voice. If he showed a hint of weakness, if he even blinked, Hammers would move in for the kill.

"What's going on?" Hammers voice grew toneless. His biceps tensed up; pythons, preparing to strike.

"Don't even think about it," Cage warned. "Move." He motioned towards the door.

Hammers stared. He tried to determine if the good doctor had the stomach for murder.

Worriment flooded Cage's eyes. The worst was happening. Hammers refused to comply. The prospects of having his face blown off at pointblank range had no more effect on him than a fly buzzing around his eyes that needed to be swatted. He didn't buy the performance.

"You really think you can pull the trigger?" Hammers asked. "Go ahead. Pull it."

Sweat gullied up on Cage's brow. His life dangled by a thread. He had to remain in control. People who ranted didn't mean business. Not to mention they made mistakes. It's the quiet ones who needed to be watched. They were cool. Balanced and focused. They were ready to take action at a moment's notice.

Cage twisted the cold barrel of the gun tighter against Hammers' throat. Leaning in he whispered, "Listen asshole. It won't take long for the company to figure out what I've done. In short that means I'm already dead. I don't care who joins me in the slaughterhouse." His finger twitched at the trigger. "Now are you gonna move or do I split your head open with a bullet?"

Hammers turned from coolness to hesitation. Shades of doubt overshadowed his face. If nothing else he considered the idea that Cage just might be crazy enough to shoot him.

"You got three seconds Johnny. Then you die." Cage breathed deep. "One," he counted. "Two…"

52

Sealing the Crypt

Colin Fibbs looked up and blinked in disbelief. Sam Cage pushed Johnny Hammers up the corridor. A gun crushed in on his throat. Fibbs instantly reached for the alert button underneath his desk.

"Freeze!" shouted Cage. "One wrong move and I'll put a bullet in both your heads."

Fibbs raised his hands faster than someone grabbing a kettle of boiling water.

"Open the front door," Cage ordered. "Now!"

Fibbs stared blankly. The guard always figured this day might come. Guys like Cage were on overload. Sooner or later their brains turned to mud. That's what must have happened to Cage. He blew a fuse and embarked on a trip to Fantasy Island.

"I said open the door!" He repeated and jammed the gun tighter against Hammers's neck.

"Do as he says," Hammers conceded. He shifted his gaze to Cage. "You won't get away with this. You know that, right?" For an instant Hammers's face loosened up in sympathy. "You're screwed old friend. See you at the bottom of an ocean."

Fibbs punched in a code on the panel. The entrance doors slid open.

Cage nudged Hammers with the tip of his gun. "Outside."

Hammers tilted his head and stared. "I trusted you Cage. You betrayed me."

Again, Cage shoved Hammers towards the door. In any other circumstance he and the G-Man might have been friends. They might even have taken in a Flyers game or grab a cold one down at Cracker's Alehouse. Unfortunately, the things that might have been were now dead and gone. Sam Cage intended to Lucky 13 the whole damn place. If Hammers didn't get outside he'd end up a statistic on the casualty list.

Hammers stepped slowly outside the exit.

Cage turned to Fibbs and waved his gun. "You too Fibbs. Vamoose."

Fibbs didn't need to be asked twice. He looked like a man bolting for the toilet on a two second countdown.

Hammers looked at him from outside the doorway. "I'm not sure what you're doing Cage. I hope it's worth the sin. Adios amigo." He nodded.

Reaching across the security desk, Cage pressed a button. The metal doors slammed shut. Alone in the quiet, Cage stared down the empty corridor.

"Just like a crypt," he said out loud. "Nobody gets in."

A voice inside his head answered back, "Nobody gets back out alive either."

———

Time wasn't a virtue. Johnny Hammers would already be on the phone with headquarters. A lynch mob would be on the way. They'd be under orders to string him up.

Sam Cage raced back down the corridor towards the blast station. His heart banged so hard he feared that it might explode long before he ever had the chance to execute his Lucky 13 reign of terror.

When he entered the blast booth, he quickly flung open the breaker box on the rear wall. According to the crazy tech man, hitting the red switch would cut the power for ten minutes. If that turned out to be true, he'd be able to snip the wire, that blue bitch. The Agency wouldn't be able to do a thing to stop the countdown to extinction.

Ringlets of perspiration the size of oranges bunched up under Cage's shirt. His pulse raced. He reached for the red switch in the breaker box. It felt like the lever on an electric chair. Biting down on his lip, he pulled it.

At first nothing happened. He considered the idea that the tech man lied. Yup, he could almost hear him cackling. "Fooled you, didn't I dumb ass. The only thing you did was shut off the coffeemaker in the lunchroom."

That interior thought quickly changed. The lights flickered. The drone of electric that hummed in the halls died. Everything went dark. Cage stood their dumbly. Suddenly an overhead emergency light flicked on in the blast station. The crazy tech man had a lot more information than he gave him credit for.

Cage quickly removed a panel on the back of the mainframe computer that housed a mass of electrical cables.

"Time is running out. Cut the damn wire," Cage told himself and chewed at his fingernails. For a minute he had the impulse to giggle. He wondered if he was cracking up.

Cage peered into the open panel. He saw the blue wire. It sat directly in the middle of a bunch of cables. Reaching in, he yanked it. Still it wouldn't budge.

"Come on!" he shouted to nobody.

Looking around, he found a utility knife stuffed underneath some of Hammerss

' gun magazines in a drawer.

Cage raced back over to the open panel. Nervous fingers drummed on his subconscious mind. "Cut that blue monster right now. If you don't, you'd be better off driving the knife in your own heart."

Cage's hand barely fit through the open panel. Metal grating scratched his knuckles. Fishing around, he managed to get the tip of the utility knife positioned underneath the blue wire.

"Got you!" he shouted and pulled upward in a cutting motion.

The knife slipped off.

Glancing at the clock, his eyes widened. Ten minutes had

passed. The electric would go back on at any moment. If his hand was inside the mainframe thousands of volts would light him up brighter than a Christmas tree.

Cage frantically wiggled the knife. By luck or fate, the blade again landed on the underbelly of the blue wire. Crunch time. Do or die.

"NOW!" he roared. In an upward stroke he ripped it hard.

Something snapped. Cage flew backwards and landed on the floor.

"Snip, bang," he heard himself saying out loud.

Equipment suddenly began humming. The lighting came back on. Looking over at the computer, the monitor lit up in bright green colors.

WARNING… SOURCE COMPUTER COMPROMISED
ACTIVATING DETONATION CODES
ENGAGING 13 MINUTE COUNTDOWN
CENTRAL CONTROL… OVERRIDE TO ABORT?

The crazy tech man had struck dead center like an anvil. As predicted the computer sensed that someone tampered with it. It armed itself and cautioned Central Control to override the system if they wanted to avert a disaster.

Cage stared at the blue wire. It dangled lifelessly. If the computer was waiting for Central Control to send a termination code over that stupid little blue wire, it'd be waiting one hell of a lot longer than thirteen minutes.

Suddenly a panicky voice rang out over the intercom. "Hammers? What's going on down there? Hammers!" he shouted.

Cage shut the intercom off. He started laughing uncontrollably. "You have to be losing your mind, old buddy," he told himself. He wouldn't be the first person to crack under pressure. Manufacturing plants and post offices were full of them.

An intrusive mechanical voice again abruptly rang out. This time it echoed through the loudspeaker in the halls.

WARNING! DESTRUCT SEQUENCE ACTIVATED
THIRTEEN MINUTES TO DETONATE
PLEASE EVACUATE THE CHAMBER

Cage's heart wedged in his throat. If escape was even remotely possible it had to be now. Not that it mattered. If he made it out the front door a couple of armed thugs, including Johnny Hammers, would be waiting for him. It'd be a pigeon shoot. Nevertheless, he had to try.

Bolting out the door he turned left but stopped. Cold steel probed the back of his neck.

"Hello Cage," Stoner said. A grim smile caked on his face. He pushed him forward with his gun. "We're not done here yet."

53

Things You Can't Do (Central Control)

Shrill alarms rang in the stale air. Over at Central Control miffed faces stared at the system's computer with growing dread. Everyone ran back and forth and jabbered madly at each other.

"I can't get a signal. We're cut off!" Lanster said. A stunned look crossed his face as he peered down at the instrument panel.

"No we're not," Ray Stillwater said from behind his desk. "They can't do that," he insisted. His face grew whiter than an anemic ghost.

"What happened?" A confused tech man in blue coveralls walked in the room. He sipped casually at coffee in a Styrofoam cup. He noticed that the blood had drained away from Stillwater's face. Not even a mortician could capture that same look only moments after a coronary.

Lanster frantically pushed switches on the control board. "I'm telling you Mr. Stillwater, we can't get a signal. The detonation unit is live!"

"Override," Stillwater calmly announced as he sat in his chair like an Enterprise captain. His fingers drummed hard on a polished wooden desk.

Lanster again batted the override button back and forth. "No response. None at all. She's going to blow and there's not a damn thing we can do about it."

Stillwater sucked at his thumbs. It was his first command post. It would also be his last. He sat morbidly at his desk and brooded over the sad turn of events. The Allentown facility was about to erupt and blow up. Headquarters would hold him accountable for

211

the disaster. Shit always rolled downhill. As far as Stillwater was concerned, he waded in a cesspool.

"You guys are really screwed." The tech man sniggered at Lanster who looked too preoccupied with his own miserable state of affairs to notice.

Lanster banged the override switch with his fist again. "This can't be happening!"

Stillwater said nothing. His face was mirrored in reflective thoughts. The Allentown facility would prove to be a black eye on his career. He'd be demoted to hunting down drug sharks. Probably get his ass shot off in some jungle in Columbia. The Agency might even decide to get rid of him altogether. He wouldn't be the first person who disappeared and ended up in a meat grinder.

"Nobody can just turn the detonation mechanism on," Stillwater maintained. He slumped down in his chair. "Your computer must be wrong. They can't do that." Regardless of a bright composure, a bleak fence of despair eclipsed his sunken expression.

"There's no malfunction. The thing is activated." A red-faced Lanster whacked his fist on the instrument panel. "I think somebody "blue wired" the facility. She's going to blow!"

The crazy tech man stood in the corner of the room drinking his coffee. A fleeting vision of Sam Cage storming the Allentown facility in a flak jacket traveled through his head. He couldn't believe the crazy bastard actually did it.

"There goes another dollar taken off the American taxpayer," he sarcastically mumbled. "Snip. Bang." The tech man took a last swallow of coffee. Crumbling up his Styrofoam cup, he threw it in the trash basket and walked out the door.

54

Lucky 13

At gunpoint, Alan Stoner led Sam Cage through the building's empty corridors towards a room at the end of the hall.

"Inside." Stoner motioned Cage through the doorway. A small computer terminal sat idle on a desk in the center of the room. "Sit down." He pulled a chair out.

Across the room a loud mechanical voice announced:

DESTRUCT SEQUENCE ENGAGED
TWELVE MINUTES TO DETONATION
PLEASE EVACUATE THE FACILITY

The Lucky 13 countdown moved ahead, right on schedule.

"Did you really think you could pull this off?" Stoner gave Cage an angry slap on the cheek with the butt of his gun.

Cage's head flinched back from the blow. A trickle of blood spilled down the corner of his lip.

"Having a bad day?" Cage spit and looked up.

"Not half as bad as yours is about to become." Stoner reached over and punched some buttons on the computer's keyboard. A message flashed across the screen.

Identification Sequence #2032171RLE
Received and Acknowledged
Enter Next Sequence to Abort Detonation Code?

"Your turn," said Stoner. "Type your code in."

Sam Cage studied the blinking green cursor on the monitor. It was Stoner's last attempt to override the system. The computer required two pass-codes to deactivate the system. Cage was the only other viable candidate.

In the hall, a mechanical voice continued to broadcast over a loud speaker. It reminded all interested parties that in precisely eleven minutes the entire facility would be blown off the face of the planet.

"Do you really expect me to give you the code?" Cage laughed. "What fun would that be? Trust me. It's like when we were kids going to rock concerts. There are no rain dates on this event. Flak jackets aren't optional."

Stoner glared. Roadmaps of tension played on his forehead. "I'd reconsider. If you don't type in the code, you're a dead man." He put the gun to Cage's head.

Cage stared at the cursor.

Blip. Blip. Blip.

The computer seemed in no hurry as it waited patiently for a response. Alan Stoner, on the other hand, had less than eleven minutes.

It was funny. The Agency took pride in being ace magicians. They made people disappear every day. Cage intended to outdo their performance. He was going to pull off the biggest vanishing trick in the history of the company, something Houdini himself would marvel over. He'd remove the entire Allentown facility off the map all inside a lucky 13 minutes. Best of all, headquarters couldn't do a thing about it outside of grabbing a bag of popcorn and watching the fireworks.

There were some drawbacks to the plan. Odds of escaping from the facility before the blast occurred were at best, bleak. When the walls crumbled down, he'd be buried under the concrete.

"You look irritable," Cage noted. "I suppose I could type in my code. The bomb would stop ticking, but where's your sense of adventure? Justice hasn't been served," he reminded. "You're a criminal, Stoner. Man, those boys dressed in leather jackets and tattoos with skulls in the big house just love the rich prissy type, right? You should be thanking me. Instead of getting peeled open like a cold can of tuna in the state pen it's all going to end here in just about…"

TEN MINUTES TO DETONATION
PLEASE EVACUATE THE FACILITY

The mechanical voice fired off another warning shot.

Alan Stoner's eyes were concentrated down to pinpricks. "You're an idiot Cage. I guess there's no law against being stupid. I might even have a cure for it." Reaching in his pocket, he pulled out a syringe and tossed it to him. "Inject yourself."

"What?" Cage stared blankly.

"You heard me."

"You really think I'm going to stick myself?"

The two men glared in a wordless standoff.

NINE MINUTES TO DETONATION
PLEASE EVACUATE

"I'm not playing games." Stoner pointed the gun at Cage's head.

"Easy with that thing," Cage warned. "Without my code this place is going up faster than a rocket. I hope your life insurance premiums are paid up."

Stoner's face reddened. "Stop stalling."

"What good would it do to give you the code?" Cage mused. "Once you have what you want, you'll kill me anyway, right? Even if you let me live, The Agency would eventually get rid of me. In case you haven't noticed they frown on employees blowing up multi-million-dollar installations."

"There's still a way out," Stoner said. "I have connections. They'd get you out of the country. Think about it. By this time tomorrow you could be swinging on a hammock in the Caribbean."

EIGHT MINUTES TO DETONATION
PLEASE EVAC...

"Sounds interesting but I'll have to pass," said Cage. "I burn easily in the sun."

Stoner squinted. "I didn't expect your cooperation." He glanced at the needle. "Inject yourself. I'm not asking again."

"Sorry, not happening."

"Put the fucking needle in your arm!" Stoner's fiery eyes glared.

The cold barrel of the gun probed Cage's left eye. Stoner's finger trembled on the trigger.

Up to then Cage wondered if his coworker had the guts to open fire. The growing madness in Stoner's face suggested he would. Facts were facts. A bullet hole the size of a tennis ball exiting the back of his head would make for a real bad day. No matter how Cage added things up his continued existence remained in doubt. The exit door stood only a few feet away. It might as well have been in an airport in Guam. Stoner would shoot him before he got three steps.

SEVEN MINUTES TO DETONATION
PLEASE EVACUATE

"Last call," Stoner said.

Cage locked his angry eyes against his associate's cold ones. "Have it your way asshole," he conceded. Picking up the syringe he emptied it in his arm and tossed it on the floor. "Satisfied?"

A cold frost instantly crystallized in the pulsing gutters of Cage's arteries. He shivered. The ice in his blood turned to fire. The pain was so complete that it drove him off his chair and to his knees.

"I'm guessing you didn't give me a party favor." He breathed hard.

Stoner eased up. "You're very perceptive."

A single cough felt as if dynamite exploded in Cage's heart. "This hurts like hell. Thank God it'll only go on for about another…"

SIX MINUTES TO DETONATION
PLEASE EVACUATE THE FACILTY

"The stuff packs a wallop. Mike Tyson couldn't even throw a punch like that in his heyday." Stoner lowered his weapon. "The kicker is that it's even more deadly than painful. I'm guessing you'll beg me to shoot you in another minute or two."

Misery intensified. Cage's joints rusted into unmovable hinges.

A vision of the old med school days flashed in his head. During his tenure he visited a burn trauma unit. One man's scorched face was little more than a black cavity buried under a bundle of white bandages. The victim's tormented eyes were heated as steel pellets. Cage never realized the full extent of that person's anguish, at least not until now.

55

The Standoff

"It seems we have ourselves a situation," Stoner said. "I'm not a bad guy, Cage. In fact, you might say we're a lot alike. We carry out duties. The only difference is that at the moment your task is more painful than mine. That can change." Stoner pulled a small flask out of his pocket and held it up. "This is your ticket out. It'll counteract the poison. The rules are simple. Give me the code. In exchange you get the antidote."

Cage stared. Intense pain shot up his neck. It staggered him to the floor. "You'll kill me no matter what I do."

"Wrong," Stoner differed. "Believe me. I'd love to put a bullet in your head. The problem is that saving your ass is to my advantage. If you escape The Agency will be hell bent on finding and killing you. By the time they figure out I'm the real enemy I'll be bunking down in Fiji." He leaned down. "Work with me Cage. Give me the code. We can both get out of this." Nervous sweat rolled down his cheek.

FIVE MINUTES TO DETONATION
PLEASE EVACUATE

Cage clenched his teeth. "You must have one fantastic deal going on. Nobody takes a chance on screwing over The Agency."

"Harnessing telekinetic energy isn't exactly selling cotton candy on the boardwalk," he said. "Third world countries would chew their fingers off to get their hands on the stuff. Ten million would be pocket change."

Cage looked at the timer.

WARNING!
FOUR MINUTES TO DETONATION

Stoner glanced at the clock. "You've stalled long enough," he said flatly. "Give me the code." He raised the gun and dangled the antidote. "This'll take the monkey off your back. We can both walk out of here alive.

Cage swore something bit his flesh, almost as if it were being cannibalized by rats.

WARNING!
30 SECONDS TO FINAL COUNTDOWN

"Last chance." Stoner slammed the gun under the bridge of Cage's nose. "Give it to me!"

Cage stared at Stoner. The guy was insane. If he didn't relinquish the code, Stoner would kill him.

"I guess I'll have to trust you," Cage said.

20 SECONDS TO FINAL COUNTDOWN
PLEASE EVAC...

Cage leaned over. His lethargic fingers tapped the computer's keyboard. Every stroke jolted him like a train wreck. The poison in him could have stopped a rhino. Slowly he started typing, 4U...

10 SECONDS TO TERMINAL DESTRUC...

With one last effort, his fingers burning fire, Cage punched in the final letters and hit the enter button. Leaning back, beads of sweat flared up on his forehead.

"Good move." Stoner loosened up.

"What now?"

"I'm afraid it's time to part ways." Stoner held the gun up and laughed. "You idiot. You really thought I'd let you live? You made a mistake."

Cage groaned. "So did you."

Stoner glanced at the computer screen. The monitor read:

4U-leona-snip-bang

SECURITY CODE INVALID
WARNING! 3 MINUTE DETONATION IMMINENT
EVACUATE CHAMBER IMMEDIAELY

"Typing was never my strongpoint," Cage confessed.

Anger caked Stoner's face. He raised the gun.

Growling in pain, Cage leapt forward and bowled into his captor. Both men toppled over on the floor. Stoner dropped the gun and groggily shook his head. The antidote bounced off the floor like fine china.

Cage grabbed the bottle before it broke. Standing up on wobbly legs, he unscrewed the lid and drank it down.

WARNING! 2 MINUTE DETONATION IMMINENT
EVACUATE THE CHAMBER

Somewhere in the back of his mind Cage heard the distant voice of his old high school football coach barking out commands. "It's time to separate the boys from the men. Get down in the trenches. The clock is ticking. Show'em who you are!"

Ignoring pain, Cage fled out the door on rickety legs. He banged off walls as he hurried up the hall. No doubt a flock of federal agents would be waiting for him. Johnny Hammers would be leading the charge.

It didn't matter much anyway. Stoner poisoned him. More than likely the antidote he drank would turn out to be little more than colored tap water. Where would that leave him?

"Dead, that's where," the rude bastard inside his subconscious mind answered.

The exit was just at the end of the foyer. Every step grew heavier as he made his approach. Hobbling forward he stumbled against the security desk. His inflamed fingers frantically punched the buttons. The door wouldn't open of course. It was an intricate flaw in the overall plan. He didn't have the security code.

A sudden bullet whizzed close to Cage's ear. He could hear the hot wisp of wind.

"Cage!"

He turned to see Alan Stoner hurrying up the hall. Vengeance gleamed in his eyes.

"Come on!" he shouted and frantically tried combinations that might unbolt the lock on the door.

WARNING! 1 MINUTE TO DETONATION
COUNTDOWN ENGAGED
EVACUATE!

Sirens blared all around him. Cage wondered what was happening outside. Undoubtedly the crazy tech man would already be on the phone with the IRS bitching that he wasn't going to pay more tax dollars to rebuild the place. Thirty miles away, other stories were unfolding. Jonas Blackheart was on the loose. Keenan Braddock stood in a line of danger.

His train of thought changed when a hard punch slapped his shoulder. He instantly knew that he had been shot. A steady flow of blood rushed down his arm. He grew dizzy. Faint.

Cage surmised it was just another notch in the tragic conclusion in this thing called life. All things considered, maybe dying wasn't such a tough ticket. These days staying alive had been the more difficult road, one that now reached an inevitable conclusion. Still that instinct for survival, a wild bull trapped in a steel cage, continued to buck and search for an exit.

Struggling to decode the door Cage was thrown suddenly

backwards against the wall. The barrel of a gun rammed the underbelly of his throat.

"You're dead." A satisfied smile scrolled over Stoner's face as he squeezed the trigger.

———

"NO!" a rogue voiced echoed off the walls.

Someone jumped out of a side corridor. He tackled Stoner and pinned him to the floor. The gun fired harmlessly as it batted out of Stoner's hand.

Joe Ranger, the nightshift security guard, looked out from behind bruised eyes sunken in purple loops. Whatever foe he battled had apparently won the war.

"6421", he said.

"What?"

"The code to open the door," Ranger answered. "6421," he repeated. "Go now."

Cage punched the numbers in and the door slid open.

"Ranger, you've got to hurry!" Cage shouted.

"It's too late for me." His breath grew labored. Tears dripped in his eyes. He was past the point of running or even hobbling. A flower of blood spread out from underneath his shirt from where he had been shot, compliments of Alan Stoner. "Go now Doctor Cage. Hurry," he implored him.

Stoner struggled to get up but Ranger, a big man, kept the full brunt of his weight on him.

"Get off me!" he shouted. "Cage! Help. I'll give you anything. Money, is that what you want?"

Cage stared brutally into Stoner's eyes. "I want you dead."

WARNING! 10 SECONDS TO DETONATION
NINE SECONDS… EIGHT…

Cage fled out the door on legs useless as withered sticks.

"You're a dead man. Cage!" Alan Stoner's voice trailed after him from afar.

A low rumble, solid as distant thunder, emerged from inside the facility. It grew steadily louder until a fiery explosion shattered the walls. The force of the blast sent Cage reeling in the air. He bounced off a telephone pole and landed on the macadam in the parking lot. Somewhere in the dark trenches of his insensible mind, the roaring gust of explosives died away. Fire engines and police sirens sounded out in the night air.

———

"Stay breathing pal." A scruffy truck driver with tattoos and an earring tugged at Cage's blood-spattered shirt. "The ambulance is on the way. Over here!" He shouted to someone. "Hurry. I got half a corpse."

A paramedic leaned over. He checked Cage's pulse. Ripping the victim's shirt open he backed up. "What the hell?" He paused. "This guy took a bullet." He pried Cage's eyes open and shined a light in them. "He's going into shock. The poor bastard doesn't have a prayer." The paramedic looked closer. "What's he grinning about?"

Cage reached over and felt the piece of purple yarn tied around his finger. For the first time in a long time his dismal mind rested. A bright smile played over his face. Perhaps he was dying or at least having a beautiful hallucination. He swore that Leona Smatters, her face radiant as an angel, sat down and held him.

"I'm losing him!" a paramedic shouted. "We need to hurry!"

Drifting away in the arms of a lost lover, he couldn't help but to wonder what fate would befall those he now left behind. People like Jonas Blackheart and Keenan Braddock stood on some distant battlefield of their own. He wondered who would survive in the end.

"Get him in the ambulance, pronto!"

Closing his eyes, Cage passed into utter unconsciousness.

56

Big Fish in Little China

Almost as if the town sensed an unexpected corruption, a sewer pipe burst in downtown Jim Thorpe. The stench filtered through the open streets as Harry Grimm rolled down his car window. A cigarette dangled from his mouth. Turning his head, he looked the place over through mirrored sunglasses.

No doubt about it. The town lacked enthusiasm. There wasn't a porn shop or whorehouse anywhere in sight. Naïve people walked around with stupid grins spread over their faces. Rattling things up would be no more difficult than shaking a stubborn bottle of ketchup. Yup, sure as hell he was a big fish in little China.

Turning left at a traffic light, Grimm continued up Broadway. The chimes from Saint Mark's church rang out in the early evening air.

Across the road a young redhead in a lilac dress stepped out the front door of Dugan's, a local convenience store. Grimm scanned her shapely legs and full breasts.

"Ride honey?" He leaned coolly out the car window. "I'm the new kid on the block. Tote your cute little chicken ass over here. I'll give you a chariot ride."

The redhead lowered her head and quickly hurried down the sidewalk. Man, that girl? She couldn't have been more than eighteen years old. Probably a virgin. He shuddered to think what he might do with a woman like that. He'd make her squirm underneath him as he penetrated her deepest secrets. She'd be petrified. That only added to the intrigue. Afterwards he'd kill her or at the very least beat her senseless. She'd never say anything to the police about him for fear of retribution.

Harry Grimm shrugged off the fantasy. There'd be plenty of time for bone jumping later. Right now, he had a job to do. Killing a monster and abducting a boy was priority one.

Turning up Hill Road he veered right on Center Avenue towards Ashley Braddock's house. It was time to pay her another visit. Last time she bested him. Things wouldn't go so easy in this round. In fact, when all was said and done, she wouldn't even be alive.

57

Chief Gunner

"Take it easy lady," Chief Gunner told the frantic woman over the phone.

What did he know about killers and missing kids? He was a bartender over at the Little Tiger and only took a job at the police department for a pay hike plus free donuts and coffee.

The mess started earlier in the evening. Shots were fired in the alley behind Pisgah Mountain. Police hurried to the scene but the only person they found was a frightened woman hiding behind some garbage cans. Her name was Ashley Braddock. The woman claimed she was taken hostage by a man named Harry Grimm who fled the scene before he could be apprehended.

"Slow down lady. Tell me again. What happened?" Chief Gunner said.

"Aren't you listening?" Ashley shouted in the phone. Gunner stuck a finger in his ear as if he got blasted by an amplifier. "My son is missing. So are his friends. The name of the man who tried to kill me is Harry Grimm. He has something to do with this."

Gunner jotted Grimm's name down on a piece of paper and handed it to a deputy. "Run another check on this guy."

"We already did," the deputy said. "We can't find that he even exists. He must be using an alias."

Gunner tapped on his desk. "Don't panic lady." Who the hell knew if there even was a Harry Grimm or if she was just another whacko crying wolf in the streets? "Maybe your son is out with his buddies and didn't come home. Kids these days, right?"

Dread washed over Ashley. What if her son never came home?

The news reported on things like that every day. Her mind traveled back to the murdered girl on the mountainside.

"Sit tight. We'll find him." Gunner sounded uncertain as he hung up the receiver.

———

Ashley traipsed the floors of her house, room to room. The minutes went by like hours. Several times she looked out from behind closed drapes, certain that Harry Grimm would be lurking behind a hedge. She was about to dial the police again to see if they found any new clues when the phone rang.

"Miss Braddock?"

"Who is this?"

There was an awkward pause. "My name is Cage. Sam Cage."

Ashley stared at the receiver. "Do I know you?"

"It's about your son Miss Braddock."

"Pardon me?"

"Your son," he repeated. "Can I ask you something?"

Ashley's heart banged hard. "What is it?"

"Do you own a gun?"

Ashley stared vacantly at the phone. "I don't understand."

"I said do you have a weapon in the house?"

"What's this all about?" she asked.

"I don't have time to explain," he said. "What you need to know is that you're in danger. Lock the doors. Call the police. He's coming for you."

"Who's coming?" she asked. "Hello? Can you hear me? You're breaking up!"

Then the phone went dead.

Ashley stared at the receiver suspiciously. What if the phone didn't go dead? What if someone cut the line?

"Get a grip girl," she told herself and again thought about Harry Grimm, the man who tried to kill her.

Unable to stand around and do nothing she grabbed her car

keys. If the police couldn't locate her son then maybe she could. Slipping out the door, she hurried across the driveway. With one look around the landscape, she jumped in her car. Glancing in the rearview her hands froze on the wheel.

"Going someplace?" a familiar voice asked.

From the backseat of the vehicle Harry Grimm's gun pressed the back of Ashley's neck. She gasped and tried to bolt out the door. Grimm grabbed her by a chunk of hair and pulled her back. "I wouldn't do that."

Ashley froze. "What do you want?"

"That's easy," he said. "Man, your kid is more popular than a rock star at Madison Square Garden on a Saturday night. Everyone wants him."

Ashley glanced in the rearview. "Do you know where he is?"

"Maybe," Grimm said coolly. "But unless you want to find him bleeding in a gutter, you'll do everything I say, understand?"

"Why are you so interested in my son?"

Grimm reached up and yanked Ashley's head back. Her hair flew across her face. "Nobody asked you to talk." His eyes narrowed to black slits. "Right now, you probably think I'm the big bad wolf. You're wrong," he said. "That thing out there is the real devil, and if the devil finds your son before we do then it's lights out for the kid. A maniac like that?" Grimm shook his head. "Nobody can stop him. At least nobody but me."

Ashley stared at him through frightened eyes. "I still don't understand why you're doing this."

"Enough talk." Grimm slammed a knuckle against the nape of her neck. "Do as I say. If you're lucky I won't kill you. Drive."

58

The Dark Side

Harry Grimm held the gun to Ashley's head.

"Chill out," he said. "We'll find the kid but I wouldn't get my hopes up. If our friend in the woods tracked him down then he's already buried under the leaves with the maggots." He nudged her with the tip of his gun. "Turn left."

Ashley's heart pounded. She turned up the alley towards the trolley path that led up the mountainside. On the opposite side of the road sat a garbage can riddled with bullets from when she last encountered Harry Grimm. At the time she escaped an ill fate. Something told her she wouldn't be that lucky this time.

"Pull over," Grimm ordered.

Ashley parked and cut the engine. "What are we doing here?"

"Monster hunting," Grimm answered and studied the gloom. "There's a devil in the trees. He isn't far off."

Ashley stared. "What makes you think that thing is in the woods?"

"Trust me. Evil knows evil." Grimm scanned the area. "Killing is as routine as eating a cupcake for breakfast. He's good at his job. Even the FBI would be stymied."

Grimm reached in his pocket. He pulled out a small mechanical gadget. "You know what this is?"

Ashley's face was a blank slate.

"It's a device that zoologists use to track animals. Kind of a GPS," he said. "It gets implanted under the skin. If nothing else it keeps all those animal rights activists happy that think it's the end of the world unless they know where the raccoons and monkeys are shitting in the woods." Grimm hit a small switch and flicked the device on. "This does the same thing. Only instead of possums we're hunting bigger game."

"You can track that thing in the woods?" she asked.

"You're not getting it," Grimm said. "Your son is the person who's wired."

Ashley's face flat lined. "What?"

"Don't look surprised. We've been watching him for years. I could tell you the flavor of his first popsicle."

Ashley stopped walking. "Why would you follow him?"

"Does it matter?" Grimm answered. "What's important is that our friendly neighborhood fiend doesn't find him first." He nudged with his gun. "Out of the car."

———

Darkness fell. They trudged up the mountainside. Harry Grimm flicked on his flashlight.

"You still haven't explained," Ashley said. "What does my son have to do with this?"

Halting the pace, Grimm wiped a runner of sweat from his forehead. "Are we married?" he asked. "You're becoming a nag. Tell me something. Did you ever hear the name Harbor Point?"

Ashley hesitated. "Yes."

"How?"

"It's a treatment center for women. I might have had tests done there. It was a long time ago."

"What kind of tests?"

"I told you," she said. "It was a long time ago. I can't remember. It was a gynecologist's office. I don't remember anything unusual."

"Is that right?" The corners of Grimm's lips curled up. "Harbor Point is operated by an organization called The Agency. Let me guess. You fainted on the table during the examination."

A chill wiggled down Ashley's spine. It was a long time ago but also true. She blacked out. The doctors told her it could have been a minor reaction to a sedative.

"Ever read about women who walk into an exam room, pass out and wake up pregnant? That's you," he said. "When you stepped through the door at Harbor Point, you came away with more than you bargained for."

Ashley's blinked. "I was raped?"

"Rape is a strong word," Grimm said. "I'm no science buff but I think the term is artificial insemination."

"You're lying," Ashley said flatly.

"Am I?" Grimm asked. "After your son was born you took him to Harbor Point for a checkup. The doctors secretly implanted a microchip under his skin. I know," he said. "It probably sounds like a James Bond movie but we needed to keep a watch on him. For the most part he seemed normal outside of a few quirks. Kids these days," he said. "They're a pain in the ass."

Ashley stared. It sounded impossible. Still, Grimm knew her entire life history. The doctors at Harbor Point told her that she was pregnant. The news struck like lightning. Her boyfriend at the time, Jake Miles, denied everything. Not long after he skipped town and was never heard from again. After the child was born, she did the best she could to raise Keenan. One thing was certain; she never suspected that the baby belonged to anyone else but Jake.

Grimm said, "A few months back in Pittsburgh I was sent to abduct your son. The company needed to protect their investments, right? The plan was to kidnap him, run tests and see if he had a telekinetic aptitude passed on from his real father. Unluckily for your sister, she walked in at the wrong time. She got in the way. In my business people don't get in the way. They get dead. I had to kill her."

Hatred blackened Ashley's eyes. Curling her fists, she lurched forward.

"Easy or you'll be joining her." Grimm tightened the grip on his gun and stared into the woods. "You might be wondering about our friend hiding in the trees. His name is Jonas Blackheart. He worked for The Agency in their volunteer program. He was a guinea pig for mind control drugs. I'm telling you that shit made PCP look like butterscotch gumdrops. It drove Blackheart out of his mind. So, what's that thing in the woods the curious wench asks?" He turned to Ashley. "That's your son's genetic father and he's not just pissed off. He's insane. My guess is that if he finds your boy before we do, he'll kill him.

Ashley stared in disbelief. "Even if all this were true, why would he go after Keenan?"

"You're kidding me, right?" Grimm asked. "Serial killers are head cases. They want to feel a connection with the people getting their throats slit. Call it bonding. Your son is the ultimate prize.

"Blackheart is an empath," he continued. "Right now, I'm guessing his dark half is in charge of the ruling body. He didn't end up in Jim Thorpe by accident. He knows, or at least senses, his biological son is here. If he finds him, game over. The truth is you should thank me," Grimm told her. "Right now, I'm about the only person on the planet capable of stopping Blackheart." He held the tracking device up and pointed. "That way."

59

The Mineshaft

Tugger Rhodes tumbled down a rocky hill. He came to a crashing halt at the bottom of an embankment. Whatever it was that lurked in the darkness, it nearly caught him.

Groaning, he stood up and dusted off his knees. He was inside a cave. Faint traces of dreary moonlight chiseled through small fissures in the ceiling. With little light and even less courage, the boy shivered in the darkness.

"Hello?" he said, his voice echoing in the gloom.

No answer. Staring up at the breach in the wall from where he fell, whatever monster pursued him had given up the chase, or in a grimmer scenario, was searching for an alternate entrance into the cave.

Tugger shoved his hands in his pockets The flashlight he carried was gone. However, he still had a candle and matches from the *Dead Night* when he sneaked out with his friends. Striking up a match, he lit the candle.

Looking around, drippings of foul water trickled off the walls. The screech of bats could be heard fluttering in the tunnels. They sounded haunting as the cries of long dead souls lost in the darkness.

If nothing else the air felt cool when the wind moaned through breaches in the walls. The slight breeze in the musty air hinted that there must be a nearby opening that led to the outside world.

There were also interconnecting crawlspaces in the cavern. Some were caved in and impassable. Other passages veered off into unknown directions. The place resembled a burial chamber for primordial kings.

"Haunts for spiders and lizards," he thought to himself.

Tugger heard breathing and there were shuffling noises in the walls as if gatherings of rodents were on the move. Whatever the premise the conclusion seemed obvious. If he didn't find his way out quickly, the place would become his own crypt.

A rush of dread flooded over Tugger. He listened to a loud thump behind one of the walls. It occurred to him that his captor might have found an alternative route into the cave.

Whirling around, Tugger's eyes darted from corner to corner. He eyed a small passageway on the backside of the cavern. Still any hope of a fast getaway wouldn't be easy. Whatever hunted him was on the move. Running would be futile. He'd need to fight to survive.

Tugger raised his chin and took a step forward. No sense in delaying things. He'd only lose whatever smidgeon of bravery remained in his young guts. Walking towards the crawlspace he swore he heard something, perhaps labored breath, in one of the passageways.

"Is someone there?" He peered into the darkened tunnel.

All things remained quiet.

Tugger bent down and shimmied into the crawlspace. He held the candle squarely in front of him. Its flame flickered off dirty walls. For a minute he swore something tugged at the cuff of his blue-jeans. Gulping, he looked down but nothing was there. Imagination played in his head like mad gangs of teenagers with switchblades in dark alleys.

He again heard movement and put his ear against the wall. His heart jacked up to double time. Something moved again. He was sure of it.

One thing remained clear. Holding his current position would prove deadly. If something treacherous charged out of the darkness he'd be an open target. Even if he did remain hidden, nobody knew his whereabouts. AJ, Becca, and perhaps even Keenan, might be searching for him. The question remained as to how they would find him. He'd rot and die down in the damp confines of the cave before anyone found him.

Tying his sneaker, he bit down on his lip and slowly made his way through the darkened tunnels under the mountain.

60

Pisgah Mountain

Early the next morning, accompanied by Wild Bill, AJ and friends began the long climb up Pisgah Mountain. Most of the afternoon was blanketed in sunlight. Still, a continual growing darkness rested in their hearts. If Tugger was alive, he could be anywhere on the mountain. Finding him wouldn't be easy and perhaps impossible.

Hours passed by. They kept walking. Thin shards of sunlight glistened in the trees but gradually retreated into a grey haze. Every step of the march was held back not only by the rugged terrain but also a constant dread that surrounded them. It ate at their young hearts like spilled acid.

"Are you sure this is the right direction?" AJ pointed at an old trolley path overgrown with weeds. "That way looks faster."

Wild Bill stuck a wad of chew tobacco in his cheek. "Too risky," he said. "If that thing in the woods is hiding out there, we'll be easy pickings. We need to stay off the main trails." He pointed up in the sky with his shotgun. "There'll be no light left in an hour. Stay close together."

Becca kept a firm grip on AJ as they climbed. Darkness thickened with each passing step. Keenan hoisted himself over a rotted tree trunk, perhaps fallen by lightning on some ageless and stormy night.

Farther up the ridge, the ground rose and fell in fortress-like mounds of timeworn soil. Looking at it, one might have thought that the lush valley once played host to a brutal confrontation between primeval armies. Walking at times proved difficult. The ruins were clogged with shallow and stagnant ponds of wet scum. Both Keenan and Becca grimaced as they splashed through the water, socks soaked to the bone.

"You need the hoofs of a mule to get through this rubbish," AJ complained. Holding a broken branch, he poked at the bottom of the pond for leverage.

Becca's face puckered like an apple when she pinched her toes in the muck. "I'll wager this is filled with leeches and worse."

Wading in ankle deep water, finally they reached the other side and drier land. The sun had all but disappeared and most of the world's light rested in the stars and moon. It was getting late.

"Hold up." Wild Bill abruptly halted the march.

AJ's eyes widened. He stared at a towering wall of rock. Its shaved stones resembled old and weatherworn faces, watchful as if guarding the forest. Their unmoving figures seemed to whisper in the wind at the sight of the young champions.

Keenan approached the rock and put an ear against it as if listening for the heartbeat. "Tugger is close," he said. "I can feel him."

"What do you mean?" asked Becca. "It's just a rock. There's nothing here."

"Is that true?" Wild Bill stepped up. "They used to rake the hills for coal. Mineshafts are everywhere. This is one of them." He knocked his knuckles on the stone. "It's hollow inside."

Keenan said, "We need to get in."

"Are you sure you want to do that?" Wild Bill asked. "If rumor is true, most people that went in never came back out." He looked around suspiciously. "These hills are haunted by Sentries."

Becca blinked. "What are Sentries?"

"Gypsies," he said. "They wandered these mountains like homeless vagrants. Mostly they hid from regular folks. They'd make camp in the mining shafts when it got cold outside."

Becca twirled her hair nervously in damp fingers. "Are they dead?"

"Nobody knows." Wild Bill said. "Those sons-of-bitches could be watching us right now."

AJ shuddered. "You're starting to spook me."

"Maybe you should be spooked." Wild Bill stepped back from the rock. "Back when they mined these hills, there was an incident. Some miners were hauling dynamite up the mountainside when there was a huge explosion. Everyone got killed. Sometimes when the moon gets full people swear that they can still see skeletal remains hanging in trees like decapitated ghosts. Most of the locals think it was just an accident, but me? I think the Sentries killed them. They didn't like anyone else stepping foot on the mountain." He eyed the megalith distrustfully. "I still think they're hiding inside there. Stinking wretches!" he shouted and fired off a round from his shotgun. The bullet echoed in the empty canyon.

A damp rag of fear posted itself against the exposed wire of Becca's heart. She looked up at the towering rock. "If Tugger is in there, we can't just abandon him."

"It won't be easy getting in. The land isn't very stable." Wild Bill said. "The place is filled with impassable trails and marshes. Wolves also roam these woods; they travel in packs like killers in dark alleys. Our best bet is to go west, just over that ridge." He pointed. "There's an opening on the backside of the mountain. It leads inside the cave."

AJ wiped sweat off his cheek. "What makes you so sure about all of this?"

"There you go being a smart ass again." Wild Bill growled. "Years back when I was young, along with a kid named Bacon Peters, I found an opening. We decided to do some exploring. We crawled inside. Inching our way through the darkness, we found all kinds of passages and tunnels.

"Along the way Bacon dropped his flashlight," he continued. "Outside of a few splashes of light filtering through fissures in the rocks, the place looked like a mausoleum. We crawled on our hands and bellies, dirty as hogs in a pigpen. Finally, we found a crawlspace that led us outside. But you know something?" Wild Bill said. "To this day Bacon still swears that he saw something in those tunnels."

He leaned close. "Something not quite human. I'm not sure if it was the Sentries or just a big imagination. Either way, Bacon never set foot in these hills again."

Keenan stared at the wall of rock. "I don't know if there are ghosts or not in the mine," he conceded. "What I am sure of is that Tugger is nearby and probably inside. I'm not sure how I know that," he admitted. "I just do." He turned to Wild Bill. "We can't leave him for dead." He looked at AJ and Becca who both nodded.

Wild Bill scratched at his beard and shook his head. "Okay then. The opening is across the flats and around the backside." He pointed towards some trees tangled in weeds. "Stay alert. There's no telling what we'll find."

Holding firm to his shotgun, he began trudging through the woods.

61

Something Wicked

Wild Bill marched the company through gnarled branches and rotted trees that were clustered together. The ground was splashed with long grass and dabbed with roses. Other plants, yellow and dead, wilted at the roots as if the soil turned foul and discarded them.

AJ sniffed and scowled. Instead of a fresh clean scent of new green leaves, the wind blew and carried a sickly stink of rotted wood. Other times the breeze stood utterly still. Silence was like statues in a house of glass that would shatter if even a leaf dared to fall and break the calm.

Becca looked up in the sky at the sunken darkness that had arrived to reclaim the forest, swiftly as the tide retaking a beach. Even the cold yellow moon that sat high in the sky seemed watchful of their every move.

"This is Spooky," said Becca.

Squirrels leapt from branch to branch in the trees, curious at the sight of the company of misfits. Bats unfolded their wings and rodents marched on damp soil, awakened from their holes and set to reclaim the night.

Wild Bill halted the march. "Over there." He paused and stared. "That's the opening to the cave. We're entering the devil's den."

AJ walked over and put his hand on Keenan's shoulder. "Are you sure about this?"

Keenan's expression remained distant and foreboding. "I can feel him, strong as a heartbeat."

Wild Bill spit on the ground. "Listen up," he said. "Stay alert. Don't let your defenses down. There could be worse things roaming the night than that fiend out there. In the end it doesn't really matter. We'll be lucky if any of us get out of this alive."

62

A Ghost in the Darkness

Not far off, gun riding the back of her neck, Ashley Braddock wordlessly climbed the mountainside. Harry Grimm sifted through the darkness as if waiting for a rogue boulder to come crashing down. Near the top of a ridge, almost as if the wind stopped breathing, trees became immovable as stones.

"Things are too quiet." Grimm sniffed. "I'm telling you there's an elephant in the woods." He suddenly veered off a path and pulled Ashley down behind some weeds and bramble. Grabbing her by the hair, he yanked her head back and held a gun tight against her cheek. "Do you hear that?"

Ashley listened. "I don't hear anything."

"Exactly," Grimm said. "No crickets or owls. Something frightened the hell out of the local inhabitants. That something is just over that ridge, hiding behind those trees."

Ashley's eyes rolled across the landscape. "There's nothing out there."

"Trust me. There is," Grimm differed. "You just don't see him. He's like a ghost in the darkness. You're son is close by too. Our friend must be trailing him."

Ashley peered into the night. Everything looked quiet and still. Then she caught sight of something. A shadowy figure crouched behind a heap of stones.

"It's time to bait the hook," Grimm whispered. Adrenaline colored his cheeks. "Stand up," he ordered Ashley.

Confusion flooded her face. What?"

"I said stand up. Give him a thrill. Let him know mommy dearest is around."

"He'll kill me," she said.

Grimm jammed the gun tighter into her neck. "I'll kill you. You got three seconds."

Shivering, Ashley slowly stood up.

"Good," Grimm whispered. "Now take a few steps forward."

Claws of terror scratched Ashley's spine. She thought about running. That would prove futile. Grimm would shoot her before she managed a single step. She also doubted her ability to escape the darkman in the woods. He was big. Ferocious.

Ashley slowly walked forward. It only took a single twig breaking underneath her shoe to change the dynamics of the situation. The darkman stopped and turned. Much like an animal taken off guard by the invasion of civilization, his limbs stiffened. Green glitter sparkled in his eyes.

Backing up, Ashley screamed.

The darkman staggered towards her. A marked crease of tension overshadowed his face. He abruptly halted and for instant looked at the woman. A sunken glow of recognition brightened his eyes. Suddenly his expression shifted. His lips curled in excitement. Fists balled into sledgehammers, he raced towards her.

———

Harry Grimm stood up. The darkman turned and froze.

"Hey asshole!" Grimm pointed his gun. "Remember me?" His flashlight illuminated a jagged scar on the darkman's cheek. "Looks like you're still carrying my autograph. Ready for another inscription?"

Grimm pulled the trigger. Ashley hit the dirt. The darkman veered left behind thick brush. Firing off two more rounds, the bullets bounced off a heap of rocks.

"Show yourself!" Grimm demanded.

Nothing moved. Almost as if he evaporated into the dry night air, the darkman vanished.

No. Not vanished. More like relocated. Grimm caught sight of an opening to an old mineshaft. Blackheart used it as an escape hatch.

"You can run but you can't hide pal," he said out loud and glanced at the tracking device. "My guess is that your son is down in that cave," he said to Ashley, her expression painted with dread and terror.

Grimm smiled. Life was good. Hell, it was better than good. It was perfect. Right on schedule, every doorbell kept ringing and every door opened. Killing the target would be easy. In fact, it would be almost boring. Police wouldn't find the body until it was decomposed and wiggling with maggots. Long before the coroner ever matched dental records, he'd be roosting in a bar in Guam getting sauced on tequila and wooing young virgins into bed.

Only one small detail needed to be taken care of. It came in the form of Ashley Braddock. He abducted her as an insurance policy. He thought she might serve as good bait to help catch Blackheart. After all, she was the biological mother of Blackheart's son. She'd help draw him in like a shark in shallow waters. He'd come to feed. When he did, it would be an easy kill.

Logistics of the situation had changed. Blackheart was inside a mineshaft. Judging by the tracking device, the boy was there too. With everyone accounted for, Ashley Braddock, or "the bitch" as he liked to refer to her, had become expendable. Given the chance she'd also try to escape. She'd be a distraction. That could hamper his prime directive. After all, when it comes to murder, focus was crucial.

For a fleeting instant he considered raping the woman before killing her. He pictured himself shredding her blouse. Ravaging her at gunpoint. But the vision was short-lived. Desire deflated like a balloon punctured with a stickpin. The woman was soiled goods. God knows bona fide virgins were scarce. Still there were enough to go around and keep a smile on his face. He'd get himself something clean when this was all over. It wouldn't be a problem. Doorbells kept ringing. Doors kept opening.

The issue had been decided. Turning around, Harry Grimm raised his gun and pointed it in Ashley's direction. "Ring ring, open up wide and smile."

However, the only door that opened this time around came in the form of a heavy tree branch bashed across the side of Grimm's head.

———

Ashley needed to move fast.

Grimm stared into the gloom, occupied with his own thoughts. Her eyes shifted to a broken tree branch. It sat o the ground, a few feet away. The window of opportunity wouldn't stay open long.

Grimm suddenly raised his pistol and slowly turned.

"NOW!" a voice in Ashley's head screamed.

Unbolting herself from the ground, she sprung up and grabbed the broken branch. Grimm's eyes widened. Ashley swung hard as if wielding a wooden club. A direct hit. Grimm's ear became a fuselage of torn tissue. Runners of blood slipped down the side of his neck. Momentarily stunned, he dropped the gun. Still Grimm wouldn't be rendered unconscious. He whirled around with raised fists. Instead of recoiling, Ashley stepped inside the punch. Grabbing his hair, she pulled his head forward and rammed his face into a tree trunk. A loud crack of bone sounded off. He grunted and staggered backward.

"Bitch!" His fists punched at empty air. Quickly regaining his balance, he latched on to Ashley's arm and flung her to the dirt. She quickly got back up. Spun around. Threw a solid roundhouse squarely to the jaw. Grimm fell down and his head slammed against a rock. Suddenly he stopped moving.

Ashley abruptly halted the assault. Grabbing the flashlight out of the dirt, she stood up. Rage turned to dread and she redirected her attention to the cave. Blackheart disappeared inside. If Grimm had been right, her son was also in there.

Groggy and incoherent, Grimm suddenly latched on to Ashley's arm. The girl gasped and jumped backward. Her captor halfheartedly rolled over. Reached for his gun and pointed it at her.

"You're dead," his chilling voice whispered.

Ashley quickly hurried over rocks and disappeared inside the mouth of the cave.

63

Dark Matters of the Heart

Grappling with scraps of courage, Wild Bill shined his flashlight in the mineshaft. The passageway branched off into a maze of tunnels. Some were caved in and impassable.

Becca held tight to AJ's arm and hurried passed what looked like old bones, possibly human, and scattered on the floor of the cave.

Just in front of them Keenan halted his advance and craned his head around. He had the distinct sensation that someone trailed after them. Putting his ear against the wall he heard scraping noises, perhaps a foot dragging in dirt or someone rubbing against a rocky partition.

"There's something else in here," he whispered to his friends. "It isn't far off."

Wild Bill shined his flashlight around. He swore a quick moving shadow crossed the passageway. Skitters of dirt tumbled down the walls.

"Probably just bats," Wild Bill said.

"I don't think so," Becca answered. An eerie sensation hung over her heart, dark as a black moon. Something traced after them. When they moved, it moved. Even worse, heavy breathing echoed in the chamber.

AJ tightened his fists but knew his defenses were useless. Fighting didn't require strong knuckles. He needed a bayonet or a machine gun.

A large cavity in the cave's ceiling shed enough light to see movement in the passageway. Silent as a cat, their adversary slipped behind some rocks.

"He's over there," Becca whispered. "Behind those stones." Her heart pulsed in her ears. Reaching down she pulled AJ's hand closer. "Maybe if we're quiet he'll go away.

"Wicked things don't go away," Wild Bill answered. "They just get wickeder."

A sudden rush of heat gushed over AJ. A smell of lavender hung in the stagnant air. He recognized the scent immediately. Staring into the dark, a ghostly face appeared in the dark.

"Anthony James," a voice floated in darkness.

AJ rubbed his eyes with dirty knuckles. The vision of a woman with crimson hair stared back at him. Sadness pooled in her eyes. Still there was something else. A sunken anger wet her cheeks, almost as if every teardrop was a dagger ready to lash out.

"Mom?" AJ's face became a large staring eye.

The boy blinked uncertainly. "You can't be real."

Smiling, the vision took a step closer. "I am." She held out her hand. "Touch me."

AJ took a slow step forward. Becca pulled him back.

"Don't listen," Becca told him. "That's not your mother," she said. "She died years ago."

The vision of the woman glared hatefully and then just as quickly softened. "I'd never lie to you AJ. I missed you." she said, wet under the eyes. "I've missed you more than all the stars."

AJ tilted his head in confusion. The woman's face drooped almost as if her well defined features turned to melting wax. Her comeliness dissolved. For an instant her head seemed to grow, almost as if reshaping before returning again to the silhouette of his departed mother.

"Can't you see what this is doing to me?" Tears and mascara ran down her cheeks. "You're killing me."

"You're dead!" AJ shouted and pointed.

"How can you say that? Look at me." She pinched the fleshly part of her hand. "I'm your mother. Can't you see that? Do you remember the night of the accident?".

AJ stared. How could he forget? He was at his grandparent's house. The police knocked on the door. He heard his grandma crying from upstairs.

"We were coming home from the ski resort," she said. "The road was icy. We hit the brakes and the car spun and slid out of control. We went through the guardrail." She paused as if bracing for a terrible truth. "We didn't die easy. It took some doing. We laid there bleeding, wondering how you'd survive without us. It was cold that night. So very cold. I couldn't feel my fingers. Still no help came. We were dying Anthony," she said. "You were at home sleeping in a warm bed, dreaming dreams, and we were in a ditch dying."

"Shut up," AJ shouted with narrow eyes. "You're not my mother."

"It's so difficult having children," she continued. "You don't know if you're doing the right thing. That's all we were doing that night." She looked at him dead in the eyes. "We were trying to do the right thing. We were trying to escape. Get away from the pressures of being parents." She glared. "Trying to get away from you. Is that a bad thing?" Her lips curled in distaste. "If you never would have been born, we wouldn't have been on that highway. We'd still be alive."

AJ balled his fists. "I said shut up!"

"You killed us, you little sonofabitch!" Her cold eyes stared. "You stuck a knife in my heart, bone deep."

AJ's lips trembled and he lunged at the imposter.

The vision of the woman instantly dissolved, effortlessly as a sandcastle on a beach at high tide, and the darkman materialized. A long scar stretched down the length of the his cheek.

AJ locked his fingers together. Spinning around, he struck hard to the mid-section. The imposter rocked back on his heels. Regaining his balance, he hit back quickly with a solid punch to the side of the head. AJ toppled backward a few feet.

His face cemented with hate and fists clenched tight, the darkman moved in for the kill.

———

In that fiery moment, Wild Bill stepped in. He shoved AJ out of the way, raised his weapon, but stopped cold.

"Spider Lugosi." Wild Bill's eyes flooded with confusion. "You crazy bastard, is that you?"

"Damn straight," he answered in a throaty voice.

"What do you doing here?"

"Remember when we were in the army?" he asked. "You left me stranded on that island." He shifted forward a step. "I came back to settle the score."

Wild Bill stared. "You really want me to believe that you're Spider?" he asked. "Spider died in the bush."

"Is that so? You know what I think?" he said. "I think that you're chicken-shit."

"You wanna fight?"

"Come and get me."

Wild Bill let out a loud cry. Charging ahead, elbows swung and fists connected. Both parties groaned as knuckles smashed against noses. Struggling and breathing hard, neither contender gave any quarter. Wild Bill lifted his leg and landed a roundhouse kick to his rival's ribs. Still the darkman showed no signs of retreat. He continued his advance. Grabbing Wild Bill by the shirt, he slammed a fist into his face.

Wild Bill wobbled but wouldn't give up. He heard a slight "Oomph" when his fist connected with the muscled flesh of his opponent's gut. The darkman delivered one last blow to the side of his neck. Wild Bill fell to the ground. Alert of his surroundings, he rolled twice, picked up his shotgun and started shooting.

The darkman quickly turned, hurried around a corner, and disappeared from the line of fire.

Clutching at his knee, Wild Bill grimaced.

"Are you okay?" Becca knelt down and asked.

"My ankle," he said. "It's sprained or worse. I'll never keep pace with the rest of you. You're gonna have to go on without me."

Becca gasped. "We can't just leave you here!"

"Listen to me," he said. "I can take care of myself. Find your friend. Save him." Wild Bill studied the shadowy tunnel. "If that vagrant returns, I got one bullet left."

AJ bent down on one knee. "We'll circle back after we find Tugger."

"Course you will," Will Bill said and ruffled his hair. "Now hurry on." He nodded.

Taking a last look at their friend, they disappeared into the tunnels of darkness.

64

What Lies Ahead

Tugger Rhodes opened his eyes and gasped. A loud noise sounded out from somewhere in the mineshaft. He wasn't alone.

The boy had been crawling around the tunnels for hours. It was worse than a glass maze in a circus; exits were nowhere. Also, his candle was nearly spent. Curling up in the dirt and crying, he drifted off from exhaustion. When he woke, he hoped he'd find himself sleeping in the safety and comfort of his own bed. That thought quickly vanished as he brushed the spiders off him.

Tugger put an ear against the wall of the cave. Shadows of fear fell over his face. The noise from another corridor grew louder. It moved straight toward him. Looking from side to side, he chewed at his fingernails. No clear means of escape existed. The kid thought about sleeping in the comforts of his own bed or raiding the refrigerator in the middle of the night. Sadly, none of those specifics carried any weight. He was lost in a mineshaft well after midnight and struggling to survive a grim fate.

A foul stench more rank than a rotting carcass left to bake in the hot sun assaulted his senses. It wasn't the first time that he smelled it. Remembrances of the darkman's foul stench still hung in his nostrils. A cold shiver ran up Tugger's spine. He weighed the possibilities of his bleak situation.

Tugger struck a match and lit what was left of a scrap of candle in his pocket. Raising it in the air, the sunken light danced off the blackened walls of the cave as water dripped off the rocks. To the right of him was a small fracture in the wall of the cavern that led to another crawlspace.

Holding tight to the candle he crawled on bruised knees, edging his way through the quarry. The boy's eyes darted in all directions, convinced that evil lurked in the shadows. Still he had to keep moving. Not one person on the planet knew that he was traipsing around in a mineshaft. Waiting around wouldn't just get him killed by a madman. He'd starve to death in the process.

A loud thump on the wall made him jump. Clearly other things were abroad. Dangerous things. Shifting forward, he accidentally dropped the candle and the light went out, leaving him in utter darkness.

"Hello?" He risked giving away his position by calling out. There was no answer.

Feeling the walls with his hands, the passageway continued on for a few yards and then turned sharply to the right. All views of what might lay ahead of him were obstructed by fallen rock and dark chasms. Gathering his courage, he crawled on hands and knees and moved slowly through the crawlspace.

65

Dangerous Minds

AJ, Becca and Keenan hurried along in the dark. They could smell things rotting, cold and dead like a morgue filled with unburied corpses.

Keenan stopped and listened.

"What's wrong?" AJ asked.

"We're being probed," Keenan said. "Whatever that thing is, it's close."

"How do you know that?" said Becca.

"I can feel him. He's trying to get inside my mind. It's almost as if I can read his thoughts. He wants us dead."

Shivers ran down Becca's spine. She turned around and peered into the blackness. Inside the tunnel skitters of pebbles and dirt fell off a wall. Something moved. Like a black cat chasing after its dinner, they were being hunted.

"I think it's right over there, at the end of the tunnel," she said. Backing up she ran into a barrier of dirt and stones. "The opening is caved in." She felt around. "We're trapped!"

Keenan bent down on his knees. He put his ear against the wall again. "Dig," he said.

AJ tilted his head. "What?"

"It sounds hollow on the other side." He knocked his knuckles on the wall.

Turning around, he peered down the tunnel. A stir of echoes mixed with a growl that sounded nearly inhuman reverberated in the crawlspace.

"We have to hurry," he said. "Dig!"

AJ grabbed a rock and frantically tunneled in the dirt.

Becca turned her head and her heart iced up with fear. Something in the distance glared at her. Its green eyes glittered with aggression. Turning left, it vanished in the darkness again.

"Faster!" she begged her friends.

AJ and Keenan dug madly. Finally, they loosened a large rock in the wall. It tumbled to the ground with a thud.

"There's an open cavern on the other side of the wall," AJ said. He pushed more dirt out of the way, enough to creep through. "Becca. You go first."

Crawling on hands and knees, Becca shimmied through the open space. Keenan followed. When it was AJ's turn, he accidentally dropped the flashlight on the ground. The world suddenly turned pitch black, impenetrable as the darkness that lurks between two mountains on a moonless night.

"Find the light," Becca implored them. "Quick!" She thought she felt someone's cold breath on her neck. "I think something is in here with us."

Keenan stiffened. He couldn't see an inch. Still he knew they weren't alone. Someone was waiting. Watching. He sensed the presence, strong as a malignant spirit. He could smell the enemy's stench. Taste his aggression.

"I found it," AJ said. He held a rock in one hand as a measure of defense and a flashlight in the other.

A sudden scream escaped Becca.

"Something touched me!" she shouted.

AJ quickly flicked on the flashlight. He held the rock in striking position. Suddenly he stopped. His frozen eyes blinked in the darkness.

"Tugger?" AJ tilted his head. "Is that you?"

Curled up in the corner of the cavern, Tugger's ghostly face was muddied with dirt and tears. He stared at his friends, mouth shivering. Ghosts floated in his eyes. He wouldn't move or answer.

"Tugger, what's wrong?" Becca took a step closer and gasped.

Something large shifted from behind her friend, nearest the

back wall of the cavern. Silhouetted against the rocks stood the dark figure who stalked them. A knife crunched in one hand, he held an unexpected captive by a clump of matted hair, the blade tickling her throat.

Keenan stared with disbelieving eyes.

"Mom?" he said.

66

Of Men and Monsters

Tugger looked on with eyes wide and terrified. Behind him a sinister laugh, bubbling like a sewer pipe that erupted in the street, rose in the darkman's throat. "Don't move," he warned. "I'll snap her neck like a pencil." The edge of the knife scraped Ashley's throat.

Keenan stalled in his tracks.

"That a boy." Pulling Ashley's hair, he tilted her head back. "You don't want to be a hero. Take my word for it. In the end they always die."

"Leave her go," Keenan said.

"Says the sheep to the wolf," the darkman laughed.

"I'm not afraid of you." Keenan held firm, fists balled up.

"But you should be." He snapped his jaw open and closed. "Either way, you won't leave here alive." He looked around the room. "None of you will."

Ashley stared into her captor's cold eyes. "They're just children. Please." She studied the long scar on his face. "Do you remember The Agency? They're the ones who hurt you. They're the real monsters."

Blackheart held Ashley's head by a clump of hair. "Take a look around," he whispered in her ear. "Everyone here is ready to kill. We're all monsters."

"Why do you want to hurt us?" Ashley's eyes pleaded.

Blackheart stared. It was a credible question. Still he had no answer. The only certainty had been that something dark slipped into his life and refused to leave him. These days he was little more than a prisoner in a domicile he once called home.

Blackheart shifted his gaze to Keenan. The boy frightened him. He was a sorcerer. Like a malevolent spirit he had a talent for reading his mind. That didn't matter much in the grand scheme of things. Long before sunrise the kid would be tramping around the country of the dead. He wouldn't have to contend with him any longer.

Still, killing the boy presented a problem. He didn't want to commit murder. Twice he raised his fists. Twice he lowered them again. Who would have guessed that the worm of evil churning in his guts still had a dash of sympathy?

Blackheart's eyes shifted as one of the brave commandos stepped forward.

"You killed my dog." AJ pointed an accusing finger.

Blackheart glared fiercely. "I'm going to kill more than a dog before this is over," he warned and turned his head back to Keenan. "Things are winding down. Call me the timekeeper. Everyone has one."

Keenan asked, "Everyone has what?"

"A time to die," Blackheart answered. "This is yours."

Throwing Ashley to the ground, Blackheart raised his knife and lunged at Keenan.

"No!" Ashley screamed. She pulled herself up on bruised limbs. "You don't want to do this," she pleaded. "I know you."

Blackheart turned. His lips were thin and tense. "You don't know anything about me."

"You weren't always a killer. Do you even know your name?"

He stared blankly at Ashley.

"It's Jonas," she said. "Jonas Blackheart. The Agency did this to you. Please, you've got to listen."

The darkman hesitated. Distant memories played in his head. He recognized that name. The Agency. Bad people were there. He remembered that much. They did experiments on him. Altered his thoughts. But something went wrong. He changed. Somewhere in his mind a wolf in the dark woke up, insistent on hunting and killing.

"Listen to me," Ashley begged. "You're having delusions. I can get you help."

"Shut up!" the darkman shouted angrily. A migraine shot through his head. The knife quivered in his hand.

"Please," she begged again.

"I said shut up!" He grabbed Ashley and put the knife to her throat.

Ashley glanced at her son. Soulful. Passionate. Filled with tears; her face was raindrops in a rainbow, faded to black and scented with heartache. Her desperate eyes told every line of the story. She was insistent on saving her child's life even at the expense of her own.

"Please." A tear weaved down her cheek. "Kill me if you have to kill someone. For God's sake, Jonas," she said in a whisper so no one could hear. "He's your son."

The darkman stopped cold. He turned to Keenan. The boy's eyes were green. Reflective as mirrors. Suddenly things became clear. The ghost lifted off his shoulder.

"Harbor Point," he whispered to himself.

He stared at the knife in his trembling hand, almost as if confused as to why it was there. For an instant sanity grew on the corrupted vines of his mind. It wouldn't last long but perhaps long enough to evade murder.

Finally, he dropped the knife. The metal blade clanged off the ground. For an instant he felt a momentary reprieve, but it was short-lived. The sound of a bullet reverberated off the walls of the cavern and punched his arm.

J.L. Davis

67

A Grimm Return

Jonas Blackheart was jolted backward on impact.

Harry Grimm limped into the darkened passageway. His face appeared battered as a boxer after a hard night in the twelfth. Firing off another round, the bullet glanced off a rock. His eyes shifted to Ashley and Keenan.

"Well if it isn't America's prodigy and his mother. What we got here is a family affair. Don't sweat it kid." He winked at Keenan. "I need you alive. That doesn't mean you can't be damaged goods." He pivoted around, aiming from one target to the next. "As for everyone else in the house, be advised; this isn't the UN and we're not taking hostages. Expendables are out the window."

Getting off the ground, Ashley stood in front of Keenan and his friends. "Leave them go," she insisted.

"Are you serious? Things are just warming up here." Grimm laughed. "I'll tell you what I'm gonna do. First off I'll be having a little talk with our friend." He took aim at Blackheart and fired off another round. The bullet landed dead square in Blackheart's shoulder. Groaning, Jonas Blackheart dropped to one knee.

"It's a duck shoot so far, right?" Grimm twirled the gun in his fingers. "Now it's your turn," he said to Ashley. "Who's next? Give me the pecking order." He winked. "You never know. I might go easy on your kid and just take him out at the kneecaps." He took aim. "Hell, I guess it's time for that famous final scene."

Across the room, Jonas glared fiercely. Getting to his feet, he leapt forward.

Grimm whirled around. Smiling like an alligator he fired off another shot. The bullet hit solid meat near Jonas's ribs. Blackheart buckled over but refused to go down. He lumbered ahead towards Harry Grimm.

Fear and rage painted Grimm's black eyes. He again pulled the trigger on his weapon only this time the chamber was empty. Tossing the gun to the ground, he threw a hard punch to Jonas's mid-section followed by an uppercut to the jaw. Blackheart staggered but still moved forward, intent on eradicating the threat.

Back peddling, Grimm pulled himself up an embankment out of Jonas's reach.

"Get away!" he shouted. Grabbing a rock, he threw it and hit Jonas on the side of the head, slowing his advance.

Grimm scrambled up a pile of rocks that led to a ledge and an open crevice in the wall. With any luck he could crawl down to the cavern's bottom; escape and fight another day. Only next time instead of a handgun he'd bring a bazooka and blow the exits shut. Buried alive, they'd rot to the bone before anyone found them.

Grimm took another step but Jonas grabbed his ankle. The sonofabitch wouldn't quit. Kicking free, he glared at Jonas. For an instant, Grimm swore he saw a wolf's lean jaws closing in on him. Shaking off the illusion, he pulled a switchblade from his pocket and jostled the release button.

"Sorry Jonas," he said. "That hocus pocus crap isn't on my itinerary." Stabbing with the knife he sliced Jonas's upper arm. A flower of blood bloomed on his shirt.

Jonas Blackheart groaned. Still he wouldn't back off. Bulldozing ahead, he rammed Grimm's knees with his shoulder. Grimm's foot slipped off the ledge. Grappling for leverage, he managed to hang tight to a lip on a ridge of the rocks.

Grimm raised the knife again, this time aiming for Blackheart's throat. "Eat this and die." He grinned hideously but unexpectedly stopped. Looking across the far side of the cave, someone stared back at him, shotgun in hand.

Limping forward out of the darkness and shotgun in hand, Wild Bill took aim.

"See you in hell," he said. The sudden blast of Wild Bill's gun echoed in the cavern.

Grimm got tagged on the shoulder and shifted backward on impact. Shock graced his expression. His face twisted in dark corners of terror. Losing his grip on the ledge, he finally let go. His airborne limbs flapped like a bird with broken wings. Grimm bounced off an outcrop of jagged rocks. Tumbling down a steep embankment he came to an abrupt halt at the bottom of the quarry, dead on arrival.

68

The Long Walk Home

Jonas Blackheart buckled over. He slid down a bank and came to rest on the dirt floor. Clutching his arm, blood sopped his shirt compliments of a well-placed bullet by Harry Grimm.

On the far side of the cave, AJ, Becca and Tugger huddled together in fear. Keenan took a step forward.

"Is he dead?' Keenan asked his mother.

Ashley picked the flashlight up off the ground. She shined it in Jonas's face. Something changed in his expression. He looked calmer; no longer the monstrous figure that stalked them in the woods. His breath shallow, the shadow of death hung in his eyes.

"It's gone," Jonas finally said.

"What's gone?" asked Ashley.

He paused and looked around. "The voices. I can't hear them anymore."

Ashley bent down on one knee. She shined the flashlight on Jonas's injuries. Between gunshots and knife wounds, he was bleeding out fast.

"I'll get help," Ashley said.

"No," Jonas answered quickly. "I'm already dead." Blood dabbed the corners of his mouth. He looked at Keenan and then turned his gaze back to Ashley. "Listen. There are people out there. Bad people. They'll be coming for you. Understand?"

Ashley stared.

Jonas coughed. "Take your son. Hide him. Keep him safe."

Ashley swallowed hard. "It's all true, isn't it? You were at Harbor Point." She glanced at Keenan. "You're his..."

"Stop," Jonas cut her off. He squeezed his eyes shut as if batting away demons. Opening them again, he looked up at Ashley. "The boy doesn't need to know. Never tell him," he said. "Now go. I could blackout. If I do, I won't be able to control myself. There's something ugly inside me. Something sick as sin. I can feel it. Go while you still can."

Keenan stepped forward. Bending down he took his mother's hand and held it tight. "Who is he mom?" he asked. "Is he someone we know?"

Standing in the darkness, foul water dripped off the walls of the cave. Ashley remained silent. Jonas Blackheart shivered in the shadows. A tear rolled down his cheek. Breathing heavy, his eyes slowly closed.

"Mom?" Keenan asked again.

Ashley hesitated. "He's a friend."

"A friend?"

Ashley didn't answer. Standing up she said, "It's time to go."

Taking Keenan by the hand, they began the long walk home.

From the Diary of Keenan Braddock

Sometimes I hear echoes of children and monsters. The children are reflections of my youth, and the monsters, a reminder of a battle fought long ago.

After graduation at Jim Thorpe, my old alma mater, I attended Penn State University, majoring in medicine. Later I decided to move southward. I setup practice in Myrtle Beach. Frigid winter temperatures never impressed me and the northeast has its share of the white stuff. Be that as it may, I often think about Jim Thorpe, my old hometown. Maybe I'm still chasing childhood ghosts. That sometimes proves to be a chore. Youth isn't so plentiful these days and ghost hunting is often hard, especially on aged knees.

Two years ago, I returned home for a visit. After sundown I decided to climb Pisgah Mountain. That sounds crazy. Thinking about it, it is crazy. Still something in my soul never settled about what happened way when we were young. Often I find myself searching for the missing piece in that crossword puzzle.

Although shrouded in weeds, the old trolley trail that led up the mountainside is still there. During a hike I stopped in the woods and the graveside where we buried AJ's dog Taff on one lonesome and terrifying night. The makeshift cross that AJ put at the head of Taffy's grave endured many years before it finally disappeared. I wasn't surprised to find it sitting at the foot of AJ's coffin all those years later. It seems that Becca also climbed that same trail at times trying to put the ghosts to rest.

———

Speaking of ghosts, I stopped by Wild Bill's shack that was

buried in the hills. The place looked deserted. A dusty frying pan full of muck still hung over a dilapidated stove. The only thing missing from the cabin was the old hooch machine where he used to make moonshine.

To this day the whereabouts of the hillbilly remains a mystery. A few years after the incident, local entrepreneurs promoted the town as the Little Switzerland of America. With the invasion of bike trails, campers and rafters, Wild Bill packed up his belongings in a duffle bag. He was never heard from again.

I'm told that Wild Bill died of influenza during a cold winter some years ago. I happen to know differently though. The old coot was elusive as a sentry in the dark. I swear during AJ's funeral I saw him staring from up at the fence in the cemetery, He had a long beard and tattered clothes. He winked when I walked toward him, eyes shining like pennies in the sun, and then just as quickly disappeared.

———

After college Tugger Rhodes moved to New York. The fat little tumbleweed joined weightwatchers and became flab free. I'm told he opened a health food store on the boardwalk in Ocean City Maryland. It specializes in low fat yogurt. Tugger calls me every so often. There have been times he mentioned the monster in the woods, not by name but more often in a heavy silence, as if remembering something too difficult to bear.

It's hard to comprehend the terrors that Tugger might have endured during that night long ago. He rarely talked about it over the years. I suppose that's how it is for real soldiers. It's the ones who went through unspeakable battles that leave their bragging rights behind. They bury the haunted moments of a turbulent past in some darkened corner of the mind.

"What in God's name happened to us back then when we were kids?" I recently asked him during my annual Christmas call.

Tugger paused. "I don't think I was ever so frightened," he

said. "I'm still afraid of dark places," he admitted. "I can tell you this though. Outside of marrying my wife, the best moment of my entire life was seeing your faces when I was trapped in that cave."

———

It's after midnight. I'm alone in the woods and believe it or not, inside those same tunnels where we once fought the devil. Man, if these walls could talk? They'd whisper about a clash that took place here long ago when monsters roamed the hills and children became heroes.

Those that fought here in the theater of war are older now. The monsters have disappeared. In all the years since I've never had any closure or clear explanation as to why it all happened. The authorities investigated the crime scene. Harry Grimm was discovered at the bottom of gully on jagged rocks. However, the darkman's remains were never recovered. He disappeared or perhaps slipped away into some unknown passage of the cave where he silently died.

I never told anyone this, but sometimes I felt almost a strange connection with our nemesis. I was never sure why. Nor would I admit it to my friends. Perhaps it's because there were so many unanswered questions back then. These days, the ghost hunting never ends, and at times the edgy spirits of my life never seem as if they're put to rest.

———

Recently I visited Becca. We went out for coffee at the Sunrise Diner. After AJ's death, it took some time, but she finally got back on her feet. With the children grown and out on their own, she moved to Long Island. She never remarried, although I have occasionally joked that one day, I'd take her out dancing. She always smiles and answers, "I danced my last dance on a high school gymnasium floor." I smile back because that last dance came when we were kids and with AJ Samson.

"Sometimes I have nightmares," I once told Becca. "Even after all these years, I still dream about fighting monsters in the woods."

Becca sipped her coffee. "Did your mother ever talk about it?"

"No and I never asked her," I answered. "Sometimes I think she tried to protect me from something. If you remember we moved away after the incident," I said. "It's almost as if she kept me hidden away. At the time I was never sure why." I suddenly changed the subject. "Believe it or not, I wrote a novel about when we were kids. AJ made me promise that I'd do that. It's called The 7th Jackal."

Becca blinked. "That must be a scary tale," she said with a forced grin.

A momentary aura of grey settled in around her eyes. Her life had been dimmed with heartbreak. I could sense it. She was thinking about AJ in that hospital room, facing his darkest hour. She cried a lot when he died. Honest to God, nobody should ever have to cry that much. It just didn't seem fair. I guess when you love someone it's all part of the world.

"I'm sorry." Becca wiped her eyes. "Sometimes I break down. I just wish I knew why it all happened," she said. Shifting in her chair, she regained a little composure.

I paused and tapped nervously on the arm of a chair. After a minute I said, "Remember that game we used to play when we were kids?"

Becca tilted her head curiously and nodded.

"We called it the *Truth Game*. Everyone had to reveal a secret about themselves. I'd like to play that game just one more time," I told her. "It happened on the morning of AJ's funeral, at the cemetery."

———

It was a dreary day. Rain dripped off our noses as we gathered around the casket of our childhood friend. Near the end of the service Becca picked up a rose and placed it on the lid of the coffin. Whatever task God intended for AJ Samson to accomplish became suddenly final.

Pulling a tissue out of her purse, Becca dabbed at her eyes. Taking her by the arm, Tugger led her out of the churchyard.

"Keenan, are you coming?" Tugger turned and asked.

"In a minute," I answered. Bending down over the grave I said a silent prayer. When I stood back up, a mourner put a hand on my shoulder.

"Sorry about your loss," he said.

"Thank you," I told him. "I'm not family. We were just good friends."

"Good friends are always family," the stranger reminded. He looked down at the gravesite. His face was old. Weathered. Judging from his appearance, he had a difficult life.

I nodded and touched the lid of the coffin. "When we were kids you might say we once fought the devil together."

The stranger looked at me. "I never met Mr. Samson. I believe they called him AJ?"

"Oh," I said. "Sorry. I just assumed you were a relative." I looked at him closely and scratched my chin. "Do I know you?"

"You might say we're acquainted," the old man said. "I passed through here a few times over the years. You were a young man then. I wanted to be sure you were okay. One of the last times I was here you were tossing a ball in the alley with a friend." He glanced at AJ's coffin again. "That was a long time ago. Back then you were just a young boy, an entire life waiting to be discovered."

I looked at the old man quizzically. "You seem to know a lot about me." I nodded and turned to leave. "It was nice meeting you but if you'll excuse me, I've got an early plane to catch."

The old man hesitated. "I see," he said. "I'll be honest. Maybe you should think about taking a later flight."

Staring, I tilted my head in confusion. "Who are you?"

"I'm surprised you don't know, Keenan. From what I hear

reading minds is your specialty."

I abruptly stopped. "How do you know my name? How do you know anything about me?"

The old man said, "My name is Cage. Sam Cage," he said. "I know what happened back when you were a young man. It haunted you for a long time. It still does." He looked down the street at a diner. "Humor an old man. Let's have a cup of coffee."

I stared for a moment. "What exactly do you want Mr. Cage?"

He hesitated and smiled. "I have a long story to tell you."

The End

Excerpt from JONAS BLACKHEART
The 7th Jackal
a novel by J.L. Davis

Part 1
AGENT LOCKE

1
Alien Country

Hot sun beat down on the Nevada blacktop. Wind in her hair, Special Agent Emma Locke headed north on Highway 93. The abrupt shift of inner-city streets to desert terrain gave her the sensation of being transported to another world.

Emma gassed up the car at a Chevron station. She pondered rumors about travelers from distant worlds that gathered under the bright Nevada sky. It didn't take a conspiracy theorist to put a spin on the legendary road. Ever since Area 51 charted, the desolate tract of land had been a favorite destination for UFO hunters. Welcome to the Extraterrestrial Highway.

Turning left, she passed a huge cottonwood tree. The north gate of Area 51 baked in the rising mid-summer heat. Signs were posted on a barbwire fence that read:

NO UNAUTHORIZED ADMITTANCE,
VIOLATORS WILL BE SHOT

The place was surrounded by cameras and floodlights. A soldier stepped out of a guard shack. Emma hit the brakes and held a badge out the window.

Radioing for clearance, he opened the gate.

"That way." The guard pointed. "First building on the east end."

———

In the desert backdrop, radar equipment kept tabs on incoming and outgoing aircraft. Airplane hangars and helicopter ramps were setup on both sides of the road. There was also a fire station, rec center and even a Starbucks with a statue of a little green alien sipping a Frappuccino.

Emma turned into the parking lot of the MARS 1 complex. The building was painted drab gray and ringed with fenced wire. It resembled a maximum-security prison rather than a military outpost.

A guard wearing a gold earring stepped out of the entrance.

"Miss Locke?"

Emma nodded.

"Follow me."

Emma's footsteps echoed in the dingy halls of the building. Fluorescent lights illuminated the corridor. One blinked as if ready to burn out. Dull paint on the walls, gray with age, carried the burden of many untold military secrets.

The guard abruptly stopped halfway down the passageway.

"Wait here," he ordered and disappeared down the hall.

2
Cell Number 6

Alone in the corridor, Emma stared at a detainment chamber girded with a steel door. A small window was cut into the metal. She peered inside at a ten-foot windowless cell. The floor, dirty and concrete, had been furnished with a discolored mattress and a stool made of tamperproof material. An overhead camera monitored a wash basin and unscreened toilet.

"Comfortable as a lion's den," she whispered.

A detainee sat stone-still at a small table in the center of the room. Black as oil, his crusty eyes stared blankly at a wall. A ragged scar sullied his left cheekbone. Ankles shackled, his foot tapped anxiously on the cement floor.

Emma heard footsteps coming. She turned to see a man in a long dark suitcoat. Holding a manila envelope, he nodded and smiled.

"Agent Locke? We spoke on the phone earlier. I'm Lanster. Can I call you Emma?" His half-lidded eyes traced down her slim frame.

Emma pulled her coat shut. She glanced at the floor before meeting his gaze. "Agent Locke will be fine."

Lanster raised his jaw and stiffened at the woman's cold approach.

Emma looked at the cell door. "Who is he?"

"His name is Jonas Blackheart," said Lanster.

For an instant the prisoner lifted his head and glared.

"He looks feral," she said.

"Feral isn't the word. Blackheart has a resume longer than the state of California. He once shot a cashier and a hostage at a convenience store, just to teach the cops a lesson." Lanster's droopy eyes, weighty buckets of wet sand, again rolled down Emma's slender build.

Emma's shoes shifted nervously on the floor.

Early thirties, most of her friends were housewives attending PTA meetings. Instead, sometime after college she applied for a position at the CIA. An interview and polygraph later, she entered a rigorous training program. She got assigned to an office in Washington. The job was simple; monitor caseloads of suspected felons and drug lords on the hitlist. Not exactly storming a terrorist camp in Kabul but it had its moments.

The call from headquarters came unexpectedly. A VIP in the head office told her to report to Area 51. The following morning, she boarded a jet from Dulles International. After a long desert drive up the Extraterrestrial Highway, she pulled into the most controversial military base in the United States.

"I haven't been debriefed. What's this all about?" she asked Lanster.

"Maybe you better see for yourself."

Lanster nodded at a security guard who unlocked the cell door.

Stiff as nails, Emma stepped forward.

"Wait." Lanster held her arm. "Check your weapon."

"Excuse me?"

"No guns, knives or anything else hidden in a sock. No offense. You could get unnerved. Heavy on the trigger. We can't afford any slipups."

Hesitating, Emma set her Glock on a table. "Satisfied?"

An authoritative grin washed over Lanster.

Followed by Lanster and two guards with batons, Emma stepped in the room, shoes clicking against stone flooring.

Jonas Blackheart sat at a wooden table, fingers steepled in front of him.

"There's no restraints on his wrists," Emma noted.

"Trust me," Lanster said. "Handcuffs won't do any good here."

3

Behind the Iron Curtain

Lanster walked over to the prisoner and snapped his fingers in his face. "Jonas? You got a visitor. You gonna play nice?"

Jonas's savage eyes narrowed. Heavy breathing echoed against stone walls.

Emma tightened her fists and stepped closer. A long scar cut down the side of the prisoner's cheek. A deep blemish, perhaps an old bullet wound, marred his neck.

"What has he been into?" she asked.

"More than selling music in the local record shop." Lanster walked around the table. "He had a few run-ins with the wrong people. The last time nearly killed him. One of our sister agencies found him on a mountainside, busted up like a jackhammer on cement. He should be dead. We managed to revive him." Lanster bent down and looked closely at the prisoner. "Do you hear me Jonas? Wake the hell up."

Jonas shifted his weight uneasily. The guards instantly raised their nightsticks. Lanster held up a hand and ordered them to stand down.

"I read his M.O.," Emma said. "The case file didn't reveal much. Said he killed two people at a convenience store. That doesn't pay for room and board at Area 51."

"It isn't what he did," said Lanster. "It's what he can do." He uncrossed his arms and pulled out a chair, opposite the prisoner. "Sit down. Don't make any sudden moves. The last thing we wanna do is piss him off."

Emma cautiously lowered herself on the chair. Jonas remained silent. His cold eyes, dark rivers in winter, hardened on her.

"What now?" she asked.

"You're the profiler. You'll figure it out."

Grinning, Lanster motioned the guards towards the exit.

Emma tilted her head in confusion. "Where are you going? Lanster!"

Guards tracing after him, Lanster walked out and slammed the cell door shut.

Everything grew quiet. Everything except the heavy breathing of the man sitting on the other side of the table. Biting down on her lip, Emma turned around.

4
Blackheart

Jonas glared. His face was pale. Almost drab. He clearly hadn't been exposed to sunlight for a long time.

Emma steadied her trembling hands.

"Jonas Blackheart, can you hear me?" she asked.

Grimy sweat streaked the side of the prisoner's neck. Metal shackles on his ankles rattled when he suddenly moved.

Emma instinctively reached for her Glock but stopped. The gun sat on a table outside the cell.

"Lanster!" she shouted again. "Open the goddamn door!"

Jonas's lips pulled up in a sadistic grin. Settling back in his chair, he laughed darkly. Its haunting presence reverberated through the confines of the small cell.

Emma raised her badge. "My name is…"

"I know what your name is," Jonas cut her off. "CIA, right?" He studied her closely. Saliva dripped from the corner of his mouth. "You don't fit the bill of an operative. Too soft around the eyes."

Emma's fingernails dug into her palms. "You underestimate me."

"Do I?" Jonas laughed again. His stained molars, brown with corruption, opened wide. Emma couldn't help picturing an alligator waiting on dinner. "Tell me something Dick Tracey. You don't look stupid. Probably went to college. Studied hard between frat parties and midnight panty raids at the dorm. What made a girl like you join Intelligence?"

Emma stared, refusing to flinch.

Blackheart was smart. Savvy. People made the mistake of viewing killers as unintelligent. Not true. The Unabomber had a genius IQ. Bundy was no slouch either. Underestimating Blackheart wouldn't only be a mistake. It could prove deadly.

"I'll ask the questions." Emma scanned the drab cellblock. A large spider, black and yellow, hung from a cobweb on the wall. "The military doesn't lock prisoners in dungeons in the middle of the Nevada desert for murdering two people with a shotgun. What are you doing here?"

"You first," countered Jonas. "A woman like you? You should be home. Pregnant. Maybe in flipflops on a beach. Instead your trying to save the world. Isn't that right Agent Locke?"

"I told you," she said. "I ask the questions. Get used to it."

There was a frozen moment of silence, thick as mud. Emma got up and walked towards the door.

"I'll be back. We'll talk more later." She knocked on the cell door for the guards.

Jonas grinned. After a moment, "It was a hot July night, wasn't it?"

Emma stopped cold. She turned around. "What did you say?"

"Don't play stupid." He shifted forward in his chair, fingers folded. "That was the day your life turned down a dark road, wasn't it?"

A disturbing glow flickered in Emma's damp face. "You don't know what you're talking about."

Jonas stared brutally. A droplet of sweat dripped off his cheek. "Don't treat me like a fool, Agent Locke. Answer me!"

He slammed a fist on the table.

Emma flinched. Turning around, she knocked harder on the exit door. "Lanster? Open up!"

A sudden gush of heat penetrated the back of Emma's neck, almost as if the sun peaked out from behind thick white clouds. The room temperature became hot. Oppressive. She grew lightheaded. Things moved slower. She gripped the wall for support.

Jonas's gaze remained fixed. Concentrated. "Can you feel it Agent Locke? Can you feel it deep down in your bones? Time to go down the rabbit hole."

Emma's knees buckled and she blacked out on the floor.

Excerpt from ISABELLA
The 7th Jackal
a novel by J.L. Davis

Beginnings

Ethan Drake pulled into a parking lot off Airport Road in Allentown, Pennsylvania. Hitting the brakes, he exited the vehicle. Six agents were already on site. Even in the darkness, he could see them wedged against the exterior walls of a demolished building, tight as flypaper.

"Talk to me." Ethan said to Stan Emery, head of security.

Emery stood near a tree line at the edge of the property. He took a drag of his cigarette then outened it under his shoe. "We got a breach in the north wing. The guard isn't answering." He hit a button on his radio. "Forbes? You there, man? Forbes!"

Blank static.

"Anything on camera?" asked Ethan.

"Nothing," said Emery. "The power is out. We think the wires were cut. My men have the exits sealed off."

Ethan crossed his arms and tapped his foot anxiously in the dirt.

What remained of the building was surrounded by a heavily wooded area, purposely designed so that the structure couldn't be seen from the highway.

"I don't get it," said Emery. "This facility has been closed for years. The only thing left is an underground bunker with outdated file stacks. What the hell would anyone want?"

Ethan rubbed the back of his neck and said nothing. After a minute, he pulled out his Colt and took the safety off.

11

"Have your men stay in place and guard the perimeter," he said. "I don't need anyone slipping through the cracks."

Emery cocked his head. "What are you talking about? I got two snipers on site. They'll go in and flush the bastard out."

"Negative," Ethan told him. "There's sensitive material inside. Nobody enters except authorized personnel. We're going this one alone."

Disapproval penciled Emery's face. After a minute, he picked up the radio.

"Nabors," he said. "Have your men hold their positions. Keep the boundary secure. We're handling things here."

Emery signed off and pulled out his gun. "After you."

———

Ethan Drake stepped in the entrance door. Emery followed closely behind. Quiet as a whisper, they went down a set of metal steps that led to an underground bunker, better known as the north wing. Cobwebs draped the corners of support beams. The stench of decay, perhaps a dead rat in a wall, clung in the cool and damp air.

"The place is creepy," said Emery. He shined a flashlight down the hall. "Reminds me of a morgue. I wasn't even sure this still existed."

"It goes back a long way," Ethan said. "An organization called The Agency used it as a center for telekinetic research. One day they had a security breach. Some crazy bastard blew the place up. The explosion was heard for miles. This section is the only thing left of the original structure. The Agency disbanded years ago but left this area intact to store critical data in case the computers went down."

Further along the corridor, they came across a door that looked as if it had been jimmied open. Ethan gave it a push. Hinges creaked as they stepped inside. It was dark as hell. Emery again shined his flashlight around the room. Aisles of cardboard boxes and manilla folders lined the floor.

"Forbes?" Emery called out, his voice echoing off walls. "Quit being an asshole. Are you down here?" Reaching over, he flicked a light switch on, but the room remained dark. "No power. I'll check the breaker box. Maybe a circuit is tripped."

Walking towards a rear wall, Emery stuffed his gun in his trousers and opened a metal casing housing a circuit board. One of the breakers had been knocked off.

"Think I got it." He flipped the switch. "Presto!"

… and the lights came on.

Ethan froze. Emery's mouth opened wide.

In the middle of a cement floor among some toppled over boxes, the dirty little secret of Forbes's disappearance came into blazing light.

Forbes lay on the cold concrete, face up, staring lifelessly at the water-stained ceiling blocks. A small spider crawled over his cheek and dashed away across the floor. His limbs looked disjointed, as if twisted up in pretzel-like positions. A knife had been driven into his throat, bone deep. A pool of blood surrounded his head, angelic as a widening halo.

Emery's eyes swelled.

"What the hell, man," he said loudly. "We need backup!"

Ethan stared. More than fear, his expression was one of a man bracing for impact. Stepping carefully over Forbes's remains, he eyed something on the floor beside the body. Reaching down, he picked up an empty manilla envelope and pulled out his cell phone. Ethan placed a call. It took just one ring for someone to pick up.

"I've been expecting you. What's the situation?"

"I'm at the Allentown facility now," Ethan Drake answered. "There was a breach. One of the guards is dead."

"Anything tampered with?"

Ethan's gaze shifted down to the manilla envelope in his hand.

13

"I found a folder on the floor. It was beside the dead guard. If there were documents inside, they're missing."

There was a long pause.

"What's written on the envelope?" the person on the other end of the line asked.

Ethan blew dust off the cover of the folder and wiped it off with his hand. "The Jackal Project'," he said. "It must be something that The Agency worked on before they disbanded."

Another long pause.

"Is there anyone with you?" the person on the phone asked.

"Stan Emery," said Ethan. "A few other agents are guarding the perimeter outside."

"I'll have the agents outside the facility taken care of by some of my men," the person on the line said.

Ethan tilted his head. "What are you talking about?"

"Shut up and listen, Ethan. The Agency did some heavy crap in that facility, as in top secret research. It needs to stay that way. There's only one way to do that. You need to kill Emery."

Ethan blinked. "Say again?"

"Are you deaf? Kill him. We knew this day would come. It's finally here. After Emery is dead, dump the remains in a lake. Better still, bury him in the woods. When you're done, report back to me."

Ethan said, "Listen, I don't know…"

… and the phone went dead.

Across the room, Emery stared. "What did he say?" he asked.

Ethan tapped his foot as if considering.

"Hey man, you hear me?" asked Emery. "What's the order? You know headquarters. If we don't get the job done, they'll have our asses hung from a tree."

Raising his chin thoughtfully, gun in hand, he turned to face Emery. "Agreed," he said.

PART 1
Angel Wings

1

The House on Mulberry Street

Early evening rain glistened off the road. Yellow tape, "Crime Scene – Do Not Cross", marked the house on Mulberry Street.

Detective Scott Barilla leaned against a tree. The rotary lights from a police cruiser flashed against his face. He took a last swallow of coffee from a Styrofoam cup. Tossing it in a trashcan, he turned around to see an SUV pull up on the shoulder of the road.

A woman, early thirties, stepped out wearing black fishnets. A thin sheen of sweat glazed her face and neck. Dressed in a tight skirt and scanty halter top, she looked as if she just stepped off a street corner on the darker side of the Bronx. She stood in front of the SUV, staring at the house on Mulberry Street.

Barilla took a step forward. "Hey you. This is a crime scene. Keep moving."

The woman quickly hurried away. A few yards down the street, she ducked behind a hedge near a police cruiser. Two cops were jabbering, both within earshot.

"What happened?" one of them asked.

"Dead girl. Alexa Freeman. She moved into the house a week ago." The cop glanced over at a woman standing by an ambulance. "Her roommate, Natalie Trice, said she answered an ad to split expenses. A stranger was in the house when Trice got home from work. She called 911 but the suspect fled. Headquarters thinks it's the Angel Maker. The FBI is on the way."

The woman hiding behind the hedge quietly made her way to the ambulance. Natalie Trice leaned against the side of the vehicle. A sunken look of terror haunted her pale complexion. Mascara ran down her cheeks.

"Miss Trice?"

Wiping her eyes, Natalie asked, "Who are you?"

The woman hesitated. Ignoring the question, she asked, "Did you get a look at the intruder?"

Natalie sniffed and pulled nervously at her fingertips. "No. When I saw Alexa like that, I ran."

"Think closely. Was there anything else that seemed unusual."

Natalie stared. "Unusual? What the fuck, lady. Alexa is dead!"

"What I mean is, did you notice scars on the attacker's face?"

"It happened too fast," Natalie said. "When I walked upstairs, I saw someone leaning over Alexa and ran out of the house."

A cop hurried by. The woman lowered her head, then turned her attention back to Natalie.

"Is there anything else? Did you notice a temperature change in the house?"

Natalie blinked "What?"

"Did it suddenly get hot!" she asked sharply.

Before Natalie could answer, a police officer, fists crunched, marched towards the ambulance.

The woman in fishnets quickly hurried off. Keeping low to the ground, she crept alongside a white picket fence that led up a walkway to the crime scene.

House lights were on in every room. The front door stood ajar. Peering inside, police dusted for fingerprints.

The woman slipped inside. A faint trace of cheap perfume mixed with nicotine scented the air. A small container of half-eaten yogurt sat on a coffee table. Forensics and evidence techs scrubbed the room but were too preoccupied to notice her as she veered up the staircase.

Turning down the hall, she stopped at the bathroom. A wet towel lay bunched up on the linoleum floor. Water dripped from the shower. A bottle of Listerine had been tipped over on the sink; it trickled on the carpet. Black stockings and a red velvety skirt were draped over a towel rack. She glanced at a silver high-heel shoe kicked by a corner of the sink.

"Hasty exit," she noted to herself.

Stepping out of the bathroom, she walked down the corridor and approached the bedroom. Standing in the doorway, her mouth dropped.

Biting down on her lip, the woman clicked off her emotions; that central palette of feelings that cops sometimes get when dealing with horrendous crimes. Opening them again, she looked around. It was cold in the room. The air conditioner had been turned up, an old police trick to moderate lividity. Straight ahead, the point of contact slapped her face.

A young woman lay across the bed. Her one hand dangled lifelessly over the side of the metal frame. Blood stains marred her cheeks and neck. Her expression was forever cemented in fear as she gazed at a rotating ceiling fan. Strands of dark hair, still damp from the shower, blew across her lifeless eyes. Outside of cotton panties with red hearts, slightly torn, she was naked. Her white skin glistened with water droplets.

Gazing at the victim, a glow of recollection burned bright in her expression. She had seen the woman before. The other day in a supermarket she spotted her in one of the aisles. She also noticed her at Chelsi's Bar while having a drink.

Shifting uncomfortably, the woman scanned the rest of the room. Spatters of blood, red raindrops, dabbed the white drywall. A curling iron

17

and makeup kit were strewn on the floor, indicating a struggle. Multiple lacerations carved the girl's ankles and extended up her torso. Worst of all, a steak knife had been driven into the woman's throat. The killer didn't just cut her; the sonofabitch drove the blade in like a railroad spike. But it was the mirror above a vanity that left her digging fingernails into her palms. Speechless, she stared at it and stifled a quiet gasp.

"FBI is here," someone said from downstairs, breaking her concentration.

Quickly exiting the room, she crawled through an open window that led to the roof of a back porch. Hanging from it, she jumped in the grass on the side of the house, got up, and disappeared into the night.

2
Langley Virginia

A secretary opened the door and stepped aside.

"He's waiting for you," she said.

Emma Locke smiled, but it was a pasted-on smile; nervous and a little unnatural. She had been ordered to Langley and flown down that same afternoon. Hands fidgety, she sat in a waiting room for nearly an hour. Samuel Hawk, Director of Operations at the CIA, called her inside.

A large mahogany desk, dark and rich-looking, sat near the back of the office. Tables with chrome legs on rich carpet balanced the office decor. Sun filtered through a window that overlooked a grassy lawn with a mountainside in the backdrop.

Samuel Hawk sat in a leather chair behind a desk. It was no secret to anyone that he had mercury for blood. Nobody becomes Deputy Director of the CIA without crunching a few balls.

Hawk looked over the top of his glasses. "Agent Locke?"

Emma steadied herself. "Yes sir."

Hawk tossed a pen on the desk and leaned back in his chair. His eyes were arrows, targeted and never wavering from hers.

"It's pretty clear I didn't call you here to talk about the latest fashion trends." He stood up and crossed his arms. "The operation manager at the FBI contacted me. Hot shit Harry, as I like to call him. He's overseeing the Angel Maker case. No doubt you've heard of it."

The term "Angel Maker" was dreamed up by some bored and no doubt sleazy tabloid writer in Detroit. A dead man had been found near South Street in Philadelphia. His neck was snapped, and a knife rammed in his throat. The killer spread the victim's arms and legs out on a lawn like a snow angel, the kind kids make on winter days when school gets cancelled for bad weather.

"Yes sir," Emma nodded. "I found the first victim."

Leaving out a bored sigh, Hawk walked around the desk. Hair slicked back to cover a small balding spot, he eyed her suspiciously.

"The Angel Maker struck again last night. The problem is, one of the locals, a cop named Barilla, reported seeing a suspicious woman near the murder scene. She fit your description."

"Sir, I don't recall…"

"Save it," Hawk said. "You mysteriously disappeared during a field operation last night, then you were seen getting in a SUV that was stolen from a nearby convenience store. The owner of the car also described a woman that looked like you. Hell, you think you can turn up dressed like a hooker and nobody is going to notice? My question is simple. What were you doing on Mulberry Street?"

Emma stiffened. Hawk glanced at the line of perspiration on her forehead.

"Sir, I…"

"You nothing." Hawk walked back to his desk and sat down again. "I had the opportunity to read your profile, Locke. You've got quite a history. Not many people go through what you did and live to talk about it."

"Sir, if you're implying that I'm compromised because of…"

Hawk raised a finger again. Emma went silent.

"I do the talking. You do the listening," he said. "You've been turning up on murder scenes, namely the Angel Maker case, and more than once. That punches me in the gut as to being unusual." He leaned forward. "I'm going to ask one more time. What were you doing on Mulberry Street last night?"

Emma looked down at the floor then raised her head and stared. "I believe it's him, sir."

Hawk tilted his head. "Who?"

"Jonas Blackheart."

Samuel Hawk crossed his arms. An amused grin played over his lips. "And what makes you believe that Jonas Blackheart is the Angel Maker?"

Emma crunched her fists.

"I just know," she said. "The way he killed that woman with the knife on Mulberry Street..." She stopped.

Hawk's gaze remained fixed on her. "The FBI hasn't released details on the murder. How would you know the way she got killed unless you were there?"

Muscles tense, Emma answered, "You've got to listen. I know this guy. He's out there somewhere. Sometimes it almost feels as if he's watching me."

Samuel Hawk looked down the middle of his nose.

"Enough bullshit," he told her. "Over fifty percent of the population in America is female. You must be damn special to be the one that Blackheart wants to screw. That," he leaned forward, "or you're not telling me everything. Either way, the Angel Maker isn't our jurisdiction. He's the FBI's problem. I'm not giving this warning twice," Hawk said. "Keep your nose clean."

Tension creased the back of Emma's neck. She turned towards the door.

"One more thing," Hawk said. "You got accepted into the CIA despite a, shall we say, tainted history. That's right," he said. "I know about it. We typically don't employ people with that kind of background. You're an exception to the rule. Don't make Intelligence regret it. Jonas Blackheart is a ghost from your past. Do yourself a favor and leave him there."

J.L. Davis lives in Jim Thorpe Pennsylvania, the Gateway to the Poconos. He is the author of several award-winning books including The 7th Jackal and Jonas Blackheart. Between hiatuses to Ocean City MD and the California coast, currently he's working on his next novel.